from the kitchen *of* half truth

Praise for *From the Kitchen of Half Truth*

"Beautifully conveyed...delicate and magical. Happy to recommend this book!"

—*Marilyn Lustig, Wellesley Books, Wellesley, MA*

"*From the Kitchen of Half Truth* depicts a complicated mother-daughter relationship that anyone can appreciate."

—*Jessilynn Norcross, McLean and Eakin Booksellers, Petoskey, MI*

from the kitchen *of* half truth

— *A Novel* —

MARIA GOODIN

Originally published as "Nutmeg" in 2012 in the United Kingdom by Legend Press.

Published by Sourcebooks Landmark, an imprint of Sourcebooks, Inc.
P.O. Box 4410, Naperville, Illinois 60567-4410
(630) 961-3900
Fax: (630) 961-2168
www.sourcebooks.com

Library of Congress Cataloguing-in-Publication data is on file with the publisher.

Printed and bound in the United States of America.
VP 10 9 8 7 6 5 4 3 2 1

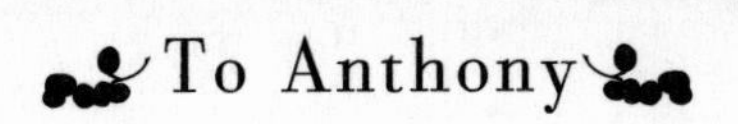
To Anthony

chapter one

I came out a little underdone. Five more minutes and I would have been as big as the other children, my mother said. She blamed my pale complexion on her cravings for white bread (too much flour) and asked the doctor if I would have risen better had she done more exercise (too little air). The doctor wasn't sure about this, but he was very concerned about the size of my feet. He suggested that next time my mother was pregnant she should try standing on her head or spinning in circles (spinning in circles on her head would be ideal), as this would aid the mixing process and result in a better-proportioned baby.

My father was a French pastry chef with nimble fingers and a gentle touch. On my mother's sixteenth birthday he led her to a cherry orchard and fed her warm custard tart under a moonlit sky. She knew it would never last, that his passion for shortcrust would always be greater than his passion for her, but she was intoxicated by his honey skin and cinnamon kisses. When they made love, the Earth shook, and ripe cherries fell to the orchard floor. My father gathered the fallen cherries in a blanket and promised my mother that upon his return to Paris he would create a cherry pastry and name it after her, but he never had the chance. Four days after his return to France he was killed in a tragic pastry-mixing accident. The only part of him still visible above the dough was his right hand, in which he clutched a single plump, red cherry. Finding herself alone with a bun in the oven and no instructions, my mother set the timer on top of her parents' fridge to nine months and waited patiently for it to ping.

Throughout her pregnancy, my mother suffered all manner of complications. She was overcome by hot flashes several times a day, which the midwife blamed on a faulty thermostat, and she experienced such bad gas that a man from the local gas board had to come and give her a ten-point safety check. Her fingers swelled up like sausages so that every time she walked down the street, the local dogs would chase her, snapping at her hands. She consumed a copious amount of eggs, not because she craved them, but because she was convinced the glaze would give me a nice golden glow. Instead, when the midwife slapped me on the back, I clucked like a chicken.

I want you to understand that these are all my mother's words, not mine. I myself am mentally stable and under no illusion that any of this ever actually happened. I have no idea what did happen during the first five years of my life, because for some reason I can't recall a thing. Not a birthday party, not a Christmas, not a trip to the seaside...not a thing. I don't remember my first bedroom, the toys I played with, the games I liked. Perhaps people don't remember much from those first five years, but I'm convinced I should remember something. Anything. Instead, all I have to go on are my mother's memories, which, in fact, are not memories at all but ridiculous fantasies that reflect her obsession with food and cooking and deny me any insight into my early years.

Am I annoyed with her? Of course I am! I want to know how I started out in this world, who my father was, what I was like as a baby, normal things like that. But however much I ask, I always get the same old stories: the spaghetti plant that sprouted in our window box on my first birthday, the Christmas turkey that sprang to life and released itself from the oven when I was two, the horseradish sauce that neighed unexpectedly…I mean, what is all this rubbish? I'm twenty-one years old, and yet my crazy mother still insists on telling me idiotic stories like I'm a baby. She's told these stories so many times that she actually believes them. The story of her pregnancy is ridiculous enough, but you should hear the story of my birth.

It was the gasman's fault I came out underdone. He'd come to deliver my mother's ten-point safety certificate in person after taking a bit of a shine to her, and my mother had felt obliged to offer him a slice of her freshly baked date-and-almond cake. They were having tea in my grandparents' kitchen when, all of a sudden, the gasman started choking. My grandfather, a member of the St. John's ambulance service, jumped up and grabbed the gasman around the waist and, with a sharp squeeze, freed the offending morsel of cake, which flew across the room, knocking the timer off the fridge. At the sound of the ping, I thought my time was up and started to push my way into the world.

Between them, my grandparents and the gasman carried my mother upstairs and laid her on my grandparents' bed.

"The baby can't come out yet!" my mother kept shouting. "It won't be properly done!"

But done or not, I was coming out, and so efforts began to make the labor as short and painless as possible.

"Go and get some butter, Brenda!" shouted my grandfather to my grandmother, mopping his brow with his handkerchief. "If she eats a pack of butter, the baby should slide out."

But a pack of butter did no good other than to turn my mother's skin yellow, so my grandmother suggested garlic.

"The baby won't like it if you eat garlic. He'll want to come out for air."

Consuming an entire bulb of garlic didn't force me out either, so my mother shouted, "Get some of that cake up here! We'll lure the baby out with the delicious smell."

And so half a freshly baked date-and-almond cake was held between my mother's thighs, and, lo and behold, I started to move.

"It's coming fast!" screamed my mother.

"Quickly, Brenda, get something to catch it in!" cried my grandfather.

In the end, it was the gasman who caught me in a heavy-based frying pan. By the time the midwife arrived, it was all over, although she insisted on poking me gently with a fork and plonking me onto the kitchen scales. She sniffed me and confirmed I was under-ripe, but as soon as she put me on the windowsill, my mother took me down again.

"She's my baby, and she'll ripen when she wants!" snapped my mother. Holding me close to her chest, she kissed the top of my head and proclaimed I tasted like nutmeg.

And so that's what I was called.

Meg.

I'm traveling home for the weekend, if you can call it home. When my grandfather died three years ago, my mother moved into the little cottage in Cambridgeshire where she grew up, the one where I was supposedly born, although I don't even know if that's true. The cottage suits her perfectly. Although it's not big, it has a long, narrow garden where my mother can indulge her love of growing fruits and vegetables. She grows potatoes and cabbages, spinach, peas, radishes, tomatoes, lettuce…and then there's all the fruit. Apart from having a small apple orchard at the far side of the garden, she also grows strawberries, plums, gooseberries, raspberries…the list is really quite endless. She spends her time gathering and cooking all these ingredients, boiling things up in big metal saucepans, frying, stewing, roasting, baking, simmering, steaming. She makes stews, pies, tarts, casseroles, cakes, soups, sauces, sorbets—you name it, she makes it. I have absolutely no idea what she does with all this food, and whenever I ask her, she's very elusive. It's my suspicion that a lot of it must get thrown away. The real enjoyment is in the cooking process itself, and what happens to the food after that is seemingly inconsequential to her. She's a flamboyant, reckless cook, throwing things around, chucking bits here and there, and leaving destruction in her wake. By the end of the day, the kitchen looks like a bomb's exploded, but I'm used to it.

My mother raised me among culinary chaos in a small North London flat. Because the ventilation was poor and my mother was constantly cooking, we survived in a haze of steam, which once got so dense that my mother lost me for forty-eight hours. She finally tracked me down in the living room with the aid of a special fog lamp. Apparently.

Because we had no TV or radio, the soundtrack to my childhood was compiled of saucepan lids banging, knives chopping, mixers whirring, and liquids bubbling. I went to school with clothes that smelled of spice and a lunchbox packed with elaborate sandwiches and homemade delicacies. The other kids thought we must be posh, but, in fact, we survived on a meager income. My mother was never too proud to take the squishy fruit or bruised vegetables that were left at the end of market day. Nothing made her happier than baking.

Nothing other than me, that is.

"Twelve minutes late," sighs Mark, staring up at the departures board. "Forty-six pounds for a train ticket, and the bloody thing's twelve minutes late. It's ridiculous. Do you realize you're spending approximately twenty-one pence for each minute you will sit on that train? That means that, in theory, they owe you two pounds and fifty-two pence for the twelve minutes you've wasted sitting on this platform. Oh, thirteen minutes now. So that makes it—"

"Mark," I interrupt, taking his hand, "you really don't have to wait with me."

He puts his arms around me and pulls me close to his chest. "I want to wait with you, babe," he says, smiling, showing off his beautifully straight, white teeth.

I take in the sharp angle of his cheekbones, the perfect line of his nose, the subtle arch of his brows. He is wonderfully symmetrical. Classically handsome. Like a child fascinated by an attractive object, I can't stop myself from reaching out and tracing the contours of his clean-shaven jawline with my fingers. His clear blue eyes sparkle with intelligence and betray a wealth of knowledge. He is always questioning, learning, rationalizing, and this thirst for knowledge, along with his heightened sense of practicality, makes me weak at the knees. When I first listened to him speak about condensed-matter physics, I knew I was in love; here was a man who, above all else, craved the same thing I did: hard, cold facts.

Mark brushes a piece of hair away from my face. "I've never noticed that little scar on your forehead before," he says, rubbing at it as if it's an imperfection he might erase.

"That's where I was bitten by a crab cake," I say casually.

"You mean a crab."

"No, a crab cake. When I was tiny, my mother made a batch of crab cakes, but she left a pincer in one of them by mistake. She told me not to touch them, but when she left the kitchen, I took one off the plate and was about to eat it when a pincer shot out and nipped me on the face. She couldn't pry it off. In the end, she got a match and held the flame underneath, and it eventually let go. The crab claw scuttled off under the fridge, and for weeks we were too scared to look under there in case it leaped out and..."

My voice tapers off as I feel Mark's arms slide from around my waist and he takes a step back. My accidental slip into this world of lunacy has embarrassed him. Again. He offers me an awkward smile, and I feel foolish, like I always do when these stories tumble out of my mouth. What he doesn't understand is they're like memories for me, so ingrained in my psyche that I sometimes forget none of it ever happened.

"Don't let your mother fill your head with too much nonsense this time," says Mark, a pleading look in his eyes. Last time I came back from my mother's, I told him how I'd apparently crawled into the freezer when I was barely a year old and had to be soaked in hot water for two hours to thaw out. I had told him with a faint smile on my lips, finding some amusement in the ridiculous image of myself—a frosty, blue baby, slowly warming through and becoming pink again as I sat in a pan full of steaming water—but Mark hadn't seen the funny side at all.

"You would have died," he had pointed out. "Or at least have suffered from frostbite. You would certainly be missing a few of your extremities."

"You're absolutely right," I had said, pulling myself together and wiping the smile from my face. "It never could have happened."

"Of course it couldn't have happened. I just don't get how you can laugh it off, though. Doesn't it annoy you, Meg? She's turned your childhood into a farce. I mean, why do you allow her to go on telling you such silly tales?"

"Because they're all I've got," I had said rather too defensively. "I'd rather have fictional memories than no memories at all. Besides, it's always been this way. I'm used to it. And anyway, it's all harmless rubbish really, isn't it?"

"Is it?"

And of course I wasn't sure. This fantastical world that had been part of my life—part of me—for so long had started to seem less entrancing, less colorful, less absorbing as I grew older. I felt confused and cheated by the stories that had once held me captivated and enthralled. Where I had once been carried away on a magic carpet into a fantastical past that I couldn't recall, I now felt irritated and patronized. A story, after all, is just another word for a lie.

"I won't let her fill my head with anything," I promise Mark, trying to redeem myself from claiming I was assaulted by a crab cake. It's still fairly early days in our relationship—only seven months in—and I desperately want to make a good impression, but every time I talk about my childhood he must think I'm insane. Or at least that I have an insane mother, which still isn't a particularly appealing quality in a girl.

"Here's your train," he says, drawing me toward him. "Have a great weekend and make sure you think of me every second that you're away."

"I will."

"I'll see you Sunday evening."

When we kiss, I breathe in the sweet scent of his expensive aftershave. He is so perfect. And he's mine!

I pick up my bag and board the train.

"And Meg," he calls after me, "I hope your mum's doing okay."

I smile appreciatively and wonder if he's talking about her wayward mind or her dying body.

It hasn't always been like this. I haven't always been ashamed of my fantastical past. When I was a little girl, I would boast to my friends about how I once ate so many apples that I started spitting seeds, or how my mother's meringues were so light that we once floated to the kitchen ceiling together after just one bite. At first the other children used to envy my extraordinary childhood and listen to my stories in awe, hanging on my every word. Their memories were so boring in comparison. Tracey Pratt's funniest memory was the day she got stuck in the loo, and Jenny Bell remembered falling off a donkey, but none of their memories ever compared to mine. And they *were* memories at that time, or at least I thought they were. I had heard the stories so many times that they had become part of me, part of my past. I could actually feel myself floating against the kitchen ceiling, half a meringue still clutched in my tiny fist, looking down on the cramped kitchen. I remembered seeing the baking tray steaming in the yellow washing-up bowl and the discarded ball of parchment paper lying on the worktop, little crumbs of meringue stuck to it. I recalled sitting in my highchair and spitting those apple pips across the kitchen, hearing them ping against the steamy window as my mother stirred something in a saucepan on the stove. As sure as the sun had risen that morning, these things had happened to me.

It wasn't until I was about eight that I first felt something was wrong. On our first day back after the summer holidays, Mrs. Partridge, in an attempt to get to know the class, had asked us to write a paragraph titled "My Earliest Memory." I knew how much everyone loved hearing about my life, so when it was my turn to share my work with the rest of Red Class, I stood up, puffed my chest out, held my head up high, and read my paragraph with pride.

> *In my earliest memory, I am very little, and I am sitting on the kitchen floor at home, and my mum is about to start chopping runner beans when they all leap up and run away. My mum says she knew she shouldn't have bought runner beans, and then she starts chasing them, and they are running in circles round me, and I am laughing. It was very funny.*

I looked up from my book and smiled at Mrs. Partridge, waiting for her to praise my work, but she didn't look pleased at all. In fact she looked positively annoyed. To make matters worse, the other children in the class were starting to laugh. Not their usual, gleeful giggles of entertainment, but scornful snickers. Something seemed to have changed over the summer; my friends seemed to have grown up, and for the first time ever, I experienced the humiliation of knowing my peers were not laughing with me, but at me.

"Meg," said Mrs. Partridge sternly, "that's a very funny story, but it's not a memory, is it? All the other children have written something that actually happened to them."

I looked around me at my classmates' faces, each of them

contorted into sneers and smirks. I heard Johnny Miller call me "dumb" and Sophie Potter whisper that I was "a big fat liar."

"Why is she always telling fibs?" Tracey Pratt whispered.

I didn't understand. Sophie and Tracey used to love listening to my childhood memories.

I felt my cheeks burning but didn't know what I had done wrong. I *did* remember the runner beans. I could still see them jogging in circles, puffing and panting as they did laps around me, and my mother chasing after them with a chopping knife and telling me to watch my head. I remembered that.

Didn't I?

"Meg May," said Mrs. Partridge sharply, "you're almost eight now. I hope this isn't how you think an eight-year-old should behave. Now, go and sit in the corner and don't rejoin Elm table until you can stop being silly!"

And so I slunk off into the corner, confused and ashamed, hot tears burning my eyes.

After that day I questioned everything. I knew beans couldn't run and people couldn't float, so how was it that I remembered these things happening? *Did* I remember these things happening? Or was it like that time I found myself telling everyone how once, in nursery school, I had spun in circles so many times that I had thrown up on the play rug?

"That didn't happen to you, silly!" squealed Jenny Bell. "That happened to me!"

"Oh, yeah!" I screamed. "That was you! I don't know why I said that!"

At the time we had nearly wet ourselves laughing, but now, after my humiliation at the hands of Red Class, the incident seemed to take on new meaning. How had I thought that something that had happened to Jenny had actually happened to me? Was it because she had told me that story so many times that I had somehow put myself in her shoes? What if being encircled by frightened, puffing runner beans was not a memory at all? And if my memories had never really happened, then what *had* happened? Memory, it suddenly seemed, was subject to distortions and could not be trusted.

"Well, *I* remember it happening," my mother said defiantly when I questioned her about it. "Those blasted things were fit as fiddles and just kept going and going. I distinctly remember that by the time I caught up with them, I was too exhausted to cook them, and we ended up having egg on toast for dinner instead."

"But beans *don't* run," I persisted.

"Huh! You try telling them that!"

Suffice it to say that by the age of eight I was confused. Could I trust my mother? Could I trust my own mind? Only one thing was for sure: never again would I humiliate myself by talking about things that might not be true. Even if there was only the *tiniest* chance that something might not be true, I would hesitate before saying it. I would weigh everything up first, use every bit of knowledge and reasoning I had, and then try to come to a sensible conclusion. Only when I was one hundred percent sure that my views were logical and right would I give voice to them. That way nobody could ever call me a liar again, and nobody would be able to laugh at me.

In a fit of overzealousness, I threw out my dolls and packed away my storybooks in an attempt to rid my life of any make-believe that might contaminate my mind. I pinched myself each time I daydreamed as a form of punishment. I listened to my mother's stories with nothing more than polite detachment and sat alone on the wall at break times, watching my classmates with disdain as they ran around pretending to be ponies and princesses. They didn't understand the danger they were in, teetering on the edge of fantasy worlds that threatened to pull them in and drag them under, sapping them of any logic and making them laughingstocks.

But I knew. I had seen the dark gulf between fiction and reality, and there was no way I was going to be dragged down into the abyss.

Without knowing it, I had already decided to become a scientist.

chapter two

One dark and magical evening, my parents' eyes first met over a tray of croissants somewhere in the middle of Cambridge city center.

"I had been at the library," my mother always tells me, "studying for my English O-level exam. I should have been home hours ago, but I had completely lost myself in *Wuthering Heights*. The romance, the anguish, the tragedy, the undying love! Well, the next thing I knew an agitated librarian was turning out the lights and ordering me to leave, fretting that she was going to miss the start of *University Challenge*. When I emerged from the library, darkness had already fallen, and knowing that I would be in for a scolding when I arrived home, I jumped on my bicycle and started to pedal as fast as I could go.

"As I was cycling alongside the river, I noticed how brightly the moon hung in the sky that evening, and how the stars seemed to be winking at me one by one. I slowed down, mesmerized by the moonlight glistening on the water, illuminating the white swans that bobbed on the surface, their heads nestled beneath their folded wings. The air was still and the night was silent, the only sound the gentle grind of the gravel beneath my tires. My skin tingled with anticipation. It felt like an evening for wizardry and wonders, ripe for magic and enchantment. I should have carried on along the river path toward home, but the bulrushes seemed to whisper to me, and the branches of a horse chestnut tree beckoned me toward the bridge. An owl hooted a warning, telling me to hurry home, but on the other side of the river a toad croaked an invitation to cross the bridge, and a single star flashed in the sky like a beacon luring me over to the other side.

"Just then the most scrumptious scent overwhelmed my senses, making me so woozy that I nearly fell off my bicycle. Hot butterscotch, toasted almonds, spiced teacake, dark rum...I tried to keep my handlebars straight, but my bicycle was like a thing possessed and started veering off toward the bridge. I tried to fight it, but the delicious scent was intoxicating, and before long I let go of my handlebars altogether, closed my eyes, and found myself freewheeling over the bridge and toward the city center, where I came to a stop in front of a huge white tent in the market square.

"I dropped my bicycle on the ground and watched the steady trickle of people emerging from side streets, making their way, trancelike, toward the tent before disappearing inside. As if in a dream, I allowed the sweet, sugary scent to engulf me as I was carried across the market square and swept in through an opening in the canvas.

"Inside was a cacophony of lights, sounds, and the most incredible smells. At one stall, a man turned the handle of a gleaming silver machine while a large woman with ruddy cheeks pulled out a long string of herby sausages. At another stall, a man flipped golden crêpes right up to the roof of the tent before watching them sail down through the air and land perfectly in the base of his frying pan. His friend flambéed the crêpes so that great orange flames shot upward with a loud whoosh and everybody gasped and clapped. At yet another stall, two women threw a large ball of glutinous dough between them, stretching it out, swinging it like a jump rope, and then plaiting it into a loaf before throwing it into the fiery pit of a clay oven.

"As I pushed my way through the crowd, I noticed the banner that hung from one side of tent to the other: *Célébration de la Gastronomie Française!* I had no idea what it meant, but I really didn't care. I was still following my nose, heading toward the source of the delicious sweet scent that had drawn me inside.

"A squawking chicken brushed my head as it flew past me, closely followed by a fat man with a meat cleaver shouting something in French. A woman with a basket of baguettes bumped into me, muttering, '*Pardon, pardon*,' as she jostled through the crowd. Someone tried to press a piece of cheese into my mouth and shouted, 'Taste, *Mademoiselle*, taste!' But I didn't notice any of it. Through a parting in the crowd I had spied the source of that intoxicating scent.

"He was handsome, with dark hair and fire in his eyes. They were reflecting the flambéed crêpes, of course, but to me it seemed they were a window to the burning passion in his soul—a passion for the dough that he was kneading with such gentle grace and dexterity, his hands moving one over the other like rolling waves. For a moment I watched him, breathing in his scent, tasting him on my lips, savoring his aroma. I had never known that anyone could be so delicious. I watched, enthralled, as he twisted the dough into perfect croissants and laid them, ever so lovingly, onto an enormous baking tray.

"He looked up and met my gaze, as if he had expected me to be there all along. He smiled, and I found myself standing right in front of him, although I think I must have hovered over to his stall, because I could no longer feel the ground beneath my feet, and I'm sure my legs were too weak to carry me there. We gazed into each other's eyes for what felt like an eternity, unable to look away. Neither of us spoke, and for a while it seemed that words were unnecessary. Then, holding my breath, I watched as his lips parted, and he whispered the most delicious sound I had ever heard:

"'Mademoiselle, où est l'hôtel de ville?'"

Où est l'hôtel de ville.

For years I thought it was the most romantic phrase in the universe. The way my mother said it, the words rolling into one another, made it sound so sensuous. She said it was a declaration of love, and I believed her. I imagined that on my wedding day Johnny Miller would gently lift my veil, lean in to kiss me, and whisper: "Meg, my darling, *où est l'hôtel de ville.*" I never considered how I would reply, seeing as I didn't even realize it was a question.

"Tell us again how your parents met," Sophie Potter and Tracey Pratt used to beg excitedly, and I would describe for them the scene of the meeting, just as my mother had always described it to me, while they hung on my every word, clutching their hearts.

"*Où est l'hôtel de ville,*" they would repeat dreamily at the end of the story. "That's *sooo* romantic."

To truly embrace my cultural heritage, I occasionally wore a red beret to school.

"Paris is the most beautiful and romantic city in the world," I would tell my friends, "and as soon as I'm old enough I'm going to go and study there. I'll probably find my father's family and live with them. They will be so excited to meet me!"

I had a map of France pinned over my bed, with a little flag stuck right in the heart of Paris. I would imagine my father—young, strong, and handsome—in a stripy T-shirt and a beret like mine, cycling through the Parisian streets on his way to work at the most prestigious bakery in France. I didn't like to think too much about the tragic pastry-mixing incident, but I had a sense that his death had been heroic. He had died in his quest to create the finest cherry tart and name it after my mother, and that was as heroic a death as I could imagine. Somewhere I had heard a phrase about the brave dying young, and I imagined whoever said it must have been talking about my father.

My mother said that my father was always there with me in spirit, and that was comforting, but also scary.

"Will he be there when I'm on the toilet?" I asked her.

"No, darling, he won't be with you then."

"Will he be there when I'm taking a bath?"

"No, darling, not if you don't want him there."

"Will he be there when I'm doing something naughty?"

"Yes, he certainly will. So you'd better behave yourself."

I would often talk to him. Seeing as he was always there (apart from when I was on the toilet or in the bath) it seemed rude not to, and I would imagine I could hear him talking back to me. No, he didn't think Tracey Pratt was as pretty as me, or that Mrs. Partridge was right for making me sit next to smelly Scott Warner in assembly. And, yes, he did agree that my mother should let me stay up until past nine o'clock. He always agreed with everything I said, which was very endearing and made me love him all the more.

And I did love him, I think, in the idolizing, dreamy way that makes it possible to love someone you have never met. He might not have been there in person, but he was part of me, and I was part of him, and somehow that gave me strength and a sense of belonging. I would look in the mirror and see a small nose and pointy chin that—because they definitely hadn't come from my mother—must have come from him. He was there in my beret, my map of France, my love of cheese triangles, and he was there in the mirror's reflection, looking right back at me.

One day, inevitably, the mirror broke. Smashed into a thousand tiny, painful splinters. If I hadn't loved him so much, perhaps it wouldn't have been so hard, but losing the respect of my peers was nothing compared to losing my father.

It happened in my first week at Millbrook Comprehensive, in Madame Emily's French class. I had never had the opportunity to learn French before, but I knew I was bound to be a natural. After all, it was in my blood.

"Right, class, who already knows some French?"

My hand shot up. I did! I did!

Finally away from the rest of Red Class, I had the opportunity to make new friends, to impress people with my knowledge instead of spouting ridiculous stories. It had been some time since I had turned my back on fiction in the pursuit of all that was good and true, but my reputation had followed me around Elmbrook Primary like a bad smell until the very end. I heard the words they whispered about me: *liar, fibber, tittle-tattle.* Now I had the chance to start again. After an agonizing wait while Christopher Newbuck stumbled through the French for "my grandmother likes Ping-Pong" and Louise Warbuck got in a muddle and told us that her father was a coconut, I finally had my chance to shine.

"*Où est l'hôtel de ville*," I said in the passionate, dreamy way that my mother had taught me.

"That's very good, Meg," Madame Emily praised, clearly impressed. "And can you tell the class what it means?"

"From what I understand," I said with such pretentiousness that I cringe to recall it, "it's not a phrase that can easily be translated. But it's a traditional French declaration of love. And it was the first thing that my father—who was an actual French person—said to my mother when they first met."

Madame Emily gave a sharp shriek of laughter.

"Well, I'm not sure where you got that from! It would be quite an odd way to express your love. It means 'where is the town hall'!"

All around me I heard my new classmates starting to giggle. I felt as if the classroom was closing in on me. *Where is the town hall?* She must be confused. It couldn't mean that. I watched Madame Emily chuckling away and glanced at the still-unfamiliar faces around me contorted with laughter. Seeing that I didn't find it funny in the slightest but was instead on the verge of tears, Madame Emily suddenly stopped laughing and asked for quiet.

"'Where is the town hall' is an extremely important phrase, though," she said as a way of compensation. "And it's probably going to be the first thing you will want to ask someone when you arrive in France, which is why it's the first phrase we learn. If you turn to page one of your textbook, everyone, you'll see that phrase at the top of the page..."

And there it was, right at the top of page one in *French Made Fun!* In the cartoon, the Englishman with the bowler hat and umbrella was disembarking from the ferry and asking a random Frenchman—identifiable by the string of onions around his neck—*Où est l'hôtel de ville?* It wasn't romantic in the slightest, and in the context of my parents' first meeting, it made absolutely no sense whatsoever. It didn't take me any time at all to realize that it was clearly the only French phrase that my mother remembered from her own school days and that she had taken advantage of my ignorance to deceive me.

"The individual words aren't important, darling," my mother said dismissively when I burst into the flat later that day and threw my new school bag on the kitchen floor in anger. "It's the sentiment that matters. Think of it like a Victoria sponge cake. You wouldn't eat any of the ingredients on their own, but mixed together with passion and love they create something—"

"What are you talking about?" I snapped at her. "This has nothing to do with a Victoria sponge cake! Why is everything always about cakes with you? Was my father even French? Was he even a chef?"

I remember my mother standing there in our tiny, cramped kitchen with plaster peeling off the ceiling and condensation misting the windows. She had her hands placed on her hips like she always did when she was angry.

"I don't know what has got into you, young lady. Just because you're at big school now doesn't mean you have to be so quarrelsome. I will not have you insulting your poor dead father's name by asking such silly questions. Your father would have loved you very much, you know. He was a talented and courageous man who met an untimely death in his quest for perfection in the pastry industry, and you constantly question—"

"All right, all right!" I shouted. "Just…just don't talk to me about him again!"

I ran to my room and slammed the door shut, throwing myself onto my bed and bursting into tears. I didn't want to insult my dead father's name. Is that what I was doing? I just wanted to know the truth, that was all. Not only was I angry and confused, but now I was also overwhelmed with guilt. I was a terrible daughter. If my father was always with me, then he must have heard me questioning his very existence. How hurt he must have felt! But my mother had clearly lied to me about their meeting, so how was I to know what other lies she had told me about him? Thinking about it logically, which was the way I tried to think about everything, was it likely that my mother had freewheeled on her bicycle into Cambridge city center one magical evening and that the scent of my father had carried on the breeze and that…oh, of course it wasn't! Nothing about it seemed likely. I couldn't believe that having so scrupulously monitored my habits, my words, and my very thoughts over the last couple of years, I had let the fantasy of my own father slip through the net. I had failed in my mission to rid myself of all non-sensible thoughts, and look what had happened. I had made myself a laughingstock once more. With tears streaming down my face, I ripped the map of France from my wall and tore it to pieces. It was all a lie. There was no one watching over me, and there never had been. The features I saw reflected in the mirror could have been anybody's. But even as I stamped on the shredded map and pinched myself for having been so deluded, I sobbed for the loss of my father like I had never sobbed before.

"Why don't you ever bring your friends home for tea?" my mother would ask me. "I'd love to meet them. I could make some lovely muffins. Or some little cupcakes."

"I don't have any friends," I would tell her grumpily, which wasn't entirely true. I had Gary, Peter, and Sarah from the lunchtime science club, but they were all united in their love of *Star Trek* and insisted in communicating in some made-up language they called Cling-On, which not only made me feel excluded, but also resulted in a lot of misunderstandings, making our lunchtime science experiments extremely hazardous. When they did speak English, we often argued about the dangers of science fiction, but three against one made it a very uneven debate. I couldn't understand how such sensible, intelligent, and rational people could allow themselves to be corrupted by a fantasy world full of flying saucers and alien beings. The very fact that they insisted on speaking in a made-up language and appeared to worship someone called Dr. Spot was evidence of their corruption. Their fictional world was destroying them day by day, like a maggot eating away at their brains.

But the truth is that even if I had wanted to invite them home, I never would have dared. I had already made the mistake of inviting Lucy Higgins home a few weeks into the new school year, and my mother had completely confused her.

"Those wretched hot dogs have been barking in the cupboard all afternoon," she told Lucy, placing our tea down on the table in front of us. "I expect they wanted to go out for a walk, but I've tried walking a hot dog before and it's very difficult to get a collar that fits. Usually they slip off the lead and jump into a muddy puddle to cool themselves down. I'm sure your mother must have the same problem."

When Lucy asked me if my mother was "mental," I decided it was probably better not to invite people home again.

Embarrassment, anger, and guilt are the main feelings I recall from adolescence, but perhaps that isn't so unusual. Parents' evenings, particularly, were anticipated with dread. I still remember the time my mother told Mr. Lees—the trainee biology teacher and object of my affection—that eating chili con carne during her pregnancy was certainly the cause of my occasional temper tantrums.

"I didn't realize I was pregnant at that point, obviously," my mother said quickly, as if she thought Mr. Lees would be outraged that she had acted so irresponsibly. Mr. Lees, though, clearly did not understand the implication of eating Mexican food while carrying a baby and just looked rather baffled.

"Chilies lead to a fiery temperament," my mother clarified in quite a patronizing tone, as if a biology teacher really should know this. "Once I realized I was pregnant, I tried to balance out the heat of the chilies by eating several bowls of guacamole, but obviously it was too late. The damage had already been done."

She looked at me sitting slumped on the chair next to her and shook her head sadly, as if I had some sort of defect. Poor Mr. Lees looked at me for guidance, but I just blushed a deep shade of crimson and stared at my feet. I felt acutely embarrassed, but not surprised. This was bound to happen. At least it helped explain why, whenever I had a fit of teenage angst, my mother would tell me to eat a tub of yogurt. She obviously thought the chili I was subjected to in the womb was repeating on me.

I learned to live with the embarrassment. I even learned to live with the anger. But what I have always struggled to live with is the guilt.

"I am just so proud of you, Meggy!" my mother exclaimed as we walked home from that very same parents' evening. "You're doing so well. You're going to do so many exciting things with your life. I just want the best for you, sweetheart. You know that, don't you? And I'll be here for you all the way. I've always believed in you."

I had already tuned out by the time she said the word "proud," overcome by feelings of guilt and self-reprobation. Why did I have to get so angry with her? Why did I have to care what other people thought? She loved me so much. Listening to her babbling excitedly about all my achievements, so enthusiastic about everything I did, I thought about Louise Warbuck's mother, who never even washed her PE clothes, and Gary's mother, who was always half drunk. I felt angry and ashamed at myself for being so ungrateful. The truth was I couldn't have asked for a more loving and supportive mother. I just wished she could be a little more...well...normal.

My idea of heaven was a place where nobody knew me. Where nobody knew about all the silly things I had said and done, the stories I had accidentally rattled off, the ways I had humiliated myself. Heaven was being surrounded by people who saw the world in black and white, who spoke the truth, who stated the facts. People who didn't confuse me, or leave me struggling with conflicting thoughts and feelings. It was a place where things were simple and straightforward.

Heaven was the Department of Science at Leeds University.

I fit in perfectly from the day I arrived. Finally I was surrounded by people whose aims were the same as mine: to understand, to make sense of, to categorize, to fact-find, and to get to the bottom of things. I sought out the companionship of the most serious and dedicated students so that even socially our conversation rarely deviated from our shared scientific interests. It meant that I rarely had the chance to slip up by talking about how I had once blown up like a beach ball after drinking too much fizzy lemonade, or how my mother once bought a bag of onions that were so strong they even made themselves cry and ended up flooding our kitchen floor. My interest in scientific study was a bonus rather than just another thing that made me an easy target. It was making me friends and earning me respect. And in my final year at Leeds, life got even better.

"Meg May, it's a pleasure to meet you. My name's—"

"Mark Daly. I know."

Our eyes met over a Bunsen burner. Perhaps, had it been on, I would have seen fire in Mark's eyes, just like my mother saw fire in my father's eyes the first time they met. Unfortunately, the gas supply had been cut off while they prepared to close the lab due to a bat infestation. Still, the very fact that Mark Daly knew my name was enough to set me trembling. He was a doctoral student and lecturer, extremely well regarded in the faculty, especially by the female students. And he was flawlessly handsome.

"I was wondering whether I could ask you..."

He paused dramatically and leaned confidently on the workbench, looking me straight in the eye.

"Yes?" I prompted, my heart fluttering with anticipation.

"I was wondering if I could ask you, could I borrow those safety goggles?"

Could I borrow those safety goggles? Now that was a phrase to start a relationship on. Safety goggles. Goggles for practical usage in keeping one safe while unlocking the truths of the universe. Had I believed in romance, that surely would have been the closest thing to it.

The evening of the awards ceremony should have been one of the best of my life, but five months later I still want to weep with guilt each time I remember it.

"So, Miss May, where do your future interests lie?"

"Yes, you must tell us so that we can battle it out to be your supervisor! I assume you will be pursuing a PhD?"

Professor Philip Winter and Dr. Larry Coldman both clutched their glasses of wine and waited for me to answer.

"Um, I hadn't really thought—"

"Of course she will," said Mark, sweeping in at just the right moment with his incredible capacity for certainty and decisiveness. He looked dashing in his suit and tie, expertly balancing a paper plate of finger food on one hand. Thank goodness for Mark. I didn't want Professor Winter, the head of the department, to think I wasn't a serious scientist. I told myself to get a grip and stop feeling so stupidly nervous. I had every right to be here. I was a prizewinner, after all, and this evening was for a handful of students like me, students who had gone the extra mile, put in the overtime, achieved the highest grades. But as I looked around at all the doctors and professors mingling so confidently in their smart suits and dresses, I couldn't help but wonder how many of them had grown up in a tiny council flat in North London or how many weren't sure who their fathers were or how many had been caught in a frying pan.

Dr. Coldman was speaking to Mark about a new state-of-the-art scanner he had ordered for one of the laboratories, but I wasn't really listening. Instead, I was looking over his shoulder to where my mother was hovering awkwardly by one of the tables of food, looking nervous and out of her depth. It touched me deeply that she was suffering so much on my behalf. She would have nothing to talk about with any of these people. She hadn't even passed her O-levels. But she had insisted on coming to see me awarded my "gift token," as she called it (which was actually a check for five hundred pounds), and was clearly determined to stick it out until the end. I was about to excuse myself to go and rescue her when Dr. Alison McFee honed in on the buffet and struck up a conversation with my mother while piling her plate with mushroom vol-au-vents.

At first I thought everything might be fine. I could hear giggling, and they seemed to have struck up quite a conversation. But I knew something wasn't right when my mother pointed to one of the sausage rolls on Dr. McFee's plate and started doing a pig impression. What on earth was she doing? What on earth was she saying? I tried to rack my brain for stories my mother liked to tell about sausage rolls. Was it something to do with pigs rolling in muddy puddles? No, no, that was hot dogs. Was it something to do with a sausage roll oinking at her once? No, that didn't sound right either. But whatever she was saying, Dr. McFee wasn't giggling anymore. Instead, she was touching her hair nervously and looking around for an escape while my mother babbled on and on, clearly enjoying herself for the first time all evening, waving her arms around as she told some long-winded story about Dr. McFee's choice of savory snack, complete with pig-like sound effects.

Out of the corner of my eye I noticed that Mark, too, kept glancing over at my mother, and he appeared to be getting edgy on my behalf. He had only met my mother once, but it was obviously enough for him to foresee a potentially embarrassing incident occurring. He had suggested not telling her about the prize-giving at all, or telling her that parents weren't invited, or even that I just didn't want her there.

"You need to be careful, Meg," he had told me. "You don't want to give the wrong impression. Not now. These people could hold the key to your future. They're the ones who will support research applications, help get papers published, open doors for you. I can understand why you might not want your mother there—"

"But of course I want her there," I had told him, feeling slightly insulted. "I would never consider not inviting her."

And I did want her there. Desperately. Because for as far back as I could remember, everything she had ever done she had done for me, and I knew that without her support I would never have even made it to university. She had worked tirelessly all her life so I wouldn't go without. She had praised me for every achievement and supported me in every choice. Even though she couldn't understand what I was studying, she thought it was wonderful that I was so interested in it. So there was no way I wouldn't allow her to be here to share my special moment.

But as I watched her excitedly enacting some fantastical story, completely oblivious to the fact that Dr. McFee was slowly backing away, a sense of panic rose in my chest. I recalled the sense of exclusion I had always felt at school, the whispers I overheard, the rumors that followed me around. I had worked so hard to fit in here. I was respected. I was liked. I was finally being taken seriously.

"So, has any of your family come tonight, Meg?" asked Professor Winter, looking around.

I felt panic surging in my chest. I didn't want to lose what I had built for myself. I didn't want to be a laughingstock. Not again.

I felt Mark's hand squeezing my shoulder, willing me to make the right choice.

"No," I said quietly, swallowing down my guilt.

I felt sick with shame.

Mark's grip loosened, and he stroked my shoulder gently. I had done the right thing.

"None of my family could make it."

chapter three

I can't hide my shock when my mother meets me at the train station. She's so thin and pale, a shadow of her former flame-haired, curvaceous self. She is wearing a sweater, even though it's the height of summer, and when we hug I can feel the sharp angles of her elbows and shoulder blades through the material. It makes me want to cry. Did she look anywhere near this bad last time I saw her? Could she have changed so much so quickly?

"Meggy!" she squeals, ignoring the look of horror on my face. She doesn't want me to say anything about her appearance, doesn't even want me to acknowledge that she's wasting away. But I'm not like my mother. I'm not a fantasist.

"My God, you look dreadful!"

She forces a little laugh and brushes some flour off her sleeve.

"Oh, I know! I was baking a treacle tart, and I suddenly realized what the time was."

"Mother, you should have stayed at home!" I snap, annoyed with her. "I could have taken the bus."

"Don't be silly, darling. Why would you do that?"

"Because you look like you should be in bed!"

"I've made lasagna for dinner. Is that all right?" she says, walking off toward the parking lot.

I stay rooted to the spot, waiting for her to stop and turn around, waiting for her to acknowledge the unsaid, but when she doesn't, I pick up my bag and follow her.

The little redbrick cottage where my mother was raised has a white front door and pink roses climbing around the windows. It is also where I spent the first six months of my life, growing up in the warm bosom of my extended family, being cared for by my teenage mother, my grandmother, and my grandfather. They were happy times, apparently, with everybody doting on me. Of course I have no recollection of any of this, but the place felt oddly familiar when I helped my mother move in here three years ago.

"Of course it feels familiar," said my mother as we unpacked the van. "You were born here."

"Yes, but I don't remember that, do I?"

"It doesn't matter whether you remember it or not. It's still part of who you are. As far as your psyche is concerned, this is where you belong. You're like a salmon that's instinctively found its way home."

"In that case I should be due to drop dead any minute now."

"I don't think *you'll* be the one doing that, dear," she muttered, struggling to unload a large potted plant.

It was the one time I heard her make reference to her illness. I wanted to stop her, grab her by the shoulders, tell her it was okay to talk about it, that I wanted to talk about it. But I was so taken aback that I just stood there hugging a deep-fat fryer while she staggered up the path, swamped under the leaves of an enormous yucca plant.

Inside, the cottage is tight and low ceilinged but extremely cozy. There's an open fireplace in the lounge, original wooden beams, and an Aga oven in the kitchen, which my mother adores. The long garden is overflowing with leafy green vegetables, fruit trees, and beanpoles. The patio is crammed with pots spilling over with berries and herbs. And past all this chaos, near the end of the garden, I can see the little orchard of apple trees with their fruit-laden boughs drooping to the ground. It's like a jungle out there.

"It's looking a little overgrown," my mother admits as we stand on the patio in the early evening sunshine, in between a ceramic pot growing arugula leaves and an old tin bucket that's spouting green peppers. "I don't know why, but I just don't seem to be able to keep up with it lately. I'll get back out there tomorrow and give it a damn good tidy up."

I'm glad my mother is home where she belongs. It's where she deserves to be. The bland North London flat we used to live in never reflected anything about her. It seemed to strain against my mother's zest for life, as if struggling to contain within its walls the energy that she radiated. It was plain and characterless, with small, square rooms and no discernible features.

Here in this cottage there are secret hiding places, there is history, there are quirks and peculiarities. Every room has a story attached to it, a personality of its own. There is fresh air, light, nature, and room to breathe. And, above all, there are roots to my mother's past, roots I hope will ground her, steadying her in reality as she faces the hard times ahead. I know almost nothing of her life before she had me, so skilled is she at avoiding any mention of it, but I know it was here where she grew up with her parents and a cat named fluffy, here where she listened to records and danced in her bedroom, and here where my father came to call for her when they were dating. All of these things I know happened here, and my hope is that maybe as she nears the end of her life, these memories—these *real* memories—will come back to her, shoving aside the fantasy world that she has created. I want my mother to be able to look back on her life with clarity so she may remember her time on this earth—good parts and bad parts—exactly as it was. No lies, no confusion, just pure lucidity and perfect understanding. What could bring her a greater sense of peace than that?

The cottage is filled with a sweet, sugary scent. My mother has been making cupcakes, and twelve of them are lined up on the kitchen work surface, each decorated with pink icing and colored sprinkles.

"This one's for you," she says, pointing at a cake that's twice as big as the others, "and I'm going to top it with all of your favorite decorations."

I look at the bowl of rainbow-colored jelly sweets sitting near the cakes and secretly tally up the number of calories that will be contained in this well-meant gift, not to mention the amount of additives and colorings. I never eat sweets these days, not after researching what's in them.

"Fantastic," I say with a smile. "And the other eleven are for...?"

"I'm taking those to the local cancer hospice." She shakes her head mournfully. "Those poor people," she sighs, as if she's not one of them.

I always find it strange walking into "my" room. It's like revisiting my childhood in a feverish dream where everything is distorted and the wrong way around. All my childhood things are here—my pink flowery duvet, my framed photo of two little bunnies eating dandelions, my music box, my little plastic handheld mirror—but this was never actually my bedroom. It wasn't here in this cottage where I bounced on the bed or played with my toys or read my books; and yet here is the bed I bounced on, the toys I played with, and the books I read. My mother keeps it like a shrine to me, albeit a shrine that has been relocated from Tottenham to Cambridge. My school certificates and prizes are lined up on one shelf; my first science set sits on another. She has even kept all my old exercise books in a box at the bottom of the wardrobe. Feeling nostalgic, I delve in and pull one out—English Literature, Year 9, Mr. Hamble—and flick through the pages, recalling the pains I took to write in such small, neat letters. Everything is beautifully presented, with the dates in the margin and the headings underlined, but the pages are half blank.

I read the assignment title at the top of one page: "Write your own myth of 500 words explaining how penguins lost the ability to fly."

In immaculate handwriting I have written: "I object to this assignment on the basis that it is fundamentally flawed. The Natural History Museum has told me there is no evolutionary evidence that penguins could ever fly."

Mr. Hamble has written "See Me" in big red letters at the bottom of the page.

After my disgrace in Red Class, I hated English, all those silly stories and poems that were full of fictional characters and unrealistic scenarios. I greatly objected to being forced to read fiction and told Mr. Hamble it would certainly rot my mind.

"It's completely unrealistic," I told him, "that Romeo would think Juliet was dead and then kill himself, and then that she would wake up, see Romeo was dead, and kill herself. What are the chances of that actually happening? I don't think that has ever happened to anyone. Ever."

At parents' evening Mr. Hamble told my mother that I was "a strange girl with an extremely underdeveloped imagination" and that I might benefit from some extra exposure to stories of a fictional nature. Huh! If only he knew!

On the shelf next to my science kit, my old reading books are lined up neatly and hemmed in by two wooden bookends made to resemble caterpillars. I scan through the titles: *Who Am I?—A Journey Around the Human Body*; *101 Interesting Facts You Probably Didn't Know;*

A Beginner's Guide to Keeping Hamsters; *Let's Explore the Solar System*; *A Frog with Your Tea?—Strange Customs from Around the World*; *The Tale of the Jiggly-Wop*. I pull this last one out and study the aged cover, wondering what a work of fiction is doing in there with all my educational books. This had been my mother's favorite book when she was a little girl, and I recall her reading it to me when I was about six years old. It was my favorite, too, back then, but I could have sworn I had thrown it out along with every other storybook I owned. It was the silliest of fairy tales, full of talking animals and other ludicrous products of the imagination that could only serve to pollute my mind and lead me astray. I thought I had dumped it in the bin along with *Alice in Wonderland*, *The Hobbit*, and every other piece of nonsense my mother had subjected me to in a bid to rot my common sense, but obviously it managed to escape my mission of destruction. I had listened to this story so many times that I can still remember the words.

"In a land far away, there lived a creature that didn't know quite what it was..."

I run my fingers over the front cover, tracing the outlines of the strange Jiggly-Wop beast: his elephant ears, his feathery cheeks, his flowing mane, his zebra-striped body, his webbed feet. For a moment, a smile plays at the edges of my mouth before I pull myself together and chuck the book into the wastepaper basket.

"No wonder children are so stupid," I mutter.

Over a dinner of lasagna with fresh salad straight from the garden, my mother twitters on about her vegetable patch and Rick Stein and sea bass and turnips, anything to prevent me from questioning her about her illness.

"Mother," I finally interrupt, "how are you feeling?"

"Wonderful," she says cheerfully, quickly standing up and clearing the table.

"Really?"

"Of course."

"You've lost a bit of weight, haven't you?" I suggest in what must be the understatement of the year.

"You know, I do seem to have lost a few pounds," she says, tugging at the gaping waistband of her long, purple skirt. "I've had to tighten the elastic on this a couple of times now." She bunches the waistband together in her fist, shakes her head, and looks genuinely baffled. "I did need to lose a few pounds, though," she says, more cheerfully. "Too many puddings. You know what I'm like."

"Have you seen Dr. Bloomberg lately?"

"Yes, just last week," she says, plonking the dishes into a sink full of lemon-scented suds.

"And?"

"And what?"

"And what did he say?"

"Oh, nothing much. You know how he waffles on. Now, I made treacle tart and chocolate mousse for dessert. Which would you like?"

I shake my head slowly, incredulously, but she refuses to look at me. "Whatever," I mumble.

The next morning I awake to the smell of sausages and bacon. For one dreamy moment, tucked up under my old pink sheets in the narrow bed with the sinking mattress, I imagine I'm a little girl again in our North London flat. I can feel the warmth of the morning sunshine stealing through the gap in the curtains, and I imagine I am running across Hampstead Heath, my mother holding her arms wide open, ready to catch me.

But suddenly I feel the hand at my throat, fingers rough and calloused against my soft skin, squeezing, constricting, pressing against my windpipe. I can't breathe. I can't breathe! And someone is shouting at me, words I can't decipher.

I sit up with a start, gasping for air, clutching at my throat ready to pry away the hands that are choking me. It's always the same, this horrible dream. I can't see anyone. There's no face, just this voice—deep and angry—and this feeling of suffocation. And the smell. The sweet, stomach-churning smell of raw meat. I almost told Mark about it the other day, such was my desire to share it with someone, but no doubt he would have thought me strange and perhaps even a little unstable. I flop back against my pillow, sweat cooling against my back and my heart pounding in my chest.

"Morning! I'm making pancakes. There's fresh coffee on the table, and the sausages and bacon are nearly ready. Now, how about eggs? Fried? Scrambled? Do you want some toast? It's fresh bread; I made it this morning."

"Mother, I can't eat all this," I say, slumping down at the kitchen table in my pajamas.

"I want to feed you up while you're here," she says, pouring batter mixture into a sizzling frying pan. "You're looking rather thin."

I watch her straining to lift the frying pan with both hands. How much must she weigh right now? A hundred pounds? Not even?

As she tips the frying pan from side to side, spreading the batter around the pan, I see her body sway slightly. She places the pan back on the stove with a heavy clatter and stands motionless, gripping the handle as if for support.

"Mother? Are you all right?"

No reply.

"Mother?"

"I'm fine," she says breathlessly.

"Let me do that." I stand up and approach the stove.

"Absolutely not!"

She turns and glares at me as if I've attempted to assault her. By suggesting she may not be capable of cooking, I have threatened her very way of life. She forces a little smile and takes a deep breath.

"Do you want syrup or sugar with your pancakes?" she asks sweetly.

Despite my protestations, my mother insists on getting out into the garden after breakfast and beginning her tidying up. For the first twenty minutes I am surprised and encouraged to find that she appears to have more energy than I do. She is a whirlwind of pruning, snipping, and trimming. As I work alongside her, stumbling through the tangle of roots and leaves, gathering the cuttings into a black plastic sack, I am foolish enough to allow a tiny ember of hope to catch alight inside me. Maybe her earlier weakness was just a momentary lapse. Surely she can't be that sick when she seems so full of beans, can she? She chatters away while she works and hums tunes from the Beach Boys, David Bowie, and Abba.

She picks various herbs and shoves them under my nose for me to sniff.

"Isn't that just delicious!" she says, beaming.

The morning is warm and bright, and the rich, earthy smell of the soil mingles with the scent of rosemary, mint, and lemon balm. The birds twitter in the trees, and for a while it's easy to forget that things aren't perfect, that this isn't just another summer like all the others we've had before. That this may, in fact, be one of our last. But despite her zealous start, it's not long before my mother starts to wane. She drags her feet and rubs her back, gazing forlornly at the overgrown garden as if overwhelmed by the prospect of having to contend with so much work. The light fades from her eyes, gradually replaced by fatigue.

"Mother," I say tentatively, pulling weeds out from between a row of lettuce plants and deliberately avoiding her eye. "I was wondering, do you think perhaps it might be a good idea to get someone in to help you with the garden? Just for a couple of hours a week?" I hold my breath, waiting for her to snap at me like she did this morning.

"Why would I want to do that?" she asks, tying an unruly bunch of runner beans onto a pole with a piece of frayed green string.

Immediately I go from being worried about upsetting her to wanting to slap her face. Her denial is starting to grate. I try to breathe deeply, but I feel like I am nearing the end of my tether.

"Because," I say as calmly as possible, "it's an awful lot for one person to manage."

"But I'm perfectly capable—"

"I know you're perfectly capable," I say, clenching my teeth, "but this garden is really a lot to cope with on your own."

"Meg May," she says, placing her hands on her bony hips and looking at me sternly. "I have been coping on my own since the day you were born. I have cooked, cleaned, scrubbed, tidied, washed, and ironed. I have sewn your dresses, done the shopping, and paid all the bills. I have fixed ovens, plastered ceilings, laid flooring, and put up shelves. Do not tell me that I cannot cope on my own. I've managed to grow vegetables in the past with not a minute left in the day and you clinging to the hem of my skirt, so if I could manage then, I can certainly manage now when I've got all the time in the world and no one else to worry about."

I know not to push this matter any further. I am defeated. There is no making her see sense. Getting her to face reality is, and always has been, like swimming against the tide. No matter how hard you struggle to reach dry land, a huge wave always comes and washes you back to where you started.

This is what Mark doesn't understand. It's all very well asking me why I put up with my mother's ridiculous delusions, but he doesn't know how exhausting it is trying to reach the distant shores of reality. Somehow it is just easier to float alongside her in a sea of make-believe.

"Fine," I say, raising my hands in surrender, "it was just an idea. I'm going inside to make us some coffee."

Chastened, I throw my gardening gloves on the ground and follow the little brick path between the sprawling vegetable patches back toward the house. But before I reach the back door I stop, racking my brain to try to throw some light on my mother's words.

"When did you grow vegetables before?" I ask, turning around.

My mother shields her eyes against the sunlight and squints at me, a trowel dangling from her hand.

"What?"

"You said you managed to grow vegetables with me clinging to the hem of your skirt. When? We moved from here when I was six months old and went to live in our flat in Tottenham. We didn't even have a garden."

My mother stares at me like she can't understand what I'm saying, as if she's trying to process the words into some sort of logical order.

"We had a window box," she says quickly.

"You grew vegetables in a window box?"

"Of course. Just small ones, obviously. Little carrots, a few radishes..."

"I don't remember."

"Well, of course you don't remember," she says tersely, "but that doesn't mean it never happened."

Rosy red patches have formed on her cheeks, and she is anxiously picking little pieces of dried mud off her trowel.

I shake my head, too hot and tired to think about whether there could be any truth in this, and turn to go inside, feeling that I have overstepped an invisible boundary once again.

As the coffee brews, I open the front door and pick up the single pint of milk that has been left on the step. There is something comforting about villages where milk bottles still appear during the night as if by magic. It's so much nicer than having to fight your way through the chaos of a twenty-four-hour Tesco, and I'm glad my mother is being spared that one stressful chore.

The little lane where she lives is quiet and peaceful. The cottages are small and modest, spaced just far enough apart to afford privacy without isolation. This is perfect for my mother, who, despite her talkative energy and eccentricity, is very much a loner. She is happy with her pots, pans, and vegetable garden, chattering away to the plants and animals or even to herself. She goes out only when it is essential, scurrying to and from the shops with her head down. I don't think she's ever spoken to any of the neighbors, insisting that all the people who lived in the lane when she was growing up have long died or moved away and that she can see no point in getting to know anybody new.

"Why would I want to talk to people?" she always says. "I already have everything I need."

Back in Tottenham, she used to connect loosely with people through food, leaving casserole dishes or baskets of muffins on our neighbors' doorsteps, but what they took for an invitation to friendship was no such thing; it was merely a desire to see others eat well. Comforting, nutritious soups were left for Mr. Ginsberg, who had lost his wife and also his teeth. Reheatable curries were left for the medical student from India who pored over his books late into the night. Healthy vegetable stews were left for Mrs. Wallace, who needed to lose weight so she could undergo a hip replacement but who had no idea about calorie control. Cakes and cookies were left for the painfully thin girl in the flat below, who my mother assumed had an eating disorder but who was in fact a heroin addict.

Yet when any of these people tried to engage my mother in conversation, she always had an excuse at the ready, some reason why she had to dash away and couldn't possibly stop. I think it made them feel awkward at first, not to mention confused. They weren't sure what my mother wanted if it wasn't their friendship, and their efforts at paying her back in some way were always rebuked. But after a while my mother's ways were simply accepted. Freshly washed dishes would appear on our doorstep every other day, sometimes with a thank-you note and sometimes without. If ever anybody ventured to knock on our door, my mother would open it with a warm smile on her face, chatter and laugh energetically for a few minutes, and then shut herself away again without inviting them in. I heard her being described as "lovely," "wonderful," "peculiar," and even "mad," but generally people learned to accept her dishes without a fuss and offer nothing in return. She wouldn't have it any other way.

As I take the milk into the house, I absentmindedly give the bottle a quick shake and examine the contents, just to make sure there are no fairies trapped inside, before I realize what I am doing and curse myself for being so stupid. When I was small, my mother and I often used to try to catch fairies in the park, tiptoeing softly around the bushes in the early morning, empty milk bottles at the ready. But logic soon taught me that this, too, was nothing but make-believe, and the next time my mother asked me to go hunting for fairies I snapped, "Stop being silly! I'm not a baby!" I thought she was doing it for my entertainment, but in fact she still went without me. And it's not just fairies she believes in; it's all things otherworldly. She's fascinated by spirits and crystals and leprechauns and aliens...anything that sparks her wild and unruly imagination.

Growing up, I always connected her bright, crumpled, flowing dress sense with the mystical nonsense she believed in, and in reaction I decided to only ever wear plain clothes in neutral colors so no one could ever accuse me of being anything less than perfectly sensible. Unlike my mother's flowing cotton skirts and brightly colored, shapeless tunics, I choose neat blouses, plain T-shirts, flat shoes, and neutral V-neck sweaters. I keep my mousy brown hair at shoulder length, wear only stud earrings, and use a hint of makeup only in emergencies. I buy my mother sensible clothes, too, clothes that I think are more suitable for her, and over the last couple of years she has actually started to wear them. Her wardrobe these days is a strange mixture of new-age hippy meets Marks and Spencer.

That evening, we eat fresh salad with Gorgonzola cheese, crispy bacon, and slices of avocado.

"One of Jamie's recipes," my mother explains. She's on first-name terms with all the celebrity chefs, so much so that for a while I thought Jamie, Delia, and Nigela must all be friends of hers she'd met since moving to Cambridge.

"Ainsley is such a card," she chuckles, soaking up some garlic-infused olive oil with her morsel of ciabatta. "He had me in stitches the other day; you'll never guess what he said..."

She loves all this modern food. "Balsamic reduction" is now one of her favorite phrases.

After eating, we lounge on the sofa, eat homemade toffee ice cream, and play a game of Scrabble, where my mother attempts to cheat by forming the word "bongle" ("It's a word! We found ourselves in a right old bongle. You can say that!"), and I pretend to be significantly less intelligent than I am ("I just don't think I can make a word from the letters C, T, and A.").

"Are you letting me win?" she asks when she's twenty-three points ahead.

"No."

"You are."

"I'm not."

"You are! I can tell by the look on your face, you cheeky monkey!" She dips her finger in the ice cream and puts a blob on the end of my nose.

"Hey!"

I wipe the ice cream off my nose and smear it on her cheek as she squeals and tries to push me away with the little strength she can muster after our hard day's work. She looks tired and has all evening, but she's trying, for my sake, to be lively.

"Meg May!" she says, laughing and wiping her face. "That's no way for a university student to behave! You're meant to be the sensible one. You won't be able to behave like that once you're a famous physicist."

"Mother!" I groan, covering my face with my hands. "I'm not going to be a physicist!"

She bites her lower lip sheepishly, knowing she's got it wrong again. According to my mother, over the past two years I have studied everything from physics to pharmacy, and just about every other subject ending in *–ology*.

"I do try, darling," she says, apologetically. "It's just that I don't understand about all these science-y things. I was never good at all that. I don't know where you get it from."

Neither do I, I nearly say, but I hold my tongue. The question of how a French pastry chef and an amateur cook produced a daughter who can barely make a piece of toast yet who can comprehend the complexities of bioscience has always been sidestepped.

"I study genetics, Mother," I tell her for the one-hundredth time. "It's not that hard to remember. DNA. The human genome. It's actually rather important."

She sighs, looking pale and worn out. "I know. I suppose I just can't get my head around it all."

"But if you'd give it a chance, you'd realize how fascinating it is. It's what makes us, us. It's all about knowing who we are."

She smiles proudly and pats me on the knee, then stands up and gathers the empty ice cream bowls.

"But you know who you are, darling," she says as she leaves the room.

I bury my head in one of the sofa cushions in despair.

"But I don't," I groan quietly. "Thanks to you, I don't have a clue who I am."

chapter four

Being born prematurely wasn't the problem. The problem was that I refused to grow. My grandfather insisted that plenty of sunshine would do the trick, so I spent the first few weeks of my life lying on a blanket on the garden patio, the same patio that is now crowded with ceramic pots sprouting mixed salad leaves, strawberries, and little green peppers.

"This baby's still not growing, Brenda," my grandfather told my grandmother one day, measuring me against the length of a garden cane. "She must have come from bad seed, I reckon."

"Would she do better in a greenhouse?" suggested my grandmother. "They work wonders for tomatoes."

My grandfather shook his head. "I'm not building a bloody greenhouse just to grow one baby. I think maybe she'd do better in partial shade."

So I was relocated to the end of the garden next to the hedgerow, where I got full sun in the morning and plenty of shade in the afternoon. But after another week, when I still hadn't grown, my mother was becoming anxious.

"Is she getting enough water, Dad?" she asked my grandfather. "It's been very dry this summer. Even the apple trees look parched."

So I was moved closer to the garden sprinkler, but extra water didn't seem to help me grow either. My mother feared I might just shrivel up altogether, so Dr. Bloomberg was called to the house as a matter of urgency. He turned me over in his large hands, pinched my arms and legs, and agreed that I was still very firm for a four-week-old baby.

"She should be plump and fleshy by now," he declared authoritatively.

He looked at my mother, still only sixteen years old, and shook his head as if this unfortunate situation had been inevitable.

"It takes the mighty oak tree no less than twenty years to produce an acorn," he said.

My mother blushed and looked at her feet. She knew what he meant. It was no wonder her baby was so small when she wasn't even fully grown herself.

But my grandfather was damned if he was going to stand by and let his daughter be insulted. "It takes the cherry tree almost no time at all to produce its first fruit," he told the doctor, putting his arm protectively around my mother's shoulders.

The doctor ignored him.

"Feed her one teaspoon of this a day," he said, handing my mother a little bottle. "It's bicarbonate of soda, a good raising agent. Then leave her in the warm water heater closet overnight."

My mother thanked the doctor profusely, in awe of his superior knowledge. "Thank goodness for Dr. Bloomberg," she said, rushing to get a teaspoon.

But another week later I still hadn't grown.

"I don't know what to do," sobbed my mother, clutching my

little body to her breast. "She hasn't risen one bit, and she's still under-ripe. In fact, I think she's turning a little bit green."

"Have you tried talking to her?" suggested my grandmother as a last resort.

My grandfather looked at her as if she were mad.

"Talking to her? What are you on about, woman?"

"Well, talking to plants is meant to make them grow, so I just thought..."

Her voice tapered off as my grandfather tutted and rolled his eyes.

My mother shook her head, confused. "But what would I say?"

"I don't think it matters, dear," said my grandmother.

Despite his skepticism, my pushy grandfather decided that if anyone was going to try it, he wanted to be the first. Barging my grandmother out of the way, he stuck his face inside my blanket, nose to nose with me.

"Hello," he said gravely. "Hello?"

"You're not talking into a telephone receiver, Bob," my grandmother huffed. "She's not going to answer you."

"Then there's no bloody point in talking to her, is there?" he retorted. "Don't listen to your mother, Valerie," he told my mother, shuffling out of the room. "She should be institutionalized. We never spoke to you when you were a baby, and you grew just fine."

"It was just an idea," shrugged my grandmother, following him out the door.

Once we were alone, my mother decided that anything was worth a try.

"I'm not sure what to say to you," she said, gazing awkwardly at me. "I don't suppose we have any of the same interests. I enjoy baking and reading. I'm not sure what you enjoy other than chewing on your blanket and gurgling. I like dancing, but I don't go out much, not now that you're here. To be honest, I'm not sure what I'm meant to do with you. But I suppose that's not your problem, is it?"

I looked up at her inquisitively and wriggled on her lap. She leaned down a little closer to my face, staring into my big brown eyes.

"Please grow," she whispered. "I might not be the best mother in the world, but I love you."

I sucked on my tiny fingers and then wiped drool all over her sweater. She let out a heavy sigh full of exhaustion and worry.

"Well, I suppose I could tell you a story," she said. "That would at least give me something to say to you."

She cleared her throat theatrically.

"In a land far away, there lived a creature that didn't know quite what it was..."

For the first time ever I gave my mother a gummy smile, and by the end of the story she swears I had grown an entire inch.

Today Dr. Bloomberg looks at me in the same way he must have looked at my mother all those years ago: with eyes full of pity and condescension, as if I am little more than a child who has failed to understand the rules of the game.

Meeting him is like finally meeting Santa Claus. He has been a fairy-tale presence in my life for as long as I can recall, and yet I was never wholly convinced that he existed. As we sit in his office, the large mahogany desk between us is the only thing that stops me from reaching out and stroking his soft white hair or tweaking his bulbous nose just to test that he is real. I try to imagine him twenty-one years younger, those large, safe hands squeezing and prodding me like I am an under-ripe melon, but I can't imagine him being any different from how he is right now. He seems like someone who has always been old, someone who has been on this earth since time began. It is strangely comforting to think that he was witness to a time I can't remember. His very existence seems to validate mine.

"I'm sorry if this has come as a shock to you," he says gently, monitoring my face with concern.

I shake my head defiantly, but when I open my mouth to speak no words come out.

"N-no," I manage to stutter. "It's not a shock. I knew she had very little time left. Of course I knew that."

Through a pain that feels like I have been hit in the stomach with a sledgehammer, I remain adamant that Dr. Bloomberg, this fellow worshipper of science and reason, shall not think that I have in any way deluded myself. I will not humiliate myself in front of someone of such intellect, and I will not make myself vulnerable to being patronized. Dr. Bloomberg is clearly a sensible man of great knowledge, and the very notion that he might see how misinformed I have been, how foolish I have been for hoping my mother might live for more than a year, is too much to bear. He may have once regarded my mother as a naïve young girl, but I will be damned before allowing him to tar me with the same brush.

"Some people find counseling very useful," he suggests cautiously, sliding a leaflet across the desk toward me. There is a photo of a pair of glasses on the front and a slogan that reads, "Helping you find a new perspective."

"I don't need counseling," I say bluntly, rummaging in my bag for a notepad and pen. "If you could just let me know what to expect."

I take down notes as if I'm at a lecture, interrupting several times and demanding specific details. Eventually Dr. Bloomberg gives up trying to wrap his words in cotton wool and tells it to me straight. There is no doubt that he is taken aback by my frankness, but I like order, rules, knowledge, and facts, no matter how clinical and unpleasant. I'm not an escapist like my mother; I don't live in a world of make-believe.

"My mother doesn't seem to understand how sick she is. It's like she's in complete denial," I tell Dr. Bloomberg, ready for his mutual indignation. Instead he nods sagely, as if what I have described is completely acceptable.

"Denial's a great defense mechanism," he says, "a coping strategy. People find all kinds of ways to deal with the things life throws at them."

He glances at my notebook, in which I have drawn a chart dividing my mother's illness into categories: symptoms, medication, hospital dates.

"So what do we do about it?" I ask.

He peers at me over the top of his spectacles, raising his bushy white eyebrows as if they risk hindering his vision.

"My dear girl, we mustn't *do* anything about it. It's probably the only thing keeping her sane."

I stare incredulously at him, watching the halo of light I have projected around him fade away. He can't be serious, can he? How can someone of such intelligence and reason possibly think it's okay for my mother to go on deluding herself? He's wrong. He has to be wrong. But I don't intend to sit here and waste my time arguing with him.

"Thank you for your time, Doctor," I say brusquely, standing up. My head feels light and my knees are trembling, but I put it down to a lack of air in the room. I hold out my hand to Dr. Bloomberg in a businesslike fashion.

He stands slowly and reaches across his desk, taking my hand gently between both of his. His eyes are full of sympathy, and I want to scream at him, "Stop it! Stop feeling sorry for me!" I feel naked and exposed before him, as if he can see what a fool I have been, as if he can tell, in spite of all my protestations, that I have been thinking of my mother's remaining time in terms of years. His hands are warm and heavy around mine, and as I gaze at the white hair on the back of his knuckles I remember that those same hands once held me, turned me over, examined me, and then passed me back into the safety of my mother's arms. Hot tears spring to my eyes and my throat starts to burn.

"Good-bye," I say curtly, fumbling to shake his hand as best I can.

"Good-bye, Meg."

I gather my bag and walk hastily from his office. But before I close the door, I glance back at him. He is already sitting down at his desk, flicking through the notes on his next patient.

"It didn't help me grow, you know," I tell him, "putting me in the water heater closet."

Dr. Bloomberg frowns at me.

"I'm sorry?"

I freeze, wondering what came over me. What on earth prompted me to say such a thing? Did I seriously hope he would remember, as if his remembering would confirm something for me, make the past real? I open my mouth to speak but find myself caught between an explanation and an apology, between wanting to jog his memory and wanting to take back my ridiculous comment. I shake my head, suddenly feeling very confused.

"Nothing," I say, closing the door behind me and hurrying out onto the street.

Walking home from Dr. Bloomberg's office, I still feel sick and shaky and can only think I must be coming down with something.

"Maybe you should find her another doctor," Mark is telling me on the phone as I stride along the hot pavement. "A psychiatrist, maybe, someone who can get her to face up to things. After all, there's all the practical stuff to deal with, Meg. Has she even written a will? What about the house, her finances—"

"Actually, Mark," I interrupt, "do you mind if we talk about something else?"

My first instinct upon leaving Dr. Bloomberg's office had been to call Mark, knowing he would share fully in my indignation at being told that my mother's state of denial must be preserved. In fact, he is even more outraged than me, immediately pointing out the practical consequences of allowing this situation to continue. I love that he understands where I am coming from, and his frustration on my behalf is touching, but suddenly I wish I had never brought this up. I want him to support me in this battle against madness and delusion, but I also want him to understand what a difficult battle it is to fight, and that's something he can't seem to comprehend. In his eyes it's simple: separate fiction from reality. But in my world things have never been that easy.

"I'm not going to be coming back for the start of term, Mark," I say. "In fact, I don't think I'll be coming back this year."

I haven't told him that my mother doesn't have as long as I thought. I don't want him knowing that I have been laboring under a misapprehension all this time. He would have checked out the facts earlier, done his research, dug beneath the surface of pretense, and armed himself with the truth. Right now he would be calling psychiatrists, funeral directors, clergymen, financial advisers, lawyers, all the things he has just told me I need to do. But I just don't have the heart to do any of these things, and suddenly I feel useless and overwhelmed. I have never displayed incompetence in front of Mark, though, and I don't intend to start now.

"I think you're right to stay there," says Mark. "It sounds like your mother needs help facing up to this. I'll bring all your belongings down tomorrow."

"Would you? Oh, that would be great." I breathe a sigh of relief that at least one thing has been taken out of my hands. My heart swells with gratitude and affection. Mark is a rock, always there for me when I need him, always capable and strong, thinking ahead, planning, making sure everything is in order. With him I feel safe and protected, and although I am perfectly capable of looking after myself, occasionally—and it pains me to say this—it feels nice to have someone to rely on.

"Have you spoken to Dr. Coldman?" asks Mark.

Over the summer I am meant to be working as Dr. Larry Coldman's research assistant, but I've barely had a chance to start. I feel terrible at the thought of letting him down, but what else can I do?

"No, I'll call him tomorrow and explain," I say.

"And have you spoken to your tutor about taking a year off?"

"No, not yet."

"And you'll need to cancel your rent. What was your rental agreement?"

"I don't know."

"What about your house key? Do you have any library books that need returning? Any outstanding assignments?"

"I...Mark, can we sort all this out later?"

"It's best to get things in order, Meg. A few late library books can quickly spiral out of control, and before you know it you've got chaos on your hands."

"Right. Of course. I'll make a list."

"Good idea. Lists are good. So I'll see you tomorrow. I'll be there by four o'clock. Or maybe quarter past if the traffic's bad. But if the traffic's good I might be there a little before; it depends. If the traffic on the ring road is flowing steadily—"

"Bye, Mark."

"Oh, bye, babe."

I always wondered how I would react if I came face-to-face with an intruder. Would I scream bloody murder? Would I attempt the "stun and run" technique learned during a single self-defense class in the university sports hall last year? Would I grab the nearest weapon—a kitchen knife, a heavy vase, a poker? Would I freeze?

It turns out I do all four, in exactly that order.

I am so startled when a scruffy young man bursts through the back door into my mother's kitchen that I scream, throw my hands up into what I think is the basic self-defense position but probably looks like I'm about to start dancing to "YMCA," grab the nearest item, which happens to be a dishrag, and then just stand there wide-eyed and terrified.

"Wh-what do you want?" I shriek, warding him off with the soggy dishrag as if it's a crucifix and he's a vampire.

He freezes, one hand still on the back door handle, a startled expression on his unshaven face. My eyes dart up and down his body, scanning for a knife or even a gun. I take in the worn jeans and frayed T-shirt, the dirt on his hands. His hair is messy, long wisps falling into his eyes, and he has a streak of grime on his chin. He can't be any older than me, maybe even a few months younger, and within five seconds I have concluded that he is living rough, certainly a drug addict, and that he is no doubt here to steal my mother's belongings and sell them for cocaine. I take in his strong, sinewy arms and quickly conclude that although he is not much taller than me, he is clearly much stronger and therefore I don't stand a chance.

"If you come any closer I'll scream this house down!"

He takes a step forward.

I shake my dishrag frantically at him.

"I swear, if you come any closer I'll…I'll…"

"Wash me?"

His face relaxes and he looks vaguely amused, eyeing me up and down with interest. I pull the collar of my blouse tight around my neck. My knees, still weak from this morning, start trembling again.

"Wh-what do you want?"

"Just a glass of water," he says calmly.

My mind flits back through episodes of *Crimewatch*, scanning for information on con artists who ask lone women for a glass of water and then murder them. I know the moment I turn my back he'll be upon me, his dirty hands grabbing at me as he pushes me down on the floor. Or maybe he'll just pull a knife from his pocket and slit my throat before running off with my mother's DVD player.

"Get out of my house!" I scream, flinging the dishcloth at him with gusto, suddenly furious. It hits him straight in the face with a wet smack.

"Hey! I surrender."

He holds his hands in the air, the dishcloth dangling from one of them.

"I'm just the gardener."

I shake my head angrily.

"No, you're not! My mother doesn't have a gardener!"

I pull a knife from the drying rack. The smirk on the man's face is quickly replaced by panic.

"Are you crazy? She hired me this morning!"

"My mother would never hire a gardener!"

"Then I guess I must have been dreaming!"

Just then I hear the front door slam.

"Hello?" calls my mother.

Suddenly my mind goes into overdrive. Should I scream at her to run? Tell her to call the police? Make a bid for freedom, grabbing my mother on the way and bundling her out the front door? I monitor the young man anxiously, watching to see if he'll turn and run or make a move to attack. Then again, I think, taking in his mud-encrusted work boots, what if…

"Ah, you two have met, then," chirps my mother, plonking a bag of shopping on the kitchen table. Her breathing is heavy and labored. She rests her hands on her hips and waits to catch her breath.

"My goodness, I'm getting unfit!" she says with a laugh. "Maybe I should start going to the gym."

She looks from me to the young man and back again, taking in the knife in my trembling, outstretched hand.

"Meg, what on earth are you doing?"

"Mother, who is this man?" I demand sharply, already aware that I have made a horrific mistake.

"He's the gardener, of course. Who else would he be?"

She takes the knife from me and casually throws it into a drawer.

"He knocked this morning looking for work, and I thought I could probably do with a hand. He's already made ever such a good start."

"But you said you didn't want a gardener!" I shout, incredulous and acutely embarrassed.

"When did I say that?"

"Yesterday!"

"Well, that was yesterday. Honestly, darling, I don't know what you're getting so worked up about. It was your idea in the first place."

She shakes her head and rolls her eyes in the man's direction as if to say, "My daughter, what a loon!"

He smiles at her.

"Would you like a glass of water, Ewan?" my mother asks politely as she starts to unpack the shopping.

"Only if it wouldn't be too much trouble," he says, looking at me with a smirk.

I want to crawl under the kitchen table and die.

"Of course not. Get Ewan some water, will you, Meg?" she asks, her head already buried inside a cupboard.

Silent in my humiliation, I pour a glass of water from the tap and hold it out to him, carefully avoiding his eye. He drinks it down in four swift gulps, wipes his mouth with the back of his grimy hand, and passes the glass back to me.

"Thanks. Very kind of you."

I glance at him briefly. His brown eyes are glistening with wry amusement, and a smile is playing on his lips. The obvious enjoyment he takes in my acute embarrassment makes me want to hit him.

"No problem," I say, forcing a smile.

I turn and leave the room, calculating how long it might take him to tidy the garden and leave so I never have to face him again.

chapter five

I almost married Johnny Miller. He was nearly mine for life. It didn't occur to me that I had only been invited to his birthday party because my mother had become notorious for providing an excellent catering service, depositing me on people's doorsteps with mountains of sandwiches, fruit jellies, fairy cakes, sausage rolls, and meringues. In my eyes, the fact that I was the only girl in Red Class to be invited to his party meant that Johnny must love me.

"He definitely loves you," confirmed Tracey Pratt as we sat writing that fateful paragraph titled "My Earliest Memory." It was the last time Tracey Pratt would sit next to me in class ever again. "Promise me I can be your bridesmaid," she said. "I want to wear a pink dress with roses on it. I'll show you."

She turned her paper over and started to draw a dress with huge puffy sleeves and hearts all over it.

"I think he's really handsome," I said, swooning and gazing across the classroom at Johnny, who was flicking tiny balls of paper at Podge Parkinson's back.

"Me too," said Tracey. "I think he's definitely the most handsomest boy in the class. You're *so* lucky he loves you!"

I was in seventh heaven and saw my whole life with Johnny stretching ahead of me like a blissful dream. I saw myself in a huge white wedding dress, doves fluttering in the sky. I saw two babies, twins perhaps, and a beautiful cottage in the country. I saw myself kissing Johnny good-bye as he set off in his big shiny car to an office where he did something important that involved wearing a suit. We would never have our gas cut off or catch leaking water in a bucket like my mother and I had to. The landlord would never bang angrily on our door, and pipes wouldn't knock in the night. We would have kittens and a huge garden, a log fire, and exotic holidays, and every evening Johnny would bring me flowers.

How could I have known that five minutes later my dreams would all be shattered? That I would be standing, red-faced and embarrassed, as Johnny Miller, the love of my life and hope for future happiness, called me dumb? That Tracey Pratt, my closest friend and prospective bridesmaid, would have turned against me and called me a liar? That for the rest of that term I would be shunned by my friends, who no longer wanted to be associated with an eight-year-old girl who believed runner beans could run?

I will never forget that day after school when I walked up to Johnny Miller at the school gates to hand him my invitation reply slip, having proudly ticked the box that read, "Yes, I would love to come to your party!"

"I'm really looking forward to it," I said politely, feeling myself blush, still clinging onto my dream of our shared future.

Behind Johnny, Podge Parkinson and Jamie Brunt sniggered into their cupped hands.

"Make sure she doesn't bring any beans," Jamie whispered. "They might run away!"

Podge burst into wheezy, asthmatic laughter.

Johnny fiddled awkwardly with the knot of his school tie.

"The party's been canceled," he said quickly, and without even looking at me, he turned and ran away.

I stood forlornly, staring at the reply slip in my hand. I had planned to wear my new blue dress and slip-on shoes with the tiny heels. I was going to use all the money in my piggy bank to buy him a Power-Splash water pistol.

I didn't need to hear Johnny's mother shout "See you Saturday!" to Jamie's mother to know the party was still on.

I had been rejected because Johnny thought I was a liar and a fool.

"You don't have to be shy, you know."

I freeze mid-step. How on earth did he hear me? I was being as quiet as a mouse. Or so I thought. I curse my mother for insisting that I bring a cup of coffee and a slice of pecan pie outside for the gardener. After all, she's paying him, so I can't believe she's expected to feed him as well. Having crept down the brick path, I had left the refreshments on the ground in between his discarded sweater and a row of cauliflower, and I really thought I could just creep back to the house without him noticing me. But just as I am tiptoeing away, his voice reaches me from somewhere in the apple orchard. The branches of the tightly packed trees are a tangle of leaves and fruit, too dense to see through, but he is obviously in there somewhere, watching me sneaking around.

"What's up? Are you afraid?"

I spin around, my eyes searching for him among the leafy branches, irritated by his suggestion. He's clearly patronizing me, mocking me for my reaction the other day when I defended myself against him with a dishcloth. Well, I'm sorry, but I don't think it's unreasonable to feel a little frightened when a scruffy-looking man bursts into your kitchen unannounced. I'm about to tell him so when he speaks again.

"Come on, don't be shy now, sweetheart. Have a bit more confidence. You know, I think you could be a right little stunner if you wanted."

My jaw drops. Sweetheart! Stunner! The cheek of him! He's obviously one of these young men who likes to think of himself as a bit of a charmer, a "cheeky chappie" or a "lovable rogue," chatting up the ladies with a naughty smile and a glint in his eye. Unfortunately for him, I find these kind of men misogynistic, irritating, and common and see nothing in the slightest bit charming about them.

"You're quite a beauty, you know that?"

His voice is soft and deep as it carries on the gentle summer breeze, and in spite of myself, just for a second, I feel a smile playing at the side of my mouth. A beauty? Really? Mark has never called me a beauty. He once said I am rather pretty when my hair is neatly tucked behind my ears, but he has never used the word *beautiful*.

But what am I doing allowing myself to be flattered? He shouldn't be talking to me in this way. If my mother insists on having him here, he's going to have to learn that he's here to cut grass and trim hedges and that's all. I push my way into the little orchard, shoving branches out of my path, trampling over a ball of string, some shears, and a wooden box, all of which he has discarded recklessly on the ground with no regard for anyone's safety. Forcefully parting the leaves of an apple tree, I find myself staring him straight in the face.

"I have a boyfriend, you know," I tell him, matter-of-factly, stumbling on a piece of green netting that has become caught around my feet. "He's a lecturer in physics."

The gardener stares at me blankly. "Good for you," he says, watching me curiously as I stumble around in front of him, kicking my feet in a bid to free myself from the netting, which seems to have tied my ankles together.

"Yes, it is good for me," I tell him. "He's a very well-respected physicist." I grab onto a tree trunk as I nearly topple over. "So I really don't think it's appropriate for you to be—"

"Do you want some help with that?" he interrupts, reaching down to untangle me.

"I'm perfectly all right, thank you," I say confidently, causing him to back away. Realizing that all my jigging about has only served to tighten the netting around my feet, I decide to lean casually against the tree trunk with my arms folded, as if I'm completely comfortable standing with my feet tied together and do it all the time.

"Anyway, I have a boyfriend," I continue as if nothing is amiss. "So I really don't think it's appropriate for you to be addressing me as 'sweetheart' and commenting on my appearance. Plus, just for the record, nothing about you scares me in the slightest, other than the fact that you burst straight into my kitchen yesterday without having the courtesy to knock."

The gardener just stares at me, bemused, as if I'm speaking another language. I try to remember if I inadvertently used any complicated words that he might not have understood. And then, slowly, a look of realization spreads across his face.

"Oh, you didn't think…I mean, I wasn't talking to you if that's what you thought."

I look around me, confused, as if there is any chance that somebody else might be hiding in the orchard. And then it dawns on me. I see what he's doing. He's embarrassed now because he knows I have a boyfriend, so he's trying to backtrack on his suggestive and rather sexist comments. He might even be afraid that my boyfriend is a six-foot-three part-time body builder, who would flatten him in a fit of jealous rage if he knew that words such as *stunner* had been directed toward me. Admittedly, the only time I have ever seen Mark in a jealous rage was when I beat him at Countdown, and even then it was less of a rage and more of a sulk, but the gardener isn't to know that.

"Oh, okay," I say, nodding disbelievingly. "You weren't talking to me. So obviously you were talking to"—I look about, pretending to be searching for someone—"this caterpillar, I suppose?"

Mark always says that sarcasm is the lowest form of wit, but to be honest I rather enjoy it. There is quite clearly no one else here he could possibly have been speaking to, so he's just going to have to admit that he was trying to chat me up and that he has completely and utterly embarrassed himself. I have never liked the phrase "out of your league" because it sounds rather arrogant, but at the end of the day my boyfriend is a physicist, and he's...well... what on earth did he think he was trying to do?

The gardener shuffles awkwardly and tries to conceal a smile I assume must be borne out of guilt and embarrassment at his own impropriety.

"No, I wasn't talking to the caterpillar," he concedes, studying the revolting, furry, yellow creature that is crawling along a nearby branch. "I'd hardly refer to him as a 'beauty.' Or as 'shy,' for that matter. I was chatting to him earlier and could barely get a word in. No, I was actually talking to this tree."

He pats the trunk of the tree he's standing next to, and I almost laugh at his ridiculous lie. Is that all he could come up with? To say he was staring at his own reflection in a mirror and talking to himself would have been more convincing. But as I roll my eyes in a way that is meant to say, "Oh, *please!*" I notice that he looks perfectly serious.

I raise an eyebrow quizzically.

"What?"

"Well, look at her," he says. "She's not bearing any fruit. All her branches are turning inward like she's trying to hide away. Her leaves are small and dull in color, as if she doesn't want to draw attention to herself. She clearly feels ashamed of who she is. She's the classic example of a shy tree."

I study his face, searching for a sign that he's joking.

"A shy tree?" I repeat, thinking that might be one of the strangest phrases I've ever heard.

"One of the most timid trees I've met. And it's a shame, because *as I was telling her,*" he says slowly and with emphasis, "she could really blossom if she just let herself go a bit. She'd be quite a beauty, in fact. I was trying to give her a bit of positive encouragement."

It takes me a moment to absorb the fact that, firstly, he is obviously completely serious, and secondly, if he is completely serious then that means…

"I wasn't trying to chat you up," he says. "Sorry if you got the wrong end of the stick."

Despite the fact that he is trying to sound sincerely sorry for my discomfort, I can see him battling with a smile, and it is clear that, once again, my mistake has provided welcome fodder for his amusement.

"I didn't think…I just," I stammer, wondering how I can cover up my mistake. I can't believe I thought he was saying those things to me! But hang on, why am *I* the one feeling silly? *He's* the one who's been talking to a tree!

"Who in their right mind talks to trees?" I ask rather harshly, trying to turn the focus back onto him and divert attention from my embarrassing mistake.

"Lots of people," he says matter-of-factly. "People have always done it. All over the world people believe they can communicate with trees. Tree spirits play a role in all kinds of cultures. Native American, Hindu, Celtic…"

"That's only because those cultures still cling to primitive ideas," I tell him authoritatively, determined that he will be the one who comes out of this feeling silly, not me. "This is twenty-first-century Britain. If you want a tree to grow, try using chemicals; don't waste time talking to it."

"Chemicals are nowhere near as effective as a few gentle words of encouragement and some stroking."

"Stroking? You're kidding."

He shakes his head. "Honestly, you can't beat it."

"And how exactly does that help a tree grow?"

He shakes his head and looks thoughtful, as if this is a question that has been a source of fascination and confusion to him for a long time. "I don't know how *exactly*—"

I let out a loud sigh of despair. If there's one thing I can't stand it's these new-age hippy types, people who go around hugging trees and banging on about vibes and spirits and souls and energy, as if they have any idea what *energy*—in the true scientific use of the word—actually means. People who claim that ghosts exist and telepathy works without ever being able to back up their argument with any proper data or scientific explanation and who base their "knowledge" on nothing more than a hunch or a feeling.

"Trees don't have souls or spirits, and they certainly can't understand you," I tell him. "It's all nonsense."

Rather than defend himself, as I would in his position, he just shrugs. Clearly my opinion doesn't matter much to him either way, and he is happy enough to persist in his unfounded beliefs in spite of me. I have never understood how people can be like that, and I find it both confusing and frustrating. Surely if someone challenges your ideas, then the aim of the game is to prove that you are right and they are wrong.

"Well," he says casually, "there's nothing wrong with a bit of nonsense now and then. I reckon we all need a bit of nonsense in our lives from time to time, don't you?"

He looks at me with a slight smile, his chestnut eyes twinkling playfully in the bright sunlight. *Of course we don't need nonsense in our lives,* I think. *What would be the point in that?* He is being ridiculous. And yet for some reason I find that *I* am the one who is blushing!

"The whole garden's in chaos," I tell him quickly. "You shouldn't be wasting your time worrying about one tree. I'm sure my mother isn't bothered about a few measly apples."

"Measly!" he exclaims in mock outrage. "How can you say that? Apples are never measly."

He gently twists off one of the small green apples hanging from the branch of a nearby tree and holds it up, watching the sunlight glisten on its waxy skin.

"Look at that," he says in the way that anyone else might marvel over an original Monet. "Perfect."

He holds it out to me in his grubby palm and I take it reluctantly, looking at it with contempt.

"People have journeyed far and wide for 'a few measly apples,' as you call them," he says. "Just look at Hercules."

"I'm not interested in comic books," I tell him.

For some reason he seems to find this comment amusing. In fact, he actually laughs. I have no idea what I might have said that's so funny, and if there's one thing I can't stand it's people laughing at me. Particularly when I don't even know why.

"What's so funny?" I ask, annoyed.

"It's not a comic book," he explains. "Hercules was a divine hero from Greek mythology who was given twelve labors, and his eleventh labor was to fetch some apples that grew in a walled garden in a far western land."

He watches my face for a sign of recognition as if I should know what he's talking about. Instead, I raise an eyebrow and look bored to show that these silly stories are beneath me. I am hardly going to feel embarrassed that I don't know about some fairy tale. In fact, I see my lack of knowledge in these areas as a sign of superior intellect, evidence that I have had far more important things to be thinking about. Anyone who knows fairy tales by heart has clearly had a wasted youth.

The gardener strokes the sickly looking branches of the timid tree and continues his story, although I'm not entirely sure if he's telling it for my benefit or talking to the tree again.

"Hercules was given a test to fetch some apples that grew in a walled garden in a far western land. On his way, he came across Prometheus, who had been chained to a rock by the god Zeus as punishment for giving fire to man. Every single day an eagle would come and eat Prometheus's liver, which would then grow in the night only to be eaten again the next day. Hercules was appalled by such suffering, so he fired an arrow at the eagle, killing it, and released Prometheus from his chains. Prometheus was eternally grateful, and he warned Hercules to be careful in his quest to fetch the apples. Any mortal man who entered the walled garden, he said, would certainly be killed by the dragon who lived inside. He advised Hercules to ask Atlas to enter the garden on his behalf, as Atlas was immortal and so could fetch the apples without fear of death.

"After a hard trek through the mountains, Hercules finally reached the walled garden. Outside he found Atlas, who was holding the heavens on his shoulders as punishment for waging war against Zeus.

"'If you go into the garden and fetch the apples for me,'

Hercules told him, 'then I'll hold the weight of the heavens on my shoulders for you while you go inside.'

"Atlas liked the idea of handing over the weight of the heavens for a while, so he agreed. He handed the heavens over to Hercules before going into the walled garden, where he fought the dragon and fetched the apples. But when he came back and saw Hercules struggling to hold up the heavens, he realized he would be mad to take that burden back.

"'You can keep the heavens,' he told Hercules, 'and I'll keep the apples.'

"Hercules had to think quickly. He pretended to agree to the deal and promised Atlas that if he would just take the heavens back for a minute while he went and got a pillow to make himself comfortable, then he would come straight back and take the weight of the heavens forevermore. Atlas, trusting that Hercules was good to his word, agreed to take the heavens back for a moment, but as soon as he did, Hercules grabbed the apples and ran away, leaving Atlas cursing after him."

The gardener strokes the tree dreamily, seemingly lost in thought. I watch him closely, registering the faraway look in his eyes, and briefly wonder what it must be like to indulge one's imagination to such an extent you are no longer conscious of the present moment. What must it be like to get lost without the fear of never being able to find your way back? To float without the anxiety of falling? Just for a second I feel the tiniest pang of something like envy. And then I wonder how, and why, people allow themselves to do it.

The gardener turns to me and smiles, back from his reverie, and I look away quickly.

"That's one of the most ridiculous things I've ever heard," I tell him.

He shrugs, as if being called ridiculous is no big deal, as if it doesn't even matter to him that I find him absurd.

"It just shows what some people will do for a few measly apples," he says.

"It doesn't show anything. In fact, it doesn't even make sense. There are so many inconsistencies. For a start, there's no evidence for the existence of gods. Or dragons. And even if you believed that heaven existed—which I don't—it certainly wouldn't exist in a tangible form that could be held on one's shoulders. Plus, nobody's liver regrows overnight. It's anatomically impossible. In fact, that Prometheus fellow would have died the first time the eagle came and attacked his liver, and if he hadn't died, he would certainly have been in need of urgent medical attention. Hercules should have been fetching the paramedics instead of worrying about a load of old apples."

The gardener is smiling, clearly finding something amusing. His eyes flit curiously across my face, as if he's trying to figure me out.

"You're right," he says, with mock approval, "those are all very sensible points. I guess whoever came up with that story hadn't really thought things through."

"People who find pleasure in such stories rarely do think things through," I tell him.

"It wouldn't make much of a story, though, would it, if you took out the gods and the dragon and the eagle and heaven? You'd really just be left with a bloke going out to pick some apples and then going home again."

"Well, what would be wrong with that?" I ask, not seeing the problem. "If people feel the need to tell these stories, then the least they can do is make them reflect real life."

The gardener frowns as if I've missed the point. "But stories are meant to take you away from real life. To help you escape from reality."

"Why would you want to escape from reality?" I ask him, feeling myself becoming annoyed.

The gardener scratches his head. "Well, because life can be tough. Sometimes it's good to escape, to just let yourself get lost in your imagination—"

"Yes, you could get lost," I tell him, adamantly. "That's exactly what could happen. Lost and not able to find your way back." I can feel my heart starting to beat faster, my voice becoming louder.

The gardener looks a little wary, and I sense this is not quite the reaction his story was meant to evoke.

"I'm not sure indulging in a bit of fantasy now and again can do much harm," he says.

I can feel anger welling up in my chest. He doesn't know what he's talking about! If he thinks a little fantasy can't do any harm, that it's simple enjoyment, then he should try living my life for a day! If he thinks you can't get lost somewhere between reality and fiction, then he should try living with my mother! But what's the point in telling him? How could I expect a man who talks to trees to possibly understand? He's already well on the wrong side of the breach between sanity and madness. I'm not going to waste any more of my time trying to make him see sense. I push the apple back into his hand.

"Keep it," I say rather haughtily. "I don't want it."

He turns the apple over in his hand, clearly baffled by my abruptness, and I turn, furious at his ignorance, ready to stomp my way out of the orchard.

Instead, I immediately fall over and end up lying facedown between the trunks of two trees, having completely forgotten about the netting tied around my feet.

"Are you—"

"I'm fine, thank you," I say before he even has time to approach me.

In frustration and embarrassment, I tear angrily at the netting, which rips loudly. I manage to free one leg so that the wad of netting is now only wrapped around one foot, where it remains stuck. Lifting myself off the ground, I dust myself off, hold my head high, and make my exit from the orchard as if sporting a trendy new fashion accessory.

"He's an absolute idiot," I tell Mark when he arrives that evening. "I mean, who in their right mind talks to trees? And then he started telling me some fairy story about apples and dragons and who knows what else!"

"He sounds like a complete fool. And how much is your mother paying him?"

"Oh, I don't know. Too much. And he doesn't seem to actually be doing anything of any use. Apparently he just knocked on the door looking for work. He probably doesn't know anything about gardening. Probably just some traveler from that site near the A10. He could be a criminal, for all we know!"

Mark uncorks the expensive wine he has brought and places the bottle on the kitchen table, while I slam knives and forks down into wonky place settings. Mark follows me around, straightening them.

"Well, you *did* say you wanted your mother to get a gardener."

"Not this one."

He places his hands on my shoulders and turns me toward him. "Forget him. How are you doing?"

I sigh and let myself fall against Mark's broad chest. I feel so safe in his arms, so protected, although of course I would never want him to know that. I barely like to admit it to myself. At twenty-one years old, I shouldn't need anyone to protect me. I *don't* need anyone to protect me. It's just that sometimes…

"I'm doing fine," I tell him, pulling myself up straight.

He smiles proudly. "Of course you are," he says, patting my back heartily. "You're the most capable girl I know."

A thought enters uninvited into my mind: *And what if I weren't capable? What if I fell apart at the seams? Would you still want to be with me?* I push the thought out of my head, wondering where it came from.

"Mark! Lovely to see you!"

My mother enters the kitchen, drying her hair with a pink towel. Since Mark arrived she has been upstairs taking a very, very long bath. Although she insists otherwise, I have always had the impression that she isn't hugely fond of Mark, not in the all-embracing future-son-in-law way that I would like. I don't understand it. He's clever, tall, handsome, and from a good (fairly wealthy) family. What else could she want for me?

"You look wonderful!" she beams, drawing him in for a kiss.

"So do you," he says unconvincingly, barely making an effort to disguise his shock at her altered appearance. He quickly draws away from her embrace, looking uncomfortable and slightly fearful. Mark has never been good with illness. It is linked in his mind with weakness, which is something he can't abide. I admire him for the importance he places on strength and resilience and like to think they are values we share, but he could be a bit more tactful.

"The flowers are for you," he says, pointing at some beautiful, delicate white lilies he has neatly arranged in a glass vase on her behalf.

"Oh, lovely!" she says, although I know she's not a fan of lilies. "It's so nice of you to bring Meggy's things down, although I can't understand why she needs quite so much. She's only extended her stay for a week, after all."

As she opens the oven door, flaps at the smoke with her towel, and examines the roast chicken, I feel Mark glaring at me. I refuse to meet his eye. I have not, as he insisted, managed to confront my mother's delusion. It has not occurred to her that I won't be going back to Leeds, given that in her eyes everything here is just hunky-dory. I know Mark thinks I should force her to face reality, but he doesn't understand how hard it is. Still, I sense his disappointment in me.

"Lay another table place, won't you, Meg?" my mother asks, prodding the chicken with a fork. "Ewan's joining us for dinner."

"The gardener! Why?"

"Because he's been working hard all day, and I insisted he should stay for a meal, that's why. And he does have a name, you know. He wasn't christened The Gardener."

"But we don't invite people for dinner. We never have."

"Well," she says, shoving the chicken back in the oven and slamming the door, "it's about time we started, isn't it?"

I don't know what makes me feel more uncomfortable, the fact that my mother gets on so fantastically well with the gardener, or the fact that Mark so blatantly hates him. Having asked the gardener to remove his boots at the back door, Mark then made no effort to disguise his horror at the state of the man's tatty socks, or the mud under his fingernails, or the rip in his faded T-shirt. There is something about Mark's manner that makes me feel uncomfortable. Yes, the gardener is scruffy, a daydreamer, naïve, and no doubt extremely uneducated, but I would never intentionally make anyone feel inferior. I would never try to make myself feel better by asserting my intellectual superiority. Would I? No, I'm sure I would never do that.

To be fair, the gardener is surprisingly polite, and for most of our meal, Mark and I appear to be superfluous. My mother is fascinated by his accounts of growing fruit and vegetables, and unless he is a very good actor, he is fascinated by my mother's accounts of cooking them.

"I never use chemical pesticides," he tells her, chewing on a mouthful of roast potato.

"I completely agree!" she exclaims, banging her wine glass down on the old oak table and sloshing wine over the rim. She is rosy-cheeked and louder than usual. Definitely tipsy. "But how do you keep slugs off your lettuce without pesticide? I've tried the trick with egg shells, but it can be a bit hiss and mit."

Past tipsy, in fact.

"Slugs respond well to honest explanations," the gardener tells her. "They have soft hearts and soft brains. They don't mean to do any harm; they just don't realize they're intruding on your turf."

My mother nods understandingly, as if this is a perfectly reasonable explanation. "I see."

Mark and I exchange looks of indignation.

"You can't seriously believe that!" scoffs Mark.

The gardener shrugs. "Sure. Just tell them you don't want them around, that they're your lettuce plants and you don't appreciate other creatures eating them. Don't get into any legal stuff about property boundaries, though; that just confuses them."

He looks Mark square in the eye, perfectly at ease. Mark, in turn, eyes him suspiciously, trying to work out if he's joking or not. Slowly, a smile spreads across the gardener's face.

"Oh, I see. You're kidding," says Mark, clearly not amused.

But the gardener shakes his head.

I have no idea if he's serious or not, and neither does Mark. The difference is that I'm not bothered, whereas Mark takes it as a personal insult if people manage to confuse him.

"I'm surprised you have any time for chatting with slugs," says Mark snidely. "Aren't you too busy talking to apple trees?"

I think the wine may also be going to Mark's head. Until now he has managed to bite his tongue, contenting himself with quiet sniggers and scornful glances. He made no comment when the gardener suggested that envy can be cured with a mixture of lavender and lemon balm, or that native Indian chants encourage rain, or that spitting on a cabbage patch can rid it of ladybugs. But he has no patience with people who spout mumbo-jumbo.

"You can talk to trees, Ewan?" asks my mother, slouching on the table, leaning close to him. "How fascinating."

"It's not fascinating; it's crazy!" Mark protests.

"That depends on how you see it," says the gardener.

"I see it from the point of view of a sane person," Mark says with a laugh, leaning back in his chair.

"I'd like to talk to trees," muses my mother dreamily.

"You should," the gardener tells her. "They like it. It helps them grow."

"No, Mother, you shouldn't," I say, angry about the suggestion. The last thing she needs is encouragement to act strangely.

"But, darling, if they like it and it helps them grow—"

"There is absolutely no scientific reason why trees should grow better just because you're nice to them," says Mark, interrupting.

"Actually," says the gardener, scratching at his stubble with jagged, grubby fingernails, "there's been quite a few studies showing that plants respond to human emotion. Cleve Baxter's report—'Evidence of a Primary Perception in Plant Life'—is probably one of the most famous. You should read it. He tested his plants on a polygraph machine and found that they react to thoughts and threats. And over a thousand different species of plants have been shown to be sensitive to human touch. Darwin started the ball rolling by suggesting that plants possess a central nervous system, based on his observations of the *Dionaea muscipula*. That's the Venus flytrap, by the way."

Mark and I stare at him, speechless.

"I might sometimes have my head in the clouds," he says, looking straight at me, "but that doesn't mean I don't have my feet on the ground."

I feel my face flush and look down at my plate. Mark, clearly annoyed at being shown up by the gardener's knowledge, takes a swig of wine.

"Isn't it fascinating?" says my mother sweetly, entirely unaware that anything is amiss. "So what made you become a gardener, Ewan? You're clearly a natural. Is your father a keen gardener?"

"Nah, Dad's not really one for gardening. He probably did inspire my love of being outdoors, though. Rocks are his thing. He often used to take me with him on his research expeditions, gathering rock samples, putting them in little bags, labeling them, taking them back and referencing them."

"Your father's a scientist?" I ask, a forkful of chicken halfway to my lips.

Ewan takes a sip of wine and gives me a wry little smile. "You sound surprised."

"Er...no, I just didn't...I...

"Well, I suppose geology is a *type* of science," mutters Mark.

While I hadn't expected the gardener to come from scientific stock at all (couldn't his father have talked some sense into him?), I really don't feel the need to undermine his father's choice of discipline by suggesting that it's one of the lower forms of scientific study, which I know Mark is trying to imply.

"And what about your mother?" I ask quickly, more to interrupt Mark's line of questioning than out of genuine interest.

"My mum? She does a lot of acting. She loves the stage."

"Oh, how wonderful!" shouts my mother, grabbing Ewan's arm. "An actress! I love a good show. Meg used to adore the theater, didn't you, darling?"

"I really don't—"

"Do you remember we went to see that one, Meg, with the lion and the witch? And there was a big wardrobe in it. What was it called?"

"*Romeo and Juliet*?" suggests the gardener.

My mother looks thoughtful for a moment, and in spite of myself, I almost laugh.

"Oh!" shrieks my mother, suddenly realizing the gardener is pulling her leg. She slaps him playfully on the arm, and the gardener gives a little chuckle while my mother hoots with laughter at her own foolishness.

Mark coughs and shoots me a look that suggests I should try harder not to encourage such idiocy. I try to suppress my smile, busying myself by neatly folding my napkin.

"Would you like some fruit salad, Ewan?" asks my mother once she has composed herself.

"No, thanks," he says, standing up and patting his stomach. "If you'll excuse me, I've got a bit of work to finish in the garden before it gets too late."

"Oh, no, you've worked so hard all day!"

"Please," he says, raising his hands in protest, "I don't like to leave jobs half done. I'll let myself out the back gate when I'm finished. Thanks a lot for dinner. It was fantastic."

By the back door he pulls his muddy boots on and thanks my mother again before heading back out into the garden.

"Well, wasn't that lovely!" she says, beaming.

Mark and I sit in silence.

My mother finally senses the tension and her smile fades. "Well, perhaps I'll go and lie down for a while," she says awkwardly, disappearing out of the room.

I start to gather up the plates and run a sink full of water. Mark sits silently at the table, sipping his wine and nursing his bruised pride, before suddenly announcing, "I've never heard of this Baxter experiment, have you? I'll look into it. Probably not a scientifically conclusive study. I'll contact John Stokes at the university; he'll know. Who is Baxter anyway? Not a name I've heard of."

I am barely listening. Instead, through the open kitchen window, I am watching the gardener digging in the dirt, pulling up weeds, and chucking them in a pile on the grass. The sun is just starting to go down, giving a golden glow to the sun-kissed skin of his sinewy forearms. I see him pick up a frog from among the beanpoles, hold it in the palm of his hand, and begin talking to it. He points at the garden gate, as if giving the frog directions, then sets the little creature gently down on the grass. It hops away and the gardener resumes digging, trusting that the frog will find its own way out of the garden. A crazy image pops into my mind of the frog packing up his little bag and shouting to all the other frogs that the gardener has politely requested they find somewhere else to hang out in the future. The other frogs would all shrug, I suppose, and off they would hop, too.

"Meg?"

I suddenly realize I haven't been listening to a word Mark has been saying and that soapsuds are about to spill over the rim of the sink. I quickly turn the taps off, trying to remember how much wine I drank at dinner.

"Sorry?"

"He's clearly a complete lunatic, isn't he? That gardener bloke?"

Gazing out into the garden again, I just catch a glimpse of the little green frog as it hops out through the open garden gate as directed.

I rub my forehead with wet, soapy hands, suddenly feeling a headache coming on.

"Oh, yes," I agree dutifully, "of course he is."

chapter six

"What keeps the clouds up?" I asked you one day.

"The sky, silly," you told me.

We were lying on our backs in our local park, side by side, finding patterns in the clouds. I remember pointing at one that looked just like a rabbit, although you insisted it was a birthday cake and that the rabbit's ears were candles. Everything always looked like food to you.

"Then what keeps the sky up?" I asked.

You were quiet for a moment. "Air," you said eventually, "like a soufflé."

"A soufflé?"

"Yes, a soufflé. Place your hand in front of your mouth and breathe on it, like this."

You breathed into the cupped palm of your hand and I copied you.

"You feel how warm your breath is? Well, with all the people in the world breathing at once, that makes a lot of warm air. And you know how warm air makes a soufflé rise?"

I nodded solemnly, pretending to know.

"Well, all the warm air from people breathing makes the sky rise in the same way."

I was young, too young to question you. You could have told me the sky was held up with safety pins, and I would have believed you. I believed everything you told me.

"What would happen if everyone stopped breathing?" I asked.

"I don't think that would happen, sweetheart."

"But what if it did? What if just for a second we all stopped breathing at once? Would the sky fall down?"

"I suppose it might."

"Then what would happen? Would we all get squashed? Would I get squashed like that ladybug when I dropped my book on it by mistake?"

"No, I wouldn't let you get squashed. I'd gather you up in my arms and run to the edge of the earth, and then I'd jump off the earth and out of the way of the falling sky."

"Would we make it in time?"

"Of course. The sky would fall very slowly, like a soufflé when you stick your fork in it and all the air goes out. Plus, I'm a very fast runner."

"You're not that fast," I said. "I'm faster than you. And anyway, what if you weren't there with me? What would happen to me then?"

You rolled over onto your side to face me and tickled my chin with a daisy.

"I'll always be there with you, silly," you said.

And like always, I believed you.

"The thing that attracted me to condensed-matter physics," Mark is telling my mother, "is that it's about the stuff that surrounds us every day. It's not about dealing with the very tiny, like particle theory, or the very large, like astrophysics or cosmology, but about all the stuff that comes in between. The good old, everyday, run-of-the-mill stuff."

"Well, that sounds fascinating." My mother smiles halfheartedly, tracing the rim of her coffee cup. "Ah, good morning, darling!"

She looks relieved to see me as I join them at the kitchen table.

"Mark's just been telling me all about quantum conductivity and super mechanics."

"Quantum mechanics and superconductivity," he corrects her.

She laughs nervously. "Silly me! I'm not very good at all this science stuff, am I, Meggy? I never understand when Meg's telling me about human gnomes."

"Human genomes, Mother, not human gnomes."

"I take it Meg didn't get her scientific mind from you, then, Mrs. May?" Mark asks my mother. He says it with a charming smile, but I know he finds her lack of scientific knowledge frustrating. "How can people not be interested in the world around them?" he is always asking me, indignant. He can't comprehend anyone who cannot grasp the complexities of physics as easily as he can.

"Oh, goodness, no, she didn't get it from me," says my mother, absentmindedly adding sugar to her coffee. "Science was her father's thing."

I stop pouring orange juice and hold the carton in midair, suspended over my glass.

"My father liked science?" I ask, astonished at this revelation. "You said he was a chef."

My mother starts spreading butter onto her croissant with such ferocity that half of it breaks off and flies across the table, landing on Mark's lap.

"There is a scientific element to being a chef you know, darling," she says hurriedly. "Weighing things. Mixing them together. Ovens. Ovens are scientific, aren't they? All those metal bits and electricity and stuff. Who would like some toast? Coffee? I'll make a fresh pot."

She stands up quickly, taking the coffee pot with her. Mark places the piece of croissant back on her plate and raises his eyebrows at me, inquiringly.

I have told Mark very little about my father, other than the fact that he is a deceased pastry chef. I have failed to tell him that this is practically *all* I know. Mark's family is so perfect that I'm sure he would find my ignorance about my own father shocking and confusing. He would tell me to demand details, access to family connections—where, when, who, why. "It's your right," he would tell me. But he doesn't understand how hard it can be, making sense of my world. He doesn't understand what it's like to come up against one brick wall after the other, to live in the murky gray somewhere between black and white.

"Well, wherever she gets her brains from, Meg will certainly be a great scientist," says Mark, stroking the back of my head affectionately.

He smiles proudly at me, and I feel my heart flutter, just like it always does when I win his approval. I have sat in on a couple of the lectures Mark has given at the university, discussing the findings of his research, and I have seen how the female students gaze at him as if he is the source of all knowledge, the oracle. I have seen the way their hands shoot up when he asks a question, desperate for his attention, dying to impress him with their intelligence. But I am the one he has chosen. I am the one whose mind has impressed him and continues to do so day after day. This is the ultimate commendation. With Mark I know I am smart enough, bright enough, good enough. There is no way any girlfriend of Mark Daly—soon to be Dr. Mark Daly—could ever be considered laughable.

"She'll be wonderful at whatever she does," agrees my mother, pouring hot water into the coffee pot. "She has so many skills. She used to love writing and painting, you know. And craft work and acting—"

"I was dreadful at all those things!" I scoff, knowing Mark has very little time for the arts. "I was terrible at anything that involved any sort of creativity at all."

"Only once you stopped trying. When you were very little you used to adore dressing up and playing at make-believe. Don't you remember?" She sits down at the table again, smiling at the memories that are flooding back to her. "You used to dress up in green tights and my frilly red blouse and pretend you were a rose. You looked so pretty!"

I frown at her, a warning to be quiet. I don't want Mark thinking I was some sort of idiot child, the sort who have imaginary friends and believe the bogeyman lives under their bed.

"I must have looked ridiculous," I tell her. "You shouldn't have encouraged me."

"One Christmas, you knocked on every door in our block dressed as Santa Claus and told all our neighbors that you'd come from Bethlehem to find the baby Jesus."

"I was obviously confused. You shouldn't have let me wander around on my own like that talking such rubbish."

"I didn't even notice you'd gone until old Mr. Ginsberg brought you back by the hand. Oh, poor Mr. Ginsberg! One day you startled the life out of him by dressing up in my big, brown woolly sweater and growling at him as he stepped out of the elevator. Apparently he thought you were a bear, although I'm not sure why he thought a bear would be wandering around on the fourth floor!"

Suddenly I can't help myself. I clamp my hand over my mouth and let out a loud snort as I try to suppress my giggles.

"Oh, you do remember, don't you?" laughs my mother, grabbing my arm.

I nod and cover my face with my hands as tears of laughter spring to my eyes. I have vague memories of that itchy brown sweater pulled up over my head and Mr. Ginsberg's look of terror as I pounced at him. I peek through my fingers at Mark, who isn't laughing at all.

"You could have given the poor man a heart attack," he says seriously.

I bite my lip hard. "It was very silly. I was only little, though. And it *was* funny."

"It wouldn't have been funny if the poor man had dropped

down dead. Over two hundred and thirty thousand British people die of heart attacks every year," he informs me.

I compose myself and nod seriously. "You're right. It wouldn't have been funny at all if I'd killed him."

My mother stops laughing and takes a sip of her coffee. Mark takes a bite of his croissant and chews slowly while I fold my napkin into little squares.

"Anyway," says my mother, "you suddenly lost interest in anything creative. Just like that. One day you came home from school, put all your toys in a box, and declared it was time to grow up." She shakes her head and smiles wistfully. "You must have been all of eight years old. I really don't know what happened."

I gaze into my coffee, suddenly feeling rather sad. Eight years old sounds so young to want to grow up, to want to put aside the magic of childhood.

"Waste of time, the arts," declares Mark.

I see my mother's lips tighten. She loves art, music, theater, poetry. She says they "take her out of herself," whatever that's supposed to mean.

"Oh, I don't think they're a waste of time," she says with a polite smile.

"No artist is ever going to find a cure for cancer, and no actor is ever going to discover the secrets of the universe. Meg, on the other hand, is going to be able to make a real difference to the world."

"She already does," says my mother sharply. Mark looks up at her, surprised by the edge to her voice. She smiles quickly.

"Of course she does," he agrees. "I understand her end-of-term paper caused quite a debate in the faculty, and if you can get people thinking, you're halfway there. She's a very intelligent girl."

He squeezes my knee, and I smile lovingly at him.

"And a funny, compassionate, and sweet girl, too," adds my mother.

Mark nods distractedly as he picks at the crumbs on his plate. My mother watches him closely, waiting for his agreement.

I want to intervene, to change the subject and stop them discussing me like I'm not here, but instead I find myself also waiting for Mark's reply. What *does* he think of me? I mean, apart from finding me smart and intelligent and intellectually challenging? What does he actually think of *me*? Bizarrely, I realize he has never said, and, even more bizarrely, I realize I have never wondered.

"Oh, yes, she's lovely," he says, realizing it's his cue to speak. He takes a napkin and wipes his mouth. I watch him, waiting, wanting more, but when he leans back in his chair, sighs, and pats his stomach, I realize he's finished.

My mother reaches across the table and rubs my hand, smiling indulgently. "She always was a sweet girl. When she was little she was so sweet I used to dip her toes in my tea. It saved me a fortune on sugar. I used to lend her out to the neighbors. 'Don't bother buying sugar,' I used to tell them, 'my daughter's the sweetest thing around, and she doesn't rot your teeth.'"

"Mother," I scold sharply, pulling my hand away from hers.

"The neighbors would knock on our door at all hours of the day with cups of tea or coffee, and they'd say, 'Can we get some sweetener?' and I'd dip one of Meg's tiny fingers or toes into their cup—"

"Mother!"

I can feel my cheeks burning with embarrassment. It's bad enough that Mark knows my mother is insane without his having to witness her rantings firsthand.

"Then one day I noticed that Meg's middle toes were starting to wither away. Have you ever noticed, Mark, how Meg's middle toes are a little too short? It was all that dipping them in hot drinks that was the problem. Well, when I realized what was happening, I had to stop—"

"Mother!" I snap angrily. "Mark doesn't want to hear any of your ridiculous stories. Stop embarrassing yourself!"

My mother stares at me, silent and abashed. I am so ashamed. Whatever must Mark think of us? Why must she do this? Why must she make us look like such fools?

Slowly she stands up, her cheeks flushed, her hands fumbling to gather up her cup and her plate.

"I must go and get on with things," she says quietly. "You don't want your silly mother sitting here rambling on all day." She gives an embarrassed chuckle and goes to leave, but just before she gets to the door she turns to me. "I just thought Mark might like to know something more about you."

"He already knows everything about me that matters," I say, annoyed.

She gives a little smile, and I wonder why, when she is the one who talks such nonsense, I am the one who feels like a liar.

Once she has gone, Mark shakes his head in disbelief. "Blimey, what a story!" he laughs. "I'm relieved to hear you take after your father, because your mother is crazy!"

I feel hurt. How am I meant to respond to that? She might be a little strange, but she is still my mother. I look at Mark shaking his head in dismay, his gorgeous, pearly white smile conveying his amusement. He is so intelligent, so confident, so everything I would like to be.

I force myself to laugh with him.

"Yes," I agree. "She is crazy."

Nothing feels right for the rest of the morning. My mother and I tactfully avoid each other. I feel annoyed with her for humiliating me, but also guilty for my outburst. Then I decide I shouldn't have to feel guilty for my outburst, and my annoyance with her doubles. In order to get out of the house, I take Mark into town, where we eat stodgy sandwiches in a cheap café. I try my best to be interesting, adding what I think are fairly astute observations to our discussions about the latest political crisis, but my heart's not really in it.

To make matters worse, our return to the house perfectly coincides with the gardener's arrival. Mark usually insists on parking his perfectly buffed and shined car in the driveway, just in case anybody should see fit to steal it, but today, for some reason, he pulls up right behind the gardener's rusty, clapped-out van, looking strangely satisfied. Unfortunately, the new parking arrangement does not seem to work quite so well for the gardener, who taps on Mark's window just as we are unfastening our seat belts.

Mark opens his door slightly, looking annoyed and muttering something about the filthy smudge that the gardener has left on his window.

"Do you mind backing up a bit?" asks the gardener. "I need to open the back doors of my van."

Mark doesn't respond, so engrossed is he in examining the streak of dirt the gardener has left on his window. I feel slightly embarrassed and want to whisper to Mark that it really doesn't matter, that we have plenty of Windex inside the house and that I will be more than happy to clean the dirt off later. But I don't think that would help matters.

"Didn't expect to see you back so soon," says Mark. "I expect you need to work every day, though, don't you, to make your line of work pay?"

I feel impressed and relieved that Mark has adopted such a friendly and sensitive tone. For a moment there I thought he was going to be insulting.

"Just on my way back from another job," the gardener says. "Thought I'd swing by and finish off the staking. Ran out of bamboo yesterday."

"Stretching the job out," Mark says with a nod. "Very clever."

They stare at each other for what feels like an embarrassingly long time, and I shift awkwardly in my seat, thinking that Mark can't possibly have realized the implication of his comment. But the gardener just smiles.

"I'm not charging for it," he explains. "I just don't like leaving a job unfinished."

Mark nods slowly, and I can see his mind whirring while he thinks of a response to this.

"We'll reverse a bit," I say quickly, wanting to end this exchange.

"Be careful not to scratch my hood when you take your tools out, won't you?" says Mark, going to close the door.

"Right you are, governor," says the gardener, giving a little salute. "Miss." He winks at me and gives another little salute before giving the top of the car a hearty pat and walking back toward his van, pretending to tip his imaginary cap. I try to suppress a smile, telling myself there is nothing funny about this insolent little comedy routine, while Mark shakes his head, disgruntled, and puts the car in reverse.

Mark isn't terribly good with heights, which is why, later that day, I am the one perching precariously at the top of a ladder with my head inside the loft hatch while he passes up my suitcases.

"What's that?" I hear him ask from the landing below.

He suddenly tugs so hard on the case I am struggling to hoist into the loft that I am forced to let it go or come tumbling down the ladder with it. It is only by grabbing onto the edge of the loft hatch that I manage to stop myself from falling and breaking my neck. I hear a cry of pain and look down to see Mark holding his head, the old, battered leather suitcase at his feet.

"Meg," he says, looking up at me, "can you try to be less clumsy?"

"But you—"

"You could have killed me."

"Sorry," I say, thinking if anyone could have been killed, surely it's me.

"What's that?" I ask, looking at the piece of paper Mark is examining.

"Just looks like an old flier for some rock band," he says, rubbing his head. "It was sticking out from the seam of the suitcase. I thought it might be important. Not so important I wanted to risk my life for it, though."

"What do you mean, a flier?" I ask, intrigued. I descend the ladder and take the piece of paper out of Mark's hand.

> *The Frog and Whistle, King's Cross, presents* CHLORINE *(nearly featured in* That's Music! *magazine). Tickets at the door.*

The date is the year of my birth.

"Probably something from your mother's crazy teenage years," Mark says. "Was she into bands? I can imagine she was. Probably did drugs. That would explain a lot..."

I turn the piece of paper over. On the back, in my mother's faded handwriting, is an address: 15 Gray's Inn Road, London.

"...drugs fry the brain. That's probably the problem, you know. Irresponsible behavior always takes its toll sooner or later..."

I'm not really listening to anything Mark is saying. All I can think is that I am holding a piece of my mother's past in my hands. A real, concrete item from the year I was born that has transcended the passage of time and ended up here, now, today, between my fingers. It feels rather surreal.

"It must have worked its way into the lining of the case," says Mark. "You should just get rid of this old thing. Look at the state of it."

I touch the piece of paper as if it is a priceless museum piece.

"This belonged to her," I say thoughtfully, "around the time I was born. Maybe even before I was born."

"Mmm. So do you want to keep this case, or shall we throw it out?"

Mark clearly has no idea what this means. Despite everything I have told him about my past—or lack of it—he still doesn't really grasp the extent of the void. And how could he? How could anybody? No one understands what it feels like to have a hole where a life should be.

"Do you think it's important?" asks Mark, spying the intrigue on my face.

Whose address could this be? I wonder. Could it be family? Could it be an old friend of my mother's? Could it be the address of my father's family, who might not have been French at all? Could it be the address of my father?

"It's probably nothing," I say.

Mark eyes me closely.

"Are you sure? Because if you do think this is important in some way, then you need to—"

"Oh, no," I say, waving my hand in the air dismissively. "It's nothing. I'm sure of it."

I haphazardly fold the paper and stuff it in my back pocket as casually as possible, as if I'm merely going to keep it there until I can reach a bin. I don't want Mark making a big deal out of this, because I know exactly what will come next. He'll tell me to ask my mother, to search out the facts, to make her talk...but he just doesn't understand. And I don't need that kind of pressure right now. So it's better to be nonchalant and to pretend that finding a scrap of my mother's past is something that happens all the time, that my heart's not pounding, that my mind's not whirring, and that I'm not having visions of myself knocking on a house on Gray's Inn Road and screaming "Daddy!" before flinging my arms around the neck of my long-lost father.

"Right, shall we try that again?" I ask, quickly scrambling back up the ladder before any more can be said about the matter.

"I'm afraid I won't be able to come down next weekend," Mark says as we stand by his car. "James has an award ceremony in London on Saturday evening, and I promised I'd be there."

"That's fine," I reassure him, thinking I could have done without this reminder of Mark's family. They are all incredibly sane and successful. His brother, James, is a microbiologist who seems to keep making amazing discoveries, and his parents are both doctors. I have only met his parents once. They were very smart and respectable, and neither of them felt the need to invent ridiculous stories about their son's childhood.

"I'll come down the following weekend, though," Mark says.

"That's fine," I say again.

If the truth be told, I am quite keen for Mark to get in his car and go, which is a terrible thing to admit. I really do appreciate everything he has done for me, and it was very good of him to pack up all my belongings and bring them down, but I can feel the flier in my back pocket, burning like a hot coal through the denim of my jeans, in need of urgent attention.

I'm sure it's nothing. But what if it is? What if this could lead me to someone or something from my past? My mother is so scrupulously secretive. She has woven her web of lies so carefully that no trace has ever existed for me to follow. But now I have something. A little scrap of paper with an address on it. It might mean nothing. But then again…

Mark cups his hands around my face and plants a firm kiss on my lips. "Talk to your mother," he advises me, wisely. "She really needs to start facing the truth about what's going to happen. Get some more advice from the doctor. And call a lawyer, won't you? You don't want to just leave things; you need to plan ahead. If you want, my parents have a great attorney—"

"It's fine," I say quickly, squeezing his arm. "I'll sort it out."

He smiles at me.

"I know you will. That's the thing I really admire about you, the fact that—"

"Oh, Mark, look at the time! You're going to miss the car wash. It closes at five."

Mark checks his watch, looking as panic-stricken as I have ever seen him.

"Does it? Right. Better go, then."

As Mark slowly drives down the road, I wave to him and tap my foot restlessly on the hot pavement, feeling rather guilty for wanting him gone. By the time his car reaches the end of the road and stops at the intersection, its turn indicator flashing, I have already pulled the flier from my pocket and am clumsily unfolding it with one hand while continuing to wave to Mark with the other. Even though there is never any traffic on these roads, I know Mark will be checking—left, right, left again, right again—just like he always does. By the time he carefully turns the corner, I have managed to convince myself that this little scrap of paper is the key to the universe, and I can't wait a moment longer.

"Right," I tell myself, already halfway up the garden path. "Time for the truth."

"I was never very good at making toad in the hole. I could never get the toads to stay in the batter long enough to get the dish in the oven. They knew what was coming, you see. As you know, toads don't much like the heat, so the moment I opened the oven door they'd be off, hopping across the work surface, leaving little batter footprints everywhere."

I hover behind the blackberry bush, listening to my mother's ravings. She must be talking to the gardener. I am surprised at how sociable my mother is being; usually she avoids other people like the plague. Unfortunately, it seems that finally she has found someone willing to endure her nonsense for hours on end.

"Trying to catch those toads was impossible!" she is saying. "They're slippery enough as it is, but when they're covered in batter you haven't got a chance!"

I close my eyes and resist the urge to scream. Or cry. It's bad enough having Mark think she's a lunatic, but when it's a complete stranger…

"Maybe you should have used frogs instead, Valerie. I know toad in the hole is more traditional, but the thing is toads are really smart creatures, whereas frogs, well, they're not so bright."

"Really?"

"Sure. Why do you think the French eat so many of them? They're easy to catch, no coordination. Toads, on the other hand, they'll be off and out of sight before you know it."

"Well, I never knew that. That would have saved me many an hour running around the kitchen after those wretched toads. Actually, to you tell the truth, even when I caught them I never put them in the oven. They had a way of looking at me with their big sad eyes—"

"I know just what you mean. Toads are real emotional blackmailers."

I put my hands over my face in despair. My God, they're both as crazy as each other! He's just encouraging her. Out of all the gardeners in the world who could have knocked on our door…

"Hi, there."

I peek through my fingers at the gardener, who is standing in front of me with a bamboo stake and some twine in his hands, looking at me curiously.

"Are you okay?"

I take my hands away from my face and straighten my blouse.

"Yes, thank you. I was just looking for my mother."

"Hello, darling," she says, emerging from behind the bush in an enormous straw sunhat and sunglasses that swamp her face. Her voice has lost the excitement of a moment ago, and she looks slightly nervous, as if she is waiting for me to tell her off again like I did this morning.

I feel horrible. I didn't mean to make her feel bad. Seeing her looking so timid—and so ridiculous in those glasses—my heart softens, and I wonder whether I should question her about the flier after all. Wouldn't it be easier just to smooth over the events of this morning with a nice glass of lemonade and a chat, lying side by side on the lounge chairs? I'm sure she's got some recipe she wants to tell me about, and it's such a lovely day...but no! If this could mean something, if this could be a link to the past, then I need to know.

"Mother, what is this?" I ask, holding the piece of paper out to her. "It was in the lining of your old suitcase."

My mother takes the paper from my hand and examines it, turning it over and reading the address. An expression I have never seen before suddenly clouds her face. She looks like she's just opened her own death warrant. Her hand flutters at her throat, and the color seems to drain from her rosy cheeks.

"I don't...I really...I have no idea," she stammers.

"Whose address is that?"

My mother touches her lips nervously.

"I don't know, darling. I really don't know. Is it yours?"

I stare blankly at her.

"Oh, no, no, you don't live in London. Not now. You did. We did. But now I live here. And you live in Leeds. What was the question again? I'm sorry; I seem to be getting a bit confused. I think it's the heat."

"Are you all right?" asks the gardener, stepping forward.

My mother takes her enormous glasses off and rubs her forehead. I notice her hands are shaking.

"I'm feeling a little light-headed. Too much sun, probably. Maybe I'll go inside for a bit."

She takes a couple of unsteady steps, veering into the blackberry bush.

The gardener is at her side before I am, steadying her by the elbow.

"Do you need to sit down?" he asks.

"Goodness, no!" she laughs, rather too shrilly. "I'm fine. Just the heat getting to me. It's such a hot day, isn't it? What's this?"

She looks at the flier in her hand again as if she has never seen it before.

"Is this yours, darling? Does it need signing?"

"I'll take that," I say gently, taking the paper from her, suddenly very worried.

"Are you sure you're all right?" asks the gardener.

"Yes, yes," she says, wandering off down the garden path. "Don't you worry about me. It's just the heat. It gets to me sometimes. I'll be back out to help you soon!"

"That's really not necessary—"

"Nonsense! Two pairs of hands are better than one!"

If I had my wits about me I would follow her, but I am so baffled that instead I just stand there, gazing after her. I turn the flier over in my hands. Did this little piece of paper cause that reaction? Surely not. My mother does sometimes suffer in the sun, after all. And she has been out here all day, trying to keep out of my way. But then again, she also tends to go a bit funny when there is any mention of the past, so maybe…

"She's some woman, your mother," says the gardener, breaking the silence. "She's been telling me the most incredible stories."

Baffled, I fold up the flier and put it back in my pocket. "I bet she has," I say distractedly.

He nods up at my mother's bedroom window. "She was telling me how you were born up there. Caught in a saucepan, I hear."

"It was a frying pan."

He laughs. "And the first thing you did was cluck like a chicken. Too many eggs, she said. And then the gasman—"

"Please, don't encourage her," I interrupt.

He stops laughing. "Encourage her?"

"Yes. I heard you telling her all that rubbish about how frogs are easier to catch than toads, and how toads are really smart."

"I was just telling her the truth."

I fold my arms and roll my eyes. "Oh, please."

"A recent study from the American Institute of Zoology showed that in general, frogs have a slower reaction time than toads when faced with the threat of predators."

"Oh," I say, slightly taken aback, "I see. Well, anyway, I'd rather you didn't pretend you're interested in my mother's ridiculous stories. If you do, she'll just keep telling them."

"But I am interested. They're cool stories."

"They're lies," I say, correcting him.

He shrugs. "Does that matter?"

"Of course it matters. People can't just go around lying."

"There's a very fine line between the truth and a lie, isn't there?"

"No, there isn't. One is real, the other is not. It's extremely simple if you think about it."

I am aware that my words sound patronizing, but it's turning out to be a bad day and I am already upset and annoyed without some gardener talking nonsense at me.

He smiles, his eyes half closed against the late afternoon sun. I notice that one of his teeth is slightly chipped, and for some reason it annoys me that he hasn't had it fixed. There's no need for imperfections when cosmetic dentistry is so widely available.

"I don't think that's the way life is," he says thoughtfully. "I think life is a mass of lines that are always being crossed. A patchwork of shapes that are constantly shifting. There are so many different ways of seeing the world. How can we say where fiction ends and reality begins, who's right and who's wrong?"

"Well, the person with the correct information is right," I tell him tersely, "and the person with the incorrect information is wrong. Look, I understand that to someone who enjoys talking to trees my mother's stories must seem quite amusing, but I really would appreciate it if you'd try not to indulge her. She can get a little…well…out of control."

"And what's wrong with that?" His hazelnut eyes flit over my face, flecks of gold glistening playfully in the light. "Don't you ever want to get out of control?"

For the first time I notice the tiny dimples that appear at the corner of his mouth when he smiles. Suddenly I am starting to feel rather warm.

"No," I tell him, forcing myself to look away. "I don't."

He chuckles. "Now, why doesn't that surprise me?"

"What's that supposed to mean?"

"Nothing. I just think you're a very self-controlled person, that's all. I suppose I have difficulty imagining you really letting go."

"I can let go!" I snap.

"I'm sure you can," he says. "I can just imagine you running wild with a pie chart, going crazy with an encyclopedia, blowing off steam with a test tube—"

"At least I don't waste my time talking to lumps of wood!" I exclaim, pointing toward the apple trees.

"You could have fooled me," he mumbles.

"Sorry? Are you referring to Mark?"

He tries to suppress a guilty smile and holds his grass-stained hands up in apology.

"Sorry, that was—"

"I'll have you know that Mark is a very intelligent, articulate, and educated man, who is held in very high esteem."

"So I see."

"Not just by me! Everybody in the faculty knows how bright he is."

"Brightness can be blinding."

"And insolence can be annoying."

"I'm starting to get the impression that everything about me annoys you. Am I right?"

"Pretty much, yes."

"In which case, I have nothing to lose."

"Except your job, obviously."

"To be fair, you don't employ me; your mother does."

"I'm sure I can make her change her mind."

"You seem to want to change a lot of things about her."

I gawk at him. "How dare you judge me! You don't know anything about me."

"Don't I?" He points to the upstairs window. "I know you were born upstairs in that room and caught in a frying pan."

"I wasn't! I mean, I was…I might have been. I—"

"You don't know?"

"Of course I know! It's just…it's complicated."

"How can it be complicated? You either were or you weren't. It's extremely simple if you think about it."

I stare at him, outraged. How dare he use my own words to mock me? How dare he try to show me up? I open my mouth, ready to spit a sarcastic comment back at him, but I can't think of anything. Infuriated, I do the only thing I can think of.

"I'm sure you must be finished by now," I tell him, taking a twenty-pound note out of my pocket and chucking it on the grass by his feet. "Keep the change."

I turn my back on him and stride back toward the house, fuming.

"Mother!"

I burst into the kitchen, all guns blazing, but she isn't there. Fueled by the gardener's insolence, I am determined to say my piece. How can I not even be sure where I was born? I don't even know if I was caught in a frying pan or not! I will not be a walking target for other people's ridicule. I will not be made to look stupid. Not again. Forget the flier. Forget the address. I shouldn't need to be scrabbling around after clues like Sherlock Holmes. I deserve to simply be told the truth! It's my right!

"Mother!"

She can't do this to me! Mark's right, it's not fair. I have a right to know the truth about who I am. And the gardener's wrong; life is not a patchwork of shifting shapes. There are truths and there are lies, and I need to know which is which.

I burst into the lounge.

"Oh my God!"

I fall on my knees next to where she lies unconscious by the fireplace, her right arm twisted beneath her. My shaking hands fumble to push her long hair away from her face. Her skin is white, as if all the blood has drained from her body, and her face feels cold.

"Mother? Can you hear me?"

In a blind panic I run to the kitchen door and scream at the top of my lungs:

"Help!"

He is standing exactly as I left him no more than two minutes ago, turning the twenty-pound note over in his hand.

"It's my mother! Please come quickly!"

He starts to run toward the house. I rush back through to the lounge, and seconds later he is there, crouching by my side, listening to my mother's heart.

"Has this ever happened before?" he asks me.

"I don't know what happened. I came in and she was just lying here. What do we do?" I shout, my voice shrill. "I don't know what to do!"

"Does she have any medical conditions?"

"Oh my God! What's wrong with her?"

"Meg, does she have any medical conditions?"

I look at him blankly, unable to understand anything he is saying to me, such is my state of panic. All I can think is that his boots are getting mud all over the rug. "I…what shall I do? Mother?"

"Where's the phone?"

"Is she going to be okay?"

He calmly puts his hands on my shoulders. "Where—is—the—phone?"

"What? I don't know! Why are you asking me? What shall we do?"

I cover my face with my hands, my head spinning. When I look up, the gardener has the phone in his hand.

"Ambulance, please."

I watch him as he gives our address calmly and coherently. He explains how she was found unconscious only moments ago. No, he doesn't know if she has any medical conditions. No, he doesn't know if she's taken anything.

I am frozen, unable to do or say anything of use. I can only watch as events unfold around me in slow motion, and someone else—the last person I would have expected—steps up to the mark and takes control where I cannot.

"Has she been ill at all?" the gardener asks me.

He holds the phone between his shoulder and his ear as he clasps my mother's wrist, monitoring her pulse.

I swallow hard and nod. "She's dying."

He stares at me, speechless. I can hear the voice of the telephone operator coming from the earpiece.

"Please, come quickly," he tells them.

chapter seven

I try to imagine a world without you in it. A world where I have no one to call when I can't remember the recipe for chicken soup; where no one bakes my favorite chocolate cake on my birthday; where no one rings me on a cold winter's morning just to check if I have warm socks on; where I have no one to tell me my hair needs cutting, or to stand up straight, or that I'm working too late into the night. A world where no one worries if I don't eat my greens, or if I read in a dim light, or if I don't take a raincoat. A world where no one says, "Do you remember when…?" or "When you were little…"

I try, but I can't imagine it at all.

I can't imagine coming home to a house that doesn't smell of stews and buns and pies, where you're not there to greet me with your cheery sing-song voice and breathless tales of what you've baked and what you've burnt. I can't imagine not curling up with you on the sofa in front of the fire, opening Christmas presents and feigning surprise as we both unwrap the gifts we asked for. I can't imagine not finding that a hot water bottle has been secretly placed beneath my duvet, or that you have recorded my favorite programs, or that you have sewed up a hole in my sweater without my even mentioning it was there. I can't imagine not seeing your face, sharing the life we made, having you here with me.

And the times when I can, the pain is almost too much to bear.

"It's all a lot of fuss about nothing," I hear her tell Dr. Bloomberg. "I just had a little too much sun, that's all. I'll be right as rain in half an hour."

"Even so," he replies, "I'd rather you just stayed in bed for the rest of the day."

I hover on the landing outside her room, listening to their conversation. The stress of my mother's collapse has given me a headache, and my hands still feel shaky. I stuff them into the pockets of my jeans and chastise myself for having failed to take control.

"You really must take it easy, my dear," I hear the doctor say.

"I don't need to take it easy, Doctor, I'm perfectly all right. Meg's the one I'm worried about. She looks rather drained, don't you think? And she's delayed going back to university until next week, which isn't like her at all. I think she works too hard, you know. She's forever studying, and to be honest"—she lowers her voice to a loud whisper—"I wonder if it might be her way of avoiding something."

I roll my eyes heavenward. My poor mother, thinking *I* am the one who is avoiding something! I wait to hear the doctor tell her she's wrong, that I'm perfectly fine, and that *she's* the one who needs to face the truth.

"You could be right," he says.

My mouth falls open.

"It's not necessarily unhealthy, though," he continues. "It's just her way of coping. I wouldn't worry about it, although I suppose you might try talking to her."

I shake my head in disbelief. The things he will agree with to keep my mother happy!

"It's rather difficult to talk to her about certain things," my mother tells him. "She is of a very particular mind-set."

"Yes, she's a determined girl, all right. Stubborn baby as well, I seem to remember. Just would not grow, if I recall correctly."

Oh, Mother, I think, *please don't remind the doctor about how he advised putting me in the water heater closet. He will probably whisk you away and have you locked up in an asylum!*

"Doctor, would you like another cup of tea?" I ask, swiftly entering the room.

They both turn toward me, guilty to have been caught red-handed discussing me behind my back. My mother's face is pale and tired, gazing up at me from her pillow, and the doctor peers sheepishly over his glasses at me from a chair by the bed.

"Thank you," he mumbles, heaving his heavy old body off the chair and gathering up his battered leather bag, "but I'm just off." He pats my mother's hand. "I'll come and see you in a few days," he says, smiling gently.

"Oh, don't bother yourself. I'll be all right, Doctor," says my mother.

"Will she be all right?" I ask as I reach the bottom of the stairs. Dr. Bloomberg is descending slowly behind me, clinging to the banister and treating each step as if it is a dangerous obstacle. By the time he joins me at the bottom, he is breathing heavily, and for a second it occurs to me that at least my mother will never have to grow old.

"She'll be fine for now," he says, "but you did the right thing calling the ambulance immediately. Good job. You're so levelheaded."

I bite my lip, ashamed. Do I tell him what a failure I was? How I couldn't even compose myself enough to remember the location of the telephone? Surely he would find me ridiculous. After all, this is a man whose job consists of dealing with emergencies, saving lives, making life-or-death decisions. Perhaps I blurt out the truth because I am having a moment of weakness, or perhaps I am looking for reassurance. Either way, my confession is out before I know it.

"Actually, I wasn't very levelheaded at all. I panicked. I couldn't think straight. I'm usually very much in control. I don't know what happened. It wasn't me who called the ambulance." I stare at my feet and shuffle awkwardly. "It was the gardener." As soon as it's out, I wish I hadn't said it. He probably thinks I'm completely incompetent.

Dr. Bloomberg smiles sympathetically at me. "Sometimes we all need a little help, Meg," he says gently, "whatever form that help might come in."

I tuck a strand of hair behind my ear and nod, feeling foolish.

"Give my regards to the gardener, then," he says, turning the doorknob, ready to leave.

"Ewan," I say quickly.

"I'm sorry?"

The name sounds strange on my tongue, and I realize this may be the first time I have ever said it.

"Ewan," I repeat. "His name is Ewan."

Ewan may have been the one who saved the day, but I can't help feeling annoyed by his sudden disappearance shortly after the ambulance arrived. Admittedly, it hadn't taken long for my mother to regain consciousness, but the moment she did Ewan was gone, leaving me to contend with two paramedics, a disoriented mother, and a phone call to Dr. Bloomberg. Obviously his helpfulness only stretches so far.

I am therefore rather surprised when I walk into the kitchen to find him at the stove, boiling something in a steaming saucepan. It smells familiar, slightly herby, like something from my university apartment.

"Are you cooking yourself Super Noodles?" I snap, annoyed by his audacity and still hurt by his abandonment.

He frowns at me over his shoulder. "Super what? No, I'm making herbal tea."

"You're making herbal tea? Now? I don't know if you realize, but there's just been a rather distressing incident, so if you want a cup of tea—"

"It's for your mother," he interrupts. "I've been out gathering herbs from the garden. Everything's so overgrown, though, that it took forever to find what I wanted."

I peer suspiciously at the boiling yellow liquid in the saucepan. "What on earth is that?" I ask, thinking there is no way I am letting my mother drink some gypsy concoction full of leaves and twigs.

"Mint to ease her headache, marjoram and thyme to give her strength, and lemon balm to help her relax."

I sniff it doubtfully.

"And before you say anything," he adds, "no, this recipe has not been scientifically proven, and no, I don't have a PhD in the medicinal properties of plants."

"I wasn't about to ask you either of those things," I say defensively, wondering how he read my mind.

He pours the steaming liquid from the saucepan into a cup.

"You do know what you're doing, though, don't you?" I ask cautiously. "It won't hurt her, will it?"

He turns to me, his face serious with no trace of his usual cheeky smile. "Why don't you just stick to your science and leave me to mine?"

And before I even have a chance to argue with him, he has picked up the cup and walked out of the kitchen.

When I was little and I'd done something wrong, I'd go to the garden and pick my mother a bunch of flowers. I'd leave them on her bedside table in a jam jar, and not another word would be said about it. The awkward silence would be broken, the crime and punishment forgotten. The flowers I take her this evening, though, are not only to say sorry for snapping at her; they are for so many other things that I can't find the words to say.

Ewan is sitting on the chair by her bed in grubby frayed jeans and an old red T-shirt that bears the slogan "Max Out." I have no idea what it's supposed to mean. Outside, the light is fading, casting a serene yellow glow into the bedroom. He has opened the window a little bit, just the way my mother likes it, and a cool breeze is blowing a ripple through the net curtain. I hover by the doorway, unseen by them both, and listen. Ewan is telling her a story, his voice deep and soothing.

"In the beginning there was only blackness, and because nobody could see anything, everybody kept bumping into each other. So they said, 'What this world needs is some light.' Fox said that he knew some people on the other side of the world who had plenty of light, but they were too greedy to share it with anyone else.

"'I'll go and steal it and hide it under my bushy tail,' said Possum.

"So Possum trekked to the other side of the world, and there he found the sun hanging in a tree. He picked out a tiny piece of light and hid it in his tail, but the light was hot and burned all the fur off, revealing him as a thief.

"'Let me try,' said Buzzard. 'I'll carry the light home on my head.'

"So Buzzard flew to the other side of the world, grabbed the sun with his claws, and put it on his head. But it was so hot that it burned all the feathers off the top of his head and he dropped it.

"Grandmother Spider, thinking both Possum and Buzzard were useless, said, 'Get out of my way and let me try.'

"She made a pot out of clay and spun a web reaching right across to the other side of the world. She was so tiny that nobody noticed her coming, and quick as a flash she snatched up the sun, put it in her pot, and scurried back home. Now her side of the world finally had light, and there was a huge party to celebrate. The Cherokee Indians say that this little spider brought them not only the sun, but also the art of making pottery."

I hear my mother laughing quietly.

"What a wonderful story!" she says, her voice sounding weak but full of enthusiasm. "I will never look at a little spider in the same way again!"

I enter cautiously.

"Oh, hello, darling."

My mother's auburn hair is splayed out across her pillow, and her cheeks are tinged with pink. Her eyes look brighter than they have for a while.

"How are you feeling?" I ask.

"I feel rather good, actually," she says with a smile. "My headache's completely gone."

I spy the empty cup on the bedside table. The little bunch of flowers I am clutching in my hand suddenly seems rather pointless in comparison to Ewan's healing tea. I stand awkwardly, feeling useless.

"Ewan's been telling me some wonderful stories," says my mother, quickly filling the silence.

I smile meekly at Ewan, a peace offering, but he looks down at his feet, wriggling his toes in his threadbare green socks. My mother looks from me to Ewan and back again, trying to gauge the situation.

"I should go," he says. He stands and hoists up the waistband of his jeans.

My mother smiles up at him. "Thank you for the tea."

He nods. "No problem. I'll leave the garden this week, give you some peace and quiet. I'll come back next Wednesday if you like."

"Wonderful. Thank you."

He passes close to me at the foot of the bed but doesn't look me in the eye.

"I think this belongs to you," he says quietly as he passes, holding out his clenched fist. He pushes something against my palm: the twenty-pound note I threw at him earlier.

"Keep it," he says, walking out of the room. "I don't want it."

I feel tears of shame welling in my eyes. How could I have been so rude as to throw money at him? Who am I to treat him as if he is beneath me? What on earth is the matter with me?

I swallow hard, listening to his steps disappearing down the staircase.

"These are for you," I say quickly, pushing the small bouquet of flowers into my mother's hand, trying to prevent the tears from coming. For one horrible second I have an image of her handing them back to me. "Keep them," I imagine her saying, "I don't want them." I'm sure it would be no more than I deserve.

Instead, she touches my hand and smiles. "Thank you, sweetheart."

"Are you in love with Mark?" my mother asks me.

It's late now and I have drawn the curtains, switching on the little lamp that sheds a reddish glow over the room. I am sitting in a ball on the end of my mother's bed, my feet entwined with hers underneath the covers. We have been chatting for almost an hour, discussing barometers and cheese and cats and glassblowing. We can talk for hours like this, my mother and I.

"I think I am certainly learning to love Mark," I say earnestly. "I respect him. He's kind to me. We get on well. We never argue. He's very interesting and intelligent and handsome."

My mother looks at me curiously, as if she asked me the capital of Spain and I told her it was Bermuda. I know this isn't the answer she wants, but life is no fairy tale.

"I don't believe in falling in love," I tell her. "Not in the fireworks and stars-in-your-eyes kind of way, in any case. It's just not realistic."

She plays with a piece of her auburn hair, twisting it lazily around her finger, and gazes up at the ceiling from her pillow.

"I saw stars in your father's eyes the evening we met," she says, "thousands of them, twinkling away. At first I wondered where they all came from, but when I looked up at the night sky—"

"—it was empty," I interrupt. "I know, you've told me a hundred times."

"I could hear his heart beating from three feet away, pounding like a kettle drum. And the moment he kissed me a bolt of lightning shot across the sky, leaving crackling electricity in its wake. A nightingale burst into song, and a glittering cloud of stardust engulfed us both. He tasted of cinnamon and strawberries, the most delicious taste you can imagine. And afterward, when I licked my lips, I found they were—"

"—covered in sugar, I know."

"They call it falling in love because that's just what happens, you know; you fall slowly for a long, long way. I started falling the moment your father held me in his arms, and I carried on falling for days. I thought I'd never feel the ground beneath my feet again. You feel weightless and free, like you're sailing through the sky, but it's also frightening because you don't know when it will end."

Her eyes are vacant, her voice dreamy. I have heard these stories so many times before, and every time my head fills with questions. In a bid to make the facts fit, I want to stop her and ask about dates, times, and places. I want to point out all the inconsistencies. And yet, for some reason, I never do. Instead, I hug my legs to my body and lay my head on my knees, listening to her talk. I see my parents' first evening together just as my mother describes it: the full moon shining overhead, a nightingale singing in the trees, the scent of apple blossom and ripe cherries lingering in the air.

"At night, I used to stand just there," she says, pointing at the window, "and wait for him to appear on the lawn below. If the breeze was blowing in the right direction, his scent reached me long before he did: honey and cinnamon, sugar and vanilla, toasted almonds, and warm spiced wine. I would run downstairs and sneak out the back door as my parents slept. He would take my hand, leading me into the fields at the end of the garden, where we would lie among the wheat, feeding each other Turkish delight."

She gazes at the narrow sliver of white moonlight that is piercing through the curtains.

"The day he returned to Paris, I cried tears as bitter as the juice of any lemon. I longed for his return, and yet I knew he had died before they even told me. Everything had already lost its taste, you see. I couldn't tell sweet from bitter, salty from sour. My taste buds never tingled, and my mouth never watered. That's when I knew he was gone."

She turns to me. "That's what falling in love is like, and one day it will happen to you."

I try to imagine this feeling of weightlessness, of being outside of yourself, of seeing stars where there shouldn't be any. But that's just not how I've found meeting the man of my dreams to be.

"When I first saw Mark," I tell her, "he was giving a talk on developments in cryogenic technologies. I'd stumbled into the wrong lecture, of course, but by the time I realized it, I was already hooked. He spoke with such absolute confidence and conviction, such clarity and understanding. Here he was talking about something so complex and potentially confusing, and yet he made it sound like it was the simplest thing in the world. He has this ability to make everything sound manageable, reducing it down to categories and rules and facts. Above all, I thought, here is someone who understands the way the world works."

I lean my head back against the wall and study the shadows on the ceiling. "With Mark, it's not like falling; it's the opposite, in fact, like being picked up and set firmly back down on the ground. Everything is suddenly clear. Every why has a reason, and every mystery has an answer. It's like being found when you're lost or given the solution to a puzzle that has baffled you for ages. The earth doesn't spin; it stops spinning."

I look at my mother, who is watching me intently, slightly sadly.

"Maybe falling in love can be like that, too," I say.

Later, while my mother sleeps upstairs, I call Mark to tell him about my mother's collapse.

"The doctor agreed it was probably just too much sun. Although I'm starting to think he'll agree with anything she says just to keep her quiet."

"You don't think it was that?"

"Well, she's getting weaker. Maybe things like this are just part of the illness. I really don't know."

I can hear the weariness in my voice. I feel absolutely drained. "And then there was the flier. I thought maybe it had upset her for some reason, but then I thought maybe that was just in my head."

"The flier? The one from the suitcase?"

I rub my eyes and try to suppress a yawn. "Yes. I showed it to her and she went quite weird. But then, she is quite weird anyway, so it's hard to tell—"

"Weird how? What did she do? Do you mean she seemed defensive? Like she was disturbed by it?"

My feeling of exhaustion doubles. Why on earth did I mention the flier? In all the stress and commotion of my mother collapsing, I had actually forgotten all about it. I'm not sure I really want Mark setting an agenda for me right now on how to harangue my mother into a confession.

"I don't know, Mark. It was probably all just a coincidence."

"You mean you showed it to her and about five minutes later she fainted?"

"Well, no, I showed it to her and she started to get dizzy. And very confused. And then she fainted."

"And you think that's a coincidence? Meg, that's not a coincidence. That's evidence!"

I really, *really* wish I hadn't mentioned the flier.

"That address clearly means something to her. It's a clue, Meg. You need to find out what's behind this. You need to get to the bottom of it."

"But it's not that easy. I've told you before—"

"Nothing in life that's worth having is easy, Meg. DNA wasn't discovered by people just waiting for it to fall into their laps, was it? You have a clue here. It's a starting point. You need to think methodically about how you're going to pursue it. You're meant to be a scientist."

"I *am* a scientist."

"Then think like one. Think about how you're going to use this—"

"But, Mark," I interrupt, wondering why I brought this up, "she's ill right now. If her fainting had something to do with the piece of paper I showed her, then the last thing I want to do right now is—"

"What do you mean, if it had something to do with it? It clearly *did*. In fact, she was probably just faking. She probably pretended to feel dizzy just so she wouldn't have to discuss it any further with you."

"Oh no, I don't think—"

"This is a woman who is capable of lying to her daughter day in, day out, and you don't think she's capable of feigning a fainting fit?"

"But she was unconscious. And the ambulance came. And even Dr. Bloomberg said—"

Mark sighs as if I am completely missing the point.

"She caused a commotion, in other words. And what happens when there's a commotion? People get distracted. I bet you forgot all about the flier, didn't you?"

I don't answer him, but my silence clearly says it all.

"Exactly. She's the greatest liar who ever lived. There are trained spies who have given more secrets away than your mother. She's cunning, Meg. Very cunning."

Cunning? My mother's not cunning. She's strange and confusing and exasperating, but she's not cunning. And she couldn't have feigned being ill. Could she? No. Absolutely not. But I suppose Mark's right, I did forget about the flier. I rub my tired eyes, feeling confused, and do what I often seem to do these days when my head is in a muddle.

"What should I do, then?" I ask Mark.

"Cut to the chase, Meg. If she's not going to talk, then go to that address. Find out who lives there. Who lived there at the time. Find out whatever you can."

"Do you think so? But it feels so deceitful. I'd rather she just told me—"

"Deceitful! You think you're the one being deceitful?"

I can see his point. "Maybe I should try talking to her again. Maybe this time…"

I leave my own sentence unfinished, knowing I am only fooling myself. I lay my head down on the kitchen table, exhausted by the effort of thinking, and watch as a tiny spider scurries past me toward the fruit bowl. *Of course spiders would be good at pottery*, I find myself thinking sleepily. *All those arms to smooth the clay. And such lightness of touch.*

"You need to do something, anything," Marks tells me, "to bring this ridiculous situation to an end, Meg. And you need to do it now. Because soon—"

"I know," I interrupt him.

I can't stand for him to say the words. But Mark doesn't avoid the truth. He doesn't allow for excuses, or evasion, or shying away from the facts.

"Because soon it's going to be too late."

chapter eight

There are carrots as pallbearers and zucchinis as choirboys. The vicar is an eggplant, complete with dog collar and an ill-fitting toupee. I watch from the pews as the carrots, their green hair neatly slicked back, carry the coffin down the aisle of the church and lay it gently on the altar. In front of me, a piece of asparagus reaches beneath her black veil and wipes her eyes with an embroidered handkerchief. The little zucchinis stop singing and stand solemnly, heads respectfully lowered, in a huddle at the front of the church. They look beautifully neat in their pressed white gowns, and I can't help thinking their parents would be proud.

The vicar begins to speak, but I can't understand what he is saying. All the other members of the congregation are listening intently, nodding in agreement, wiping at their eyes. I strain to understand the vicar, but the words all blur into one long, monotone sound. I turn to the figure next to me, a fat potato in a black jacket, and ask him, "What is he saying?"

The potato whispers something to me, but I can't understand him. Before I can ask him to repeat himself, he pulls a handkerchief out of his pocket and blows his nose loudly.

Then there is a mass movement toward the front of the church. The coffin lid is open, and everyone moves forward to pay their last respects.

"I should be first," I say out loud, but nobody listens.

I try to work my way toward the front, becoming increasingly desperate to have a glimpse inside the coffin, to lay down the flowers that I now seem to be carrying, but suddenly I am engulfed by a wave of vegetables. They are all clamoring to reach the front, shoving me out of the way. A turnip elbows me in the ribs, and a stick of celery wearing high heels steps on my foot. Neither of them even bothers to apologize. I am almost crushed between an inconsolable cauliflower and a sobbing cucumber before being tossed around among a group of hysterical mushrooms. Suddenly the noise is unbearable. There are hundreds of them, all wailing and crying, pulling at each other's stems in an attempt to reach the coffin while I seem to be getting pushed farther and farther back.

"I should be first!" I cry.

Suddenly my feet slip from under me, and I find myself lying on the cold, hard church floor surrounded by pulp. I look up and see that the vegetables are going soft, turning to mush, their squishy insides leaking out from their split skins, mixing with their tears and running through the metal grates in the aisle.

I can only watch in horror as they wail and lament, gradually turning to soup.

"Cut the celery into slices," orders my mother, handing me a knife.

I examine the celery stick closely and then viciously chop it in half, the knife slamming against the chopping board.

"That's for treading on my foot," I snarl.

"Sorry, darling?"

"Nothing," I mutter, "just a strange dream I had last night."

"And when you've done that, you can dice the lamb."

She slides a dish along the worktop to me, a cold, red, bloody shoulder of lamb inside it. I turn away and cover my mouth, almost retching.

"You know I can't stand raw meat," I tell her. "I'm not touching it."

"Don't be such a baby! How are you ever going to cook meat if you can't even touch it? It's no different from when it's cooked. It's the same meat."

"It's the smell; you know that. It makes me nauseous."

I've never told my mother about my nightmares and how they smell of raw meat. She would only worry.

My mother rolls her eyes impatiently and lifts the lamb out of the dish to dice it herself.

"When you've chopped the celery," she continues, "add it to the pan with the potato and mushrooms, then you can pour on the stock. You bring that to a boil, add the *bouquet garni* and some seasoning…Meg, are you listening to me?"

I rub my eyes sleepily. We have been at this for four hours now. Under my mother's watchful eye and clear instruction, I have made spinach-and-nutmeg soup, chocolate-and-blueberry flapjacks, Gruyère cheese straws, and now we are on to lamb stew.

She apparently decided, during her short period of bed rest, that the time has come for me to learn her recipes, and she's on a military-style mission to teach me.

"I could put off teaching you for another year, and then another year, but what's the point?" she said yesterday. "I don't want to wait until I'm an old lady to teach you."

I came down this morning to find the work surfaces packed with ingredients and a schedule of what we will be cooking over the coming week stuck to the refrigerator. She has literally crammed the next seven days full of cooking lessons. I'm not sure I understand the schedule correctly, but she doesn't seem to have left us any time to eat or sleep.

"I'm really tired. Can we have a rest?"

"We can rest once we've made the maple-syrup-and-pecan muffins."

"But I don't need to know all this stuff," I say wearily.

"Cooking is not a matter of need, Meg. It's a matter of desire, of passion. You don't just cook because you have to; you cook for the pure joy of it. Now, have you sliced the potatoes?"

"But maybe we could just cook one thing a day."

"That's not going to teach you anything. There are so many lovely recipes I want you to learn. We have so many to cover."

"Couldn't you just write them down?"

"That's not the same! I need to show you personally. You need to know how to make the perfect passion fruit cheesecake and the sweetest grape-and-white-wine jelly. It's all in the mixing; it's all in the blending. How can I write that down? I can't. I need to pass it on properly. I need to show you myself!"

My mother is scaring me. She seems frantic, crazed, grabbing the celery and the knife from me and chopping at a hundred miles an hour, sending pieces of celery flying through the air and scattering across the worktop.

"You need to listen to me, Meg. You need to watch and learn."

"But why?"

"Because you need to, that's why! You need to know how to do these things. You need to know all the things I have learned. You need to remember!"

She bangs the knife down on the chopping board, frustrated, suddenly looking close to tears.

"Remember what?" I ask.

She is breathing fast, her face flushed and full of distress. She stares at the tiny pieces of celery scattered across the chopping board as if she is trying to decipher some sort of pattern.

I gently touch her shoulder. "I will remember," I say softly.

She closes her eyes and takes a deep breath, the tension slowly leaving her body. Then she turns to me, searching my face as if she doesn't understand what I have just said, as if she can't remember what just happened.

I carefully pick up the knife. "Tell me what to do next."

If I could capture time, I would put it in a bottle, and I would keep this summer trapped forever inside. The flavor of our cooking lessons, the color of the roses that bloom around our front door, the breeze that blows gently through the open kitchen window, the scent of the Columbian coffee my mother drinks in the mornings... I would keep it always bottled inside a glass prison, mine to keep for the rest of my life. Every now and then I would carefully lift the cork, just enough to hear my mother's laughter as she listens to Jonathan Ross on the radio, or to breathe in the heady scent of her perfume, or to taste the strawberries we pick from the garden and eat with French toast on the sun-drenched patio in the mornings.

But time is not a willing captive. The days pass too soon, slipping through my fingers like sand. I grab for a moment, only to find it is no longer there. I take a photo with my mind, only to find it is already fading. I try to slow the hands of time by doing less during the day, insisting that my mother and I bake for only two hours at the most. The rest of the time I make sure we sit in the garden, read, talk, eat, anything that might stretch out the hours. My mother snoozes on her sun lounger, listens to the radio, reads a novel, pots plants, picks berries, and flicks through recipes. I try to keep as still as possible, knowing that the moment my attention is diverted another hour will pass me by.

It's no good, though. The sun continues to rise and set, the world continues turning, and in this battle against Old Father Time, I know I am destined to lose.

One day, out of the blue, my mother asks me, "When are you going back to university, darling? Surely you're missing too many lectures."

We are munching on our lunch of Brie-and-grape baguette, sitting in front of the television watching Nigella prepare a three-course dinner party for thirty guests. Apparently it can be done in twenty minutes with no more than a packet of frozen prawns, some flat-leaf parsley, and a seductive pout.

"I'm not going back," I say as casually as possible, despairing that she should even ask me such a question.

My mother looks genuinely shocked.

"Not going back? Why ever not?"

For a moment it goes through my mind that I could lie to her. I could tell her I'm not enjoying the course, that the university burned down, that I've decided to quit scientific research and join the circus. It would be easier for both of us, but it wouldn't be right. Carefully, I put my plate down on the coffee table.

"Because you're sick, Mother, and I'm staying here to look after you," I tell her calmly.

"Oh, don't be silly. I'm fine!"

I dig my fingernails into my thigh.

"No," I say clearly, as if talking to a child, "you're not fine. You're very unwell."

"I've just been a little under the weather! You must go back to university. You've worked so hard. I won't hear—"

"I'm staying here!" I snap, losing my patience.

"Meggy," she says with a laugh, "I really don't think that's necessary."

"Mother, look at yourself!" I cry, unable to hold back my emotion. "You're sick! How in God's name can you go on pretending like this? Like nothing's wrong? How do you do this? How do you make up these incredible lies and convince yourself they're the truth?"

She frowns and shakes her head slowly. "Lies? I have no idea—"

"You're always lying! You never tell me the truth about anything! You've been doing it since I was tiny, telling me all these ridiculous stories. How my first tooth was so sharp you used me as a can opener. How I drank so much milk you bought a cow and kept it by my cot. We lived in a flat, Mother! As if the council would have allowed us a cow! You turned my whole infancy into a lie, just like you're turning your illness into a lie!"

My mother's cheeks have turned pink, and her eyes are wide, full of hurt. She looks so fragile and childlike curled up on the big red sofa that I immediately regret my outburst, but I just can't handle this anymore. I just can't.

"I...I don't know what to say," she says meekly.

"The truth," I plead. "Just say the truth."

She runs her fingers through her brittle hair and looks contemplative. I swallow the lump in my throat and sit on my hands, afraid that I will either burst into tears or throttle her.

"You're right," she says sadly. "I haven't been very honest with you."

When she draws her hand away, six or seven dull auburn hairs are caught between her fingers. She examines them closely.

"There was no cow," she sighs. "Keeping a cow next to your cot would have been ludicrous. I don't know why I told you that. I suppose I thought it sounded more interesting than the truth."

I shift to the edge of the sofa, leaning closer, longing to hear her tell me something, anything, about my infancy that's real.

"You were lactose intolerant, so drinking cow's milk was never an option," she explains.

I nod encouragingly, wondering if finally, after all this time, her lies are about to give way to the truth.

"So I bought a goat and kept her next to your cot. You were just so thirsty all the time that I couldn't keep up. You would guzzle goat milk like there was no tomorrow, and it seemed the perfect solution until you began bleating and growing tiny horns out of your head."

I stand up, walk out, and slam the door behind me.

Upstairs in my room, I take the flier out from where I have hidden it between two books on the shelf. I am so angry right now that my hands are trembling, but I'm not sure whether I'm more angry with my mother or myself. I'm meant to be sensible and rational and pragmatic, so why do I keep kidding myself that my mother is ever going to tell me the truth?

15 Gray's Inn Road. I shouldn't have to rely on a dubious clue to find out about my own life! I shouldn't have to go off behind my mother's back in search of an address to which my mother may or may not have had some vague connection! But then again, I shouldn't have to lead the farcical life that I do. Maybe I'm just being stubborn, refusing to let go of the dream that one day my mother will give up her charade and finally be honest. Maybe a stubborn baby grows into a stubborn adult. But was I a stubborn baby? Who knows. And that's just the point.

I've tried to make her talk to me. I have tried and tried and tried. And I'm sick of trying.

I pull my *London A–Z* down from the shelf.

Mark was right.

I'm running out of time.

chapter nine

"London stinks."

Under the bus shelter, perched on cold plastic seats, we watched the fine drizzle coming down against the dirty gray buildings and waited for the number 192.

"Does it, sweetheart?" asked my mother distractedly, rummaging in her purse, checking that we had enough coins to actually get us wherever it was we were going. As far as I knew, she hadn't brought any Jamaica cake with her this time, which meant she wouldn't be able to bribe the bus driver into letting us stay on board for an extra couple of stops. Had we been going in the opposite direction, then two pieces of coconut ice would have sufficed, but for the driver of the 192, it was Jamaica cake or walk the final mile. He drove a hard bargain.

"All you can smell when you live in London are cars and buses."

Right on cue, an old BMW with blacked-out windows drove past, its stereo booming, spraying muddy puddle water at our feet, and coughing a cloud of black smoke from its exhaust pipe. The smell of gasoline and oil made my stomach queasy.

"But that's not all London smells of, is it, darling?"

My mother clipped her purse shut, looking disappointed. It looked like we would be walking that final mile after all.

"There are lots of other wonderful smells, once you get past the stench of the traffic. Aren't there?"

She turned to me and I shrugged. I was into shrugging lately. Shrugging and looking miserable. It seemed to be what all the kids were doing.

"Close your eyes," my mother said.

"Nooo," I whined. My mother was always telling me to close my eyes for one reason or another. To imagine this. To visualize that. To remember the other.

"Go on. I'll do it with you."

"No!" I exclaimed, shocked by her persistent ignorance. "The last time we did that someone stole our shopping bags."

"All right, then, you do it first. And then I'll do it."

She looked so enthusiastic that I sighed and gave in, just to keep her happy.

"Now breathe in deeply," she said, "and tell me what you can smell."

"Cars and buses," I said, opening my eyes again.

"No, try harder," my mother said, giving my knee a gentle slap. "Breathe in slowly and deeply. And forget about the cars and buses. Go past that to the smells that linger beneath."

I did as I was told, inhaling slowly. "Trash bins," I said.

"And?"

I shrugged. It didn't feel as good with your eyes closed. I guessed that half the fun of shrugging was seeing the look of suppressed frustration in the adult you were shrugging at.

"More trash bins."

"And?"

"Dog poo."

My mother tutted. "Is that all?" she asked, disappointed.

"Well, what else is there?" I asked, opening my eyes and looking around me. This was Tottenham, not the Bahamas. What was she expecting me to smell? Suntan lotion and salty sea air?

My mother closed her eyes and took a deep breath. "I can smell hot chips," she said, "straight out of the fryer. And pieces of crispy chicken from Mr. Donos's shop."

"That's right at the other end of the main street," I protested.

"And I can smell the chili and ginger on the jerk chicken they cook at the Jamaican food stall. And cumin, turmeric, and curry leaves from the Raja Tandori."

"That's two roads away."

My mother took another deep breath. "And I can smell the buttery potatoes and cabbage from O'Connell's pub. And pastrami and salami from the Italian deli. Parma ham, warm ciabatta bread, and bolognese sauce..."

I could feel my mouth starting to water.

"Juicy meat from Kebab Hut, jalapeno peppers, and warm pita bread. And sweet-and-sour chicken from the Ming Che takeout. Pork balls and shrimp fried rice. Spare ribs in sticky hoisin sauce..."

By now we were both licking our lips, lost in fantasies of hot food on this cold and wet day. My mother inhaled deeply once more. "And there's fried bacon from Mrs. Brand's B&B. And hot soup from the Helping Hand soup kitchen. Potato and leek today, I think. Jam roly-poly and custard from Saint Mary's Primary

School. Sizzling burgers and hot dogs from the football stadium. Fried onions, mustard, tomato sauce…"

Bahhhh!

We both jumped in our seats as a passing car blasted its horn, startling us out of our reverie. We looked at each other open-mouthed, our eyes wide with shock, my mother clutching her heart.

And then we both burst into laughter.

Today, standing outside King's Cross station, I breathe in deeply and try to identify the mouthwatering scents of London's multicultural cuisine. But all I can smell are cars and buses.

It feels strange to be back here after almost three years. Since I moved to Leeds and my mother moved to Cambridge, I've had no reason to come back to London. The traffic. The chaos. The noise. The crowds. The stink.

I smile to myself.

It feels good to be home.

I weave my way through the crowds inside the station. People with briefcases, suitcases, bags on wheels, carryalls, cat baskets. Everyone is on their way to somewhere.

Five minutes later, I am meandering down Gray's Inn Road, wondering whether I am doing the right thing. I feel slightly sick. Perhaps it's just those stomach-churning traffic fumes, but I don't think so. I think it's nerves. I tell myself to stop being so pathetic. The chances are that nothing will even come of this ridiculous little mission. I will probably find that the house I am looking for was converted into student digs or a B&B many years ago, and then I will simply get back on a train and be back in Cambridge by dinnertime. Or maybe the house never existed in the first place. My mother is always scribbling things down incorrectly. I've never even trusted her to take down a telephone number, because she always manages to get at least one digit wrong. In fact, there are so many reasons why it might be impossible for me to find this house that when I find myself standing right in front of it, less than ten minutes from exiting the station, I am not entirely sure what to do.

It's a narrow three-story house with a grubby white exterior, wedged between a dubious-looking liquor store and a Greek café. Five or six smelly trash bags are piled up on the pavement outside, flies buzzing around them in the afternoon sun. I look at the flier I am clutching, checking the address three, four, five times. Yes, this is definitely number 15. I should already be standing on the doorstep, banging the rusty knocker. So why am I hesitating?

What if this is it? I think. *What if the person who answers the door is a long-lost relative? An aunt or an uncle I never knew I had? A cousin? What if it really is my father?* The minute I knock on that door my life could change forever. But that's exactly what I want. That's what I've always wanted.

Isn't it?

I hear my phone ringing inside my bag and rummage around trying to find it before voice mail kicks in. What if it's my mother? What if she's had another turn? What if it's the doctor saying she's collapsed? Perhaps I should just go home. Perhaps this just isn't the right time to be doing this.

But the name that flashes up isn't my mother or the doctor. It's Mark.

I hold the ringing phone in my hand, but I can't bring myself to answer it. I know that Mark would not be impressed by my hesitation. In my position, he would be banging on that door, running through a list of prepared questions with the owner, checking things off, interrogating, noting down clues, getting to the bottom of things. I hear Mark's words echoing in my mind. *You need to do something—anything—to bring this ridiculous situation to an end, Meg. And you need to do it now. Because soon—*

"I know," I hear myself say out loud. "Don't say it."

The owner of the house balances a screaming baby on one hip and eyes me suspiciously.

"I don't really get what it is you want," she shouts in an American accent over the noise of the bawling baby.

That makes two of us, I think.

She must be wondering if I'm mentally unstable, turning up out of the blue, showing her a twenty-one-year-old scrap of paper with her address scrawled on it, asking her if she ever knew my mother or—seeing as she's barely any older than myself—whether her mother might have known my mother. Or her father, for that matter. Or anyone she's related to. Or maybe it was the person who lived here before her who knew my mother. Does she know who they were? Has she ever heard of Valerie May?

It turns out that all her family live in Texas and have never been to England (which seems to be the source of some anger), that she has lived in the house for six months and has no idea who previously lived here, and that Valerie May is not a name she has ever heard of, although she does think it's very pretty.

"Are you trying to track down your mother?" she asks, looking sorry for me.

"Oh, no, I live with my mother. I'm trying to find out if she once knew someone who lived in this house."

"So can't you just ask her?"

"It's quite complicated."

"Has she got memory loss?"

"Erm...something like that."

"That's terrible," she shouts, patting the baby's back quite hard. "My grandmother had that. She kept telling everyone she was a hula-dancing champion."

I smile and give a little laugh to be polite. But then I think it might be impolite to laugh at her senile grandmother, so I stifle the laughter instead.

"Sounds like she was confused," I comment, just to sound interested.

"Oh, no, she really was a hula-dancing champion. It was just the fact that she kept telling everyone that got annoying."

The baby lets out an ear-piercing screech, but the woman seems unperturbed and just pats its back even harder.

"Oh! Is it your father you're trying to track down?" she shouts, her face suddenly lighting up as if she now understands the situation.

"Not really. Although that would be great. It's more...anyone really. Anyone who might know...anything."

"Anyone who might know anything," she repeats, looking confused.

This is ridiculous. I sound like a complete idiot.

"I'm not sure I can help you," the woman shouts over the noise of the baby. I nod gratefully to communicate that I had already worked this out but that I am thankful for her patience anyway.

What do I do now? I wonder. It would seem logical to say thank you and walk away, leaving this poor woman to get on with her day. But instead I just stand there awkwardly.

So that's it. It's all over already. There was no one at this address who could tell me anything. I didn't find my father. Or anyone who could help me. I didn't find anything at all. No matter how many times I told myself this was probably a pointless exercise, no matter how much part of me wanted to give up before I had even started, for reasons I still don't fully understand, I realize now how much hope I had. Deep down I realize I really did believe this would lead me to some answers.

"Have you come far?" the woman asks, spying the sadness in my face.

"Cambridge."

"Oh, wow! Where the university is, right? I've never been there. You've come such a long way!"

When I tell her Cambridge is only forty minutes on the train from the station at the end of her road, she doesn't believe me, so I end up getting my train timetable out and showing her. She still doesn't seem to believe me.

"I always forget what a tiny country this is!" she shouts.

She asks me about the university and the cathedral and the

famous Crown Jewels. I tell her she's thinking of the Tower of London. It turns out she hasn't been there either.

"It's been so lovely to meet you," she says ten minutes later, as if this has been a well-organized social occasion. "I'm sorry I couldn't be of any help."

"It doesn't matter," I say, and by this time I am so sick of listening to the baby screaming that I actually mean it. Any sadness about my failed quest for information has been put on hold, my main concern being to get away with my eardrums still intact. I am tempted to ask if there's something wrong with the child.

Just as I am descending the steps, the woman shouts, "You could try the landlord. Tony."

I stop and look back at her.

"You rent?" I ask.

She pulls a rubber pacifier out of her pocket and puts it in the baby's mouth. Finally he is quiet.

"Oh, yeah," she says, jigging the now-contented baby up and down. "It's not actually my house. Didn't I mention that?"

Sheltering from the noise of the traffic in the doorway of Chicken King, I dial the number for Tony the landlord. It's not an ideal place to make a phone call, with people going in and out, the smell of fried chicken sporadically wafting out the door, but I don't dare wait any longer, because I know exactly what will happen. I will start doubting myself again, telling myself there is no point to this, that it won't lead anywhere, that I should be at home. Or, alternatively, I will start getting overexcited, believing that it is the key to everything and that one single cell phone connection is all that is separating me from the long-awaited truth. I really have no idea why I have so many confusing feelings about this, and I'm getting increasingly annoyed with myself. It should be perfectly simple. I want some information. Tony the landlord might be able to give me that information. And in order to speak to Tony, I need to make this call.

"What now? I'm trying to take a shower!"

"Err…hello…is that Tony?"

"Joan?"

"Err…no. My name's Meg May. I…um…I got your number from the lady at fifteen Gray's Inn Road—"

"Oh, I thought you were the wife. You're not from the council, are you? I already said I'd sort out that smell—"

"No, no. I…I know this is a strange question, but I'm trying to get in contact with whoever lived at that property about twenty years ago. Well, twenty-one years ago, to be precise. I know it's a long time, but I was wondering if you owned the house then, and if you did—"

"Get in contact? This isn't bleedin' Friends Reunited."

"No, I just—"

"How am I meant to remember that?"

"I just…I'm sorry, I was trying to track someone down, and I came across this flier at home for some band called Chlorine, and on the back there was this address—"

"Oh, crikey! You're not a groupie, are you? Blimey, I haven't had one of you lot call me for donkey's years. Look, I'm not giving you the number for fizz, or Fuzz, or whatever the heck he used to call himself. He moved out a long time ago, and I haven't seen him since. All right? So good-bye—"

"Wait!" I shout, although I'm not sure why. Something seems to have just come together, though I haven't had time to work out what.

"So this band," I say, working it through in my head, "Chlorine. They used to live at that house?"

"Oh yeah, they used to live there all right. Might have been about the time you're saying, come to think of it. Causing a racket day and night. Smashed up the bloody kitchen. The damn drummer threw a TV out the window once and nearly killed a homeless person down on the street. And then there were these two young groupies who went and moved in with them. Right messy business, it was."

"Groupies? You mean two young women?"

"I'm hardly going to be talking about blokes, am I? Mind you, not even young women, really. Just girls. Barely out of school. And one of them had a bleedin' baby! I tried to evict the whole lot of them, but turns out the drummer had a bloody law degree and—"

"Sorry, did you say baby?"

I put a finger in one ear and moved closer to the wall, trying to block out the noise of a garbage truck passing slowly by.

"Yeah. Tiny thing it was. Poor mite."

"Whose baby was it?"

"How am I meant to know? Could have been any one of them. These lads, you know, once they're in a band, tight trousers and all that malarkey."

"But what about the mother? Who was the mother?"

"I dunno. Long as I get the rent, what do I care who bleedin' lives there? I don't know who the girls were. Just a couple of gymslip groupies, one who had obviously got herself knocked up by someone in the band. She didn't stay long, though, the one with the baby. And I don't blame her."

"Do you know where she went?"

"Do I sound like someone who gives a monkey where these people go? Look, if you want to know the ins and outs of it all, just go ask the guys yourself."

"But how—"

"You've got the flier for one of their gigs, haven't you?"

"Well, yes, but it's ancient."

I hear a deep, rasping, smoker's laugh.

"You don't really think a bunch of no-hopers like that ever moved on, do you?"

It takes me fifteen minutes to walk to the Frog and Whistle, during which time I swing from being convinced that I am on the path to finding my real father, who was probably a musician in a band called Chlorine, to being convinced that I am simply wasting my time and should probably just go home. By the time I arrive at the pub, I am sweaty, confused, and have a large ice cream stain on my top from bumping into a woman with an orange lollipop. I have been offered drugs, accosted by a beggar, and nearly run over by a taxi running a red light. Really, I just want to go home. But what if I'm getting somewhere?

I can't give up now.

The Frog and Whistle doesn't look nearly as cheerful as its name might suggest. In fact, it's old and dingy, with tinted windows and a peeling door. I linger outside, wondering whether it's really necessary to go in. *So what if a young girl and a baby lived in that house?* I ask myself for what must be the one-hundredth time. *It could have been anyone. Why on earth would my mother have been living there anyway? But then, why would she have a flier with that address on it if it didn't—*

"Oh, just go inside, you idiot!" I snap.

An old man who has been struggling to open the pub door turns and looks at me with wide, startled eyes.

"I'm so sorry. I didn't mean you," I say quickly, opening the door for him by way of an apology.

I am beginning to see why Mark gets so frustrated with me at times. There are only two ways to go: forward or backward. What's so hard about that?

Impatiently, I shuffle inside after the old man, shocked that anyone who moves so slowly still bothers to leave the house, and am immediately struck by the stench of stale smoke, beer, and urinals. I can't believe anybody would choose to spend time in here, and judging by the fact that the pub is practically empty, I'm not the only one who feels that way. The only customers (apart from the old man, who has sat down at a table in the corner without even buying a drink) are a man in a flat cap with a Rottweiler and a woman with a beer gut, a pint, and the words *Hot Stuff* printed on the seat of her tracksuit trousers. It's dim and dreary, the only redeeming feature being that at least it's cool.

I quickly approach the bar, hoping to make my visit as short as possible.

"Excuse me, do you know of a band called Chlorine?" I ask, getting straight to the point.

The barman, a flabby middle-aged man in a white-gray vest, looks up from where he is slumped across the bar, studying a photo of a scantily clad woman in a tabloid newspaper spread out in front of him.

"What's the capital of Turkey?" he asks drearily.

"I'm sorry?"

"Turkey. What's the capital?"

He places the end of a pen in his mouth and chews lazily on it.

"Ankara."

He looks down, and I realize he's actually attempting to complete the crossword.

"That can't be how you spell 'phlegm,' then," he mutters, crossing something out.

"Goal!" shouts the old man from his table in the corner.

He is staring at a large TV screen on the wall, which, much to my confusion, is showing snooker.

"All right, Jimmy?" shouts Hot Stuff from her bar stool, winking flirtatiously at the old man.

I have got to get out of here quickly.

"I heard that a band called Chlorine sometimes plays here. Is that right?"

"Yeah." The barman yawns, throwing his pen down on the bar and stretching his arms up in the air. The bottom of his vest rises up, and I try to avoid looking at the tire of white flesh that hangs over the belt of his jeans.

"I'm trying to get hold of them. You don't happen to have a contact number, do you?"

The barman nods slowly. "Yeah."

He picks up his pen from the bar, and I prepare to grab the number and leave. But instead of writing the number down for me, he puts the pen up the bottom of his vest and uses it to scratch his belly.

"Can I have the number?" I ask, feeling slightly sick.

The barman shakes his head lethargically. "No."

"Goal!" shouts the old man again.

"Shut up, Jimmy," mumbles the man with the Rottweiler in an Irish accent.

"Why not?" I ask.

"Women," says the barman, as if this is an explanation in itself.

"I'm sorry?"

"Wizz says don't give his number to women."

"Wizz?"

"The singer."

"I'm not some sort of groupie—"

"Are you after child support?"

"No! I've never even met them. I just want to contact them because they might have known my mother a long time ago, that's all."

"Is she after child support?" The barman looks me up and down lazily. "Because you might be a bit old for it."

"Nobody wants child support," I say slowly and clearly. "I just want to get in contact with one of the band. Any one of them will do."

The barman leans on his newspaper and stares vacantly at me. I wait for a response, but I'm sure his eyelids are actually closing. I think he might be falling asleep.

"So can I have a number?" I ask loudly.

His eyes snap open. "No. Can't. Women."

"No, I'm not—"

"Goal!" shouts the old man.

God, this is hopeless.

"How do you spell 'phlegm'?" drawls the barman, staring at his paper.

"I don't know," I nearly snap, "I just need a number—"

"F–L–E–M," shouts Hot Stuff.

"You sure?" says the barman, putting the end of his pen inside his ear and jiggling it around.

"Forget it," I mumble, turning and walking out of the pub.

"They're here last Friday of the month," says the Irishman with the Rottweiler as I pass his table. He's staring into his pint, so it takes me a moment to realize he's talking to me.

"I'm sorry?"

"Chlorine. Last Friday of the month, they're here, if you're trying to get hold of one of them."

"Oh."

I am so tired and confused that for a moment I'm not sure if this is a good thing or not. I had just decided to give up this wild goose chase, and now it seems the challenge is back on.

"Thank you," I tell the Irishman, "that's very helpful," although I'm not sure if it is.

As a gesture of gratitude, I lean down and tentatively pat the top of his dog's head. It growls at me, baring the sharpest teeth I have ever seen, and I jump backward, clutching my hands close to my chest in case the dog tries to bite them off.

The Irishman doesn't even look up from his pint.

"Last Friday of the month," I say, shaken, backing toward the door as the dog glares angrily at me. "That's great. What a stroke of luck."

"Not really," mumbles the Irishman. "They're here last Friday of every month. Nowhere else will have them."

Fifteen minutes later, I am on the 9:10 p.m. train back to Cambridge, eating a Cornish pastry I bought from a stall in King's Cross station and feeling strangely optimistic all over again, having worked myself up into a state of excitement.

What if I really am onto something here? What if my mother really was a groupie and Wizz is my real father? What if he's been looking for me all these years but just didn't know where to find me? Maybe my mother has been trying to hide the truth from me because my father was a hard-partying rocker living a life of hedonism, playing his electric guitar night and day, and throwing TVs onto tramps? I might have an emotional reunion with my father and discover another side to myself. Maybe I'll start throwing TVs out of windows, too. I've never demonstrated any musical talent, but perhaps that's just because I've never tried.

Through a mouthful of pastry I start to hum, measuring my voice for any possible potential. I think I at least sound in tune, until I start choking on a flake of pastry and end up coughing and wheezing while the woman next to me slaps me on the back.

By the time I walk in the front door, I am buzzing. This is it! I'm sure of it. Mark was right. He always is; I should never have doubted him. My mother's distress at seeing that flier clearly was a clue. I'm like a detective unraveling my own past. Who knows what secrets I'm about to uncover? If Wizz is my father, perhaps I'll be able to reunite him with my mother for a final reconciliation. Whatever happened in the past will surely be forgotten, and, for a short while at least, we'll be a family! Once my mother knows I have discovered the truth, there will no longer be any point in lying, and she will throw her hands up in the air, say, "All right, then, I give in!" and tell me all the missing details to fill in the gaps. And her final moments will be clear and lucid, and we'll be honest with each other once and for all, together in those final moments of peace and understanding.

On the kitchen table sits a plate of lamb chops and vegetables and a bowl of pink blancmange dusted with sprinkles. Both are covered with plastic wrap, and I feel a pang of guilt. My mother would have made the blancmange just for me. It's my favorite, but it's about the only thing she cannot stomach.

"It gives me enough wind to blow a forest down," she always says rather inelegantly.

I eat the blancmange and then tiptoe through the hallway. It's silent and the lights are all out, apart from the little lamp by the telephone, which my mother has left on so that I can make my way safely upstairs. But just as I am passing the lounge, I see her in there, lying asleep on the sofa, a tartan rug covering her legs.

I am about to switch the light on and tell her to get up, that she will get a backache sleeping there all night, when I pause, my hand lingering over the light switch.

She looks so fragile. So childlike and vulnerable. She's not the mother I once knew, who carried me on her shoulders and lifted me up every time I fell. She's not the mother who swung me around, or raced me across the park, or turned me upside down while I shrieked with glee.

She's weak now. A shadow of the woman she once was.

What am I doing? I should have been here this evening. I should have been thanking her for making pink blancmange and spooning it down while she watched me eat each mouthful as if I were still a little girl.

"I get just as much pleasure from watching you enjoy it as I would if I were eating it myself," I can hear her saying.

I listen to her breath catching in her chest each time she inhales, a sound like the tiniest bit of air being released from a balloon. She looks small underneath the rug, and I remember all the times we snuggled up on the sofa in our flat, that rug wrapped so tightly around us that we felt like one person. She seemed big then, much bigger than she looks now, and she used to tell me that it was a game, that we were pretending to be a sausage roll. As I got older, I realized we had to snuggle up because the heating had broken down again or because she couldn't afford to pay the gas bill. But I never told her that I knew. I wasn't ready to stop being a sausage roll.

What if she had fallen tonight and I wasn't even here? What if she had suffered another bad turn? Mark was right. I am running out of time. But it's time I should be spending with my mother, not running around searching for scraps of information.

What would it do to her, anyway, to destroy this world she has created for us? What would it mean to tear it all apart? They make her smile, these silly stories. They make her happy. And I can't take that away. Not now.

I feel selfish and guilty for going behind her back.

I take the flier from my pocket and crumple it into a ball, squeezing it tightly in the palm of my hand.

This clue to the past has come too late.

chapter ten

I sit at the little table on the patio, the warm midday sun on my back, looking at the rather strange flower display that my mother has created. A large serving plate full of red, orange, purple, and yellow flower heads sits in the center of the table, and I wonder why my mother has decided to decapitate all these poor flowers. She's never been a fan of formal flower arrangements, preferring the natural, unruly look, but tearing the flowers to pieces and scattering them on a plate is not something I have ever known her to do before. Perhaps she's "expressing" herself again, like the time she painted an enormous mural of an octopus on her bedroom wall, or the day she insisted on communicating only through the medium of song.

She has been strangely excited about lunch today, and when she emerges from the kitchen, squinting in the sunshine, clopping down the back steps in her flip-flops, I pick up my knife and fork in anticipation, expecting her to place some culinary delight in front of me. Instead she just plonks a decanter of vinaigrette on the table.

"Tuck in, then, darling," she says, sitting down opposite me and gesturing to the plate full of flower heads.

I stare at her, feeling suddenly rather worried. Is it possible the cancer could have spread to her brain?

"These are flowers, Mother," I tell her, as if she is a senile old woman. "Or they were, before you destroyed them."

"Now," she says enthusiastically, picking up her knife and fork and ignoring me. "Here we have the flowers of chives, marjoram, nasturtium, and marigold. And underneath are gingermint, red orach, sorrel, and rocket leaves. It looks rather pretty, doesn't it? Seems quite a shame to eat it."

"Eat it? They're flowers," I tell her again.

"Ewan says they're all perfectly edible. Honestly, darling, I've learned so many fascinating things these last few weeks. Imagine growing all these lovely flowers in your garden and not even realizing you could eat them."

I'm not surprised that this was Ewan's idea. It sounds exactly like the kind of thing he would suggest. At least that means my mother doesn't have brain cancer; she sometimes just misunderstands things.

"Are you sure that's what he said?"

"Oh, yes. Lesson number four. Edible flowers. I wrote it all down."

Over the past few weeks, my mother has taken to following Ewan around the garden, asking him questions and scribbling down his so-called words of wisdom in a little notebook. She claims they are "gardening lessons," although I'm not sure Ewan was ever consulted or given a choice in whether he wanted to be my mother's teacher. He appears to have the patience of a saint and tolerates her with infinite humor and kindness, for which I am secretly very grateful. It keeps her occupied and gives me respite from her bizarre stories, which seem to have become increasingly frequent ever since her fainting fit.

"Oh, hello there, Mr. Butterfly," my mother chirps as a red admiral flutters down into our lunch. "Have you come to join the feast?"

"I'm not eating that bit," I tell her. "He probably has dirty feet."

"Oh, and Mr. Sparrow! You like the look of our lunch, too, do you?"

A little brown bird lands on the table and eyes the dinner plate, nervously hopping back and forth.

"Of course they like the look of lunch," I tell her. "They're used to seeing it in the flower beds. Where it's meant to be."

"Oh, this is just like *Snow White*!" my mother says, beaming. "All we need now is a little deer to come trotting up to the table. Do you remember that, darling? Disney's *Snow White*, with all the animals in the forest? We watched it when you were a little girl. And there was a song. How did that song go again?"

"I have no idea."

My mother starts to hum something with no apparent tune. She has never been a very good singer, but I remember I used to love it when she sang me nursery rhymes and made up silly songs.

"*A spoonful of sugar*," my mother warbles. "Oh no, I think that was *Mary Poppins*, wasn't it? *The birds and the bees are a-humming in the trees*…no, that was something else. How did it go, Meggy? That song? *La la la*…"

I watch my mother singing away to herself, lost in thought of times gone by, of fairy stories and cartoon characters and enchanted forests. The sun brings out the red tint in her unruly hair and makes her eyes sparkle. Today even her cheeks have a rosy tint I haven't seen in a while.

Today is a good day.

Today my mother got out of bed without a problem and didn't complain that every inch of her body ached. I didn't once hear her say *There must be something wrong with my mattress; it's the only explanation* or *Perhaps I've started sleepwalking and bumping into things.* Today she's not exhausted, which means she hasn't had to say *It's the heat; it makes me sleepy* or *If I have started sleepwalking, that would explain the tiredness.* Today she doesn't feel sick or nauseous, so there has been no reason for her to ask me *Do you think there's a stomach bug going around, sweetie?* or to tell me *I think I ate too much cheesecake last night.* Today there are no symptoms and no excuses to accompany them. Today, if I ignore how thin she looks, it's almost like nothing is wrong.

But it's not today that's the problem. It's tomorrow. Because there's always a tomorrow yet to come.

"*Hi-ho, hi-ho, it's off to work we go*...that was the other one from *Snow White,* wasn't it? With the little people. Elves. No, dwarves. And there was Sneezy and Happy and Lumpy...no, was there a Lumpy? Bashful and Grumpy..."

I'm pleased I made the decision to stop running around after clues to my past. This is where I should be, sitting in the sunshine, listening to my mother babbling away, enjoying a beautifully prepared lunch of...well, sitting with her, anyway. I feel better, less guilty, more relaxed. Less like a terrible daughter out to destroy the very essence of our lives together. These past weeks, my mother and I have been enjoying our afternoons lazing in the garden, doing crosswords, playing Monopoly, and talking about all kinds of things from global warming (which my mother blames on "farting cows") to the queen's latest dress (which I thought befitting of a lady in her position, but my mother would have brightened up with a tie-dye scarf). And when my mother aches, or feels tired, or has a headache, I'm glad I'm here to put the kettle on, or to order her to sit down and rest, or to simply be around, just in case.

I didn't tell Mark what happened in London. I reasoned there was no need. After all, he would only tell me to track down Chlorine, to follow the next clue, to keep searching...and there really is no point. I am resolved now to just let things be. Instead, I told him a slightly amended version of what happened. In fact, I told him the house I was looking for had been knocked down and turned into a Chinese takeout. There was very little he could say to that. Or at least I thought there would be very little he could say to that, but Mark, being Mark, actually told me to call the council, to demand to speak to someone in urban planning or town housing or something like that, and to quote some law that gives me the right to know who lived on that site previously.

I haven't done it, though, because I no longer feel the need. I don't even think about the information that might be out there waiting for me, or whether my real father might be one of the members of that band, or who the mother and baby were who lived in that house. It doesn't cross my mind that, this coming Friday night, Chlorine will be playing at the Frog and Whistle and that a mere forty-minute train journey could be the only thing separating me from the truth. It's not important. Because, as I watch my mother's smiling face beaming at me over a plate full of flower heads, I know that all that really matters is that I'm here, watching out for her, sharing this final time together, just as it should be.

"Eat up then, darling. Don't let your salad get warm."

She laughs. I don't know why, but she always finds that line amusing.

"You go first," I tell her.

"Are you doubting my culinary skills with a flower bed?"

"Not at all. I just want you to have first pick of these delicious geraniums, or whatever they are."

She eyes the plate of flowers as if she's not entirely convinced herself before plucking a large orange flower head from the plate and popping it into her mouth. She chews slowly, a look of intense contemplation on her face, and I try not to laugh at the sight of orange petals protruding from between her lips. She continues chewing for what seems like a very long time, running her tongue around the inside of her mouth, making the expression of someone who has just bitten into a lemon, before finally she swallows.

"Was that nice?" I ask innocently.

"Umm," she nods, trying to look convincing. "Lovely."

"Liar."

A smile breaks out on my mother's face.

"I'll go and make us beans on toast," she says, and we both start to laugh.

Ewan comes twice a week. I hear him at the far side of the garden, digging, mowing, sawing, hacking, singing Paul Weller, or talking to the plants and insects. I glimpse him from my bedroom window pulling up roots, trimming back bushes, dismantling the old shed, and putting up a new one. I avoid him at all costs, the memory of the twenty-pound note and our last, frosty exchange clouding my mind, along with my shame. Each time he comes, I take him his coffee and cake, always with the intention of clearing the air, but instead of seeking him out in the orchard or between the rows of beanpoles, I leave his snack nearby where he will find it, always making some excuse to avoid him for another day. My pride, stubborn as an ox, rarely allows the word "sorry" to pass my lips.

Today I leave his coffee and banana cake on the grass near his bag—an old canvas satchel that has been left open, revealing a lunchbox, a bottle of water, and a Barbie doll dressed in pink knickers and a bra. I am staring curiously, wondering what my mother would think if she knew this young man she thinks is so wonderful has a fetish for busty blond dolls, when I hear the voice of a little girl coming from somewhere in the orchard.

Cautiously, I tiptoe into the trees, where I find a girl with honey-colored hair dressed in pink shorts, a pink T-shirt, and a pair of pink tennis shoes with flashing lights on the heels. She doesn't notice me, being so absorbed in playing her game, so I hide behind a tree and watch, wondering who on earth she can be. The thought that Ewan—with his tendency to talk to trees, his holey socks, and his clapped-out old van—might have a child is frankly terrifying. Besides, Ewan's father is a *scientist*. He may have failed to instill much sense into his son, but I have to believe he at least managed to raise his son with some common sense. Surely Ewan can't be a father at such a young age.

"Welcome to my castle, Prince Robbie!" exclaims the little girl, opening an invisible door. "What a beautiful unicorn! Leave him on the doorstep, and I will ask Rosie, my servant, to feed him a carrot. Please, come inside. Rosie, will you fetch us some tea? The prince has traveled from very far away to come and see me. But then, who can blame him? After all, I *am* the most beautiful lady in the world."

I can't help but raise a smile at the absurdity of this little girl's imagination. Easy to see how she might be Ewan's, after all.

"Now, I understand there is something you wish to ask me, Prince Robbie," says the little girl, talking to a tree. She gasps and throws her hands up in surprise. "Oh, of course I will marry you!" She extends her hand, graciously. "What a beautiful ring! This must be the only pink and purple diamond in the world. It's worth how much? One billion trillion zillion pounds? Oh, I am so lucky to be marrying the most handsomest, richest prince in the world! Now I must get some beauty sleep, for tomorrow is our wedding day and ten thousand guests will all be looking at me."

The little girl lies down on the hard ground, closes her eyes, and pretends to snore. Then, only seconds after she has gone to sleep, she jumps to her feet again, stretching and yawning. Eight hours have apparently gone by in less than eight seconds.

"It's my wedding day! Rosie, help me into my wedding dress." She pretends to pull on various pieces of clothing before adorning her head with an actual daisy chain that she must have prepared for the occasion. "Oh, I look beautiful! Look at me! Are my forty bridesmaids ready? And are they dressed in pink like I ordered? Then fetch my unicorn, who will fly me to the church. Come on, Rosie, you can ride on my unicorn with me, as you are my most best friend in the world."

She slings her leg over an invisible unicorn, checks over her shoulder (presumably to make sure Rosie is safely aboard), then runs about in circles, ducking in and out of the trees, dodging low-hanging branches, and shouting, "Giddyup!" After a few seconds, she grabs a tree trunk, swings herself around and around, and screams something about a tornado. The foolish unicorn appears to have steered them into a storm on the way to the ceremony.

I shake my head and chuckle under my breath, baffled but mildly amused by the way little girls choose to waste their time. Part of me wants to step out from behind my tree and put an end to this silly game to spare the poor child any further loss of dignity, but in spite of myself I continue watching, curious. There is just a tiny part of me that wants to know what happens next.

"Oh, Rosie, that was a terrible journey!" the girl exclaims, swaying dizzily from side to side. "Still, we are here at the church now, and here are all my guests. Hello! Hello!" She turns in circles, shaking hands with apple tree branches. "Oh, thank you. Yes, I do look beautiful! Oh, and there is Prince Robbie waiting for me."

She starts to hum the wedding anthem, takes a few slow steps, and then kneels solemnly in front of a tree trunk.

"Do you Jennifer Lucy Green, take Prince Robbie Williams to be your husband? Yes, I do. And do you Prince Robbie Williams take Jennifer Lucy Green to be your wife? Yes, I do. And do you promise always to look after her and buy her pretty things, including the new Barbie hairbrush set, and give her the last of your fizzy fish, and let her watch *Jessie and the Space Cadets* whenever she wants to? Okay, I now pronounce you man and wife."

She stands on tiptoe to plant a kiss on the imaginary Prince Robbie. Then, scooping up a handful of flower petals that she has stashed nearby, she throws them up in the air like confetti, letting them flutter down over her head. She turns slowly in circles, her face toward the sky, laughing happily as the petals fall on her closed eyelids and stick in her hair. Rays of golden sunlight pierce through the leaves of the apple trees, making her rosy skin glow and her honey hair shine. When all the petals have fallen, she scoops them up and throws them in the air again, laughing.

I watch her closely, smiling. In the hazy shafts of sunlight, I can almost see her wedding dress covered in sequins, the forty bridesmaids dressed in pink, the handsome Prince Robbie, and the unicorn waiting to whisk the happy couple off on their honeymoon to a tropical island. I even find myself wondering where they will be going.

And, just for a moment, I am taken back to a feeling I can barely recall and that I can't quite capture, like when you wake in the morning with the memory of an elusive dream teasing the corners of your mind, telling you there is a place you have been that you can't return to, another life that was in the midst of unfolding when it was cut short. What is that feeling playing at the edge of my awareness? As I watch the little girl squealing in delight as she spins beneath the falling petals, I am reminded of…something. Something good.

Beep beep beep beep…

The alarm on my watch sounds sharply, startling me. Time for my mother to take her medication. I switch the alarm off quickly, feeling irritated. What am I doing? I don't have time to waste standing here watching this child act out her silly fantasies. I have pills to count out, the doctor's office to phone, bills to sort through. In short, I have reality to deal with, something this little girl better get prepared for, and quickly. Whoever allows her to behave this way is doing her no favors at all, and someone had better help her fast.

"You can't just marry someone the day after you've met, you know," I say, stepping out from behind my tree. "It doesn't work like that."

The girl stops giggling and almost jumps out of her skin. She stands ten feet in front of me, wide-eyed and frozen, a yellow flower petal stuck to her bottom lip.

"Churches have to be booked well in advance, for one thing. And how can you have organized such a big wedding when you had no time? And anyway, you can't love someone you only met yesterday. Plus, who's ever heard of a flying unicorn?"

The girl looks around her anxiously, looking for an escape.

"And I really don't think you would go ahead and get married only moments after escaping from a tornado. Do you know the havoc tornados wreak? People lose their homes. They die. Whole families are wiped out. One minute they're in bed asleep, and the next, their roof has been ripped off, and they find themselves being flung into the air, everyone screaming, everything crashing down around them, blood everywhere—"

The girl suddenly flees as fast as she can out of the orchard, an expression of horror on her face.

"Hey, come back!" I call. "I want to talk to you about the use of servants and social inequality!"

By the time I fumble my way out of the orchard, Ewan has come to the little girl's rescue and is crouching down by her side, wiping away her tears with the back of his grubby hand. He settles her down on an upturned wheelbarrow and hands her a half-eaten slice of banana cake before striding purposefully toward me.

"Why have you been telling my niece about people being ripped screaming from their beds?"

"She seems to think tornados are some sort of game. Hasn't she ever watched the news?"

"She's six!"

"Then it's about time someone sets her straight. She seems to think people just walk out of tornados unscathed and that unicorns actually exist."

"It's *make-believe*!" he says incredulously.

"Well, of course it is! That's the problem. Aren't you worried about the damage this sort of rubbish can do?"

Confused, he rubs his forehead, leaving a streak of mud across his brow.

"Why on earth would I be worried?"

Glancing at the little girl, now happily munching on her cake, I take a step closer to Ewan and lower my voice.

"Look, it might be fake weddings and flying unicorns today, but tomorrow she'll be telling people she saw a squash dancing in the moonlight or a cauliflower racing a head of lettuce down the garden path. And then what will happen?"

Ewan frowns.

"People will laugh at her, that's what. They'll call her a liar and a telltale, and no one will want to be her friend. All the kids at school will shun her, and she'll have to sit and eat her lunch at a table all by herself because the other children will think she's odd. They'll call her a baby and won't let her join in their games, and she'll always be confused about what she's done wrong, because as far as she knows, unicorns *do* fly and marrows *do* dance in the moonlight, because nobody ever set her straight. And she won't be able to understand why nobody believes her until she realizes that everyone else must be right and that things can't have happened as she thought, and then she'll feel stupid and more confused than ever."

Ewan stares at me, bewildered. "Are you drunk? What's wrong with you? She's six, for God's sake. I know you were probably studying the periodic table at her age, but it really is very normal for her to be playing like this. It's called *imagination*."

"No, it's called confusion. And if it's allowed to continue, she'll always be confused. And when she's grown up and she tries to remember her childhood, all she'll be able to remember is castles and unicorns and dancing cauliflowers, and she'll never have any idea what really happened, because her mind will be all muddled up. And she'll resent you because you encouraged her fantasies, and that will lead to even more confusion, because even though she'll resent you, she'll love you at the same time!"

Ewan narrows his eyes and peers at me thoughtfully.

"And I guess," he says slowly, as if testing out a theory, "that maybe she'll react to her confusion by trying desperately to ground herself in reality. Am I right?"

"That could well happen!" I blurt out, pleased he's finally understanding.

He studies me carefully, his face softening as his annoyance seems to fade.

"If you want to contribute to the poor child's confusion, then fine," I tell him, "but she'll be the one to suffer, and she won't thank you for it. Do you understand?"

He nods slowly, looking at me with what appears to be sympathy. "Yes. Yes, I think I do understand."

"Good," I say, satisfied that for the first time he has backed down and reason has prevailed. "Well, I'll leave you to deal with the situation as you see fit, then."

I don't know why, but as I turn and stride victoriously back up the garden path, I can't shake the creeping feeling that somehow I have said too much and that perhaps I am not the winner after all.

chapter eleven

It's the White Giant who tries to strangle me in my dreams. He looms over me, faceless, his shoulders so far above me that his head disappears into the clouds. He's the one who smells of raw meat. A bloody steak that sits on the chopping board. A red lamb chop before it's laid on the grill. Pink worms of pork that churn out of the mincer. The innards of a chicken. I hold my breath as he comes near me, afraid that I might be sick.

I don't know what I've done, but I've made him angry. Very angry. He swoops down on me, blocking out the light, and grabs me with his enormous hands that tighten around my throat. I try to scream, but there's no air in my lungs. I can feel his calloused fingers digging painfully into my windpipe, below my jaw, under my ears, squeezing. I try to swallow, once, twice, but I can't, and suddenly I am gulping like a goldfish on dry land and there's a pressure in my head like it's going to explode. I imagine my eyes popping out of my head and shooting out across the room on springs, like in a cartoon. I try to pry the giant hands away, but they are stuck to my skin like glue. The world around me is turning gray, the colors draining away like chalk drawings on the pavement when the raindrops start to fall. The light is fading, disappearing down a narrow tunnel that keeps on shrinking until it is no more than a little white pinprick.

It is going.

Going.

Gone.

"Out! Out! Out!"

The scruffy dog sits down in the middle of the kitchen floor and wags its tail at me expectantly.

"What are you doing, you stupid creature? Get out!"

I make a move to grab it by the collar, but it seems to think we're playing a game and rolls over on its back, its long pink tongue dangling out the side of its mouth.

"Stand up!"

My experience with animals has been fairly limited to date, and I have very purposefully kept it that way. At age thirteen, I became unreasonably attached to a hamster by the name of Jeremy that my mother bought me as a birthday present. For weeks after Jeremy's death, whenever I thought of his beady black eyes and his tiny pink nose, I would feel tears welling in my eyes, and I had to repeatedly pinch myself to regain control. It was ludicrous that I should be so upset over a little animal who did nothing other than sleep all day and run around in its wheel all night, keeping me awake. It made no sense to keep thinking about him, and I hated that my feelings seemed so disproportionate to what I had lost. I decided there and then that, as animals obviously evoked irrational feelings in me, I was clearly not cut out to own one.

"You shouldn't be in here," I tell the dog. "You're all dirty; please go back outside."

I point at the open kitchen door and try to think of the command to make a dog go away.

"Leave! Go! That way!"

The dog rolls onto its front, wags its tail furiously, and barks at me.

"I see you two have made friends."

I turn to find Ewan leaning in through the open back door, an amused smile on his lips. He looks like he hasn't shaved or slept in about a week, and his hands are covered in scratches and what appear to be teeth marks.

"I assume this is yours," I say, pointing at the scruffy animal.

Ewan covers his mouth with his hand and tries to stifle a yawn.

"Yeah. But he seems to like you. I don't suppose you ever fancied owning a dog?"

"Absolutely not. Get him out of here, please."

"Are you sure? The two of you really seem to be hitting it off."

Seeing I am not in the mood for jokes, Ewan emits a short, sharp whistle, and the dog flies out through the open door, sits down on the patio at Ewan's feet, and gazes adoringly up at him. Ewan rubs his eyes and yawns again, and I am so tired myself that I find myself starting to yawn too. Ewan catches my eye and smiles.

"Mine's down to a dog that howls all night long. What's your excuse?"

"Nightmares," I say sleepily, before I even think to stop myself.

Immediately I wish I could take the words back. I have never told anybody about my nightmares. I don't want people thinking there is something wrong with me, that I can't control the crazy thoughts that invade my head night after night. I don't want anyone thinking I'm disturbed in some way.

"Oh, nightmares are horrible things," Ewan sympathizes. He crouches on the patio and rubs the dog's head so hard between his palms that I think he might do some damage, but the dog is wagging its tail furiously. "Last year I kept having this really bad nightmare where I was falling down a well. I had it for months."

"Really?" I ask, suddenly flooded with relief that I am not alone.

"Yeah, it was scary. I would wake up in a cold sweat, grabbing at the side of the bed to stop myself falling. And I could smell the slime on the walls of the well and feel cold water around my feet."

"You could smell the slime?" I ask, feeling reassured that other people can smell their nightmares.

"Yeah, it was horrible. And even when I woke up, I could still smell slime all morning."

Me too! I almost blurt out. *All day, I smell raw beef and pink sausages and uncooked chicken.*

"What was your nightmare about?" asks Ewan.

Should I tell him? I can't. I'll sound crazy. But here he is telling me about his slimy nightmares and asking me about mine, and I am so tired and I just want to get the images out of my head, to tell somebody…

"This giant man is trying to strangle me and he smells of meat," I blurt out, "and I can feel his fingers on my throat and they're squeezing and my eyes are about to pop out and fly across the room when everything goes dark and I think I'm dead."

Ewan looks startled. I stare at my feet, suddenly wishing I had a rewind facility. What on earth must I sound like, talking about meat and giant men? Ewan may also have had crazy dreams, but then Ewan's a man who talks to trees. With him, it's to be expected. He spends most of his waking life having crazy thoughts.

"That sounds terrifying," says Ewan, gazing up at me from where he is crouched with the dog. He looks genuinely bothered on my behalf.

It is! I want to shout. *I feel like I'm dying, like I'm leaving my body and I can't pry these hands away, these huge calloused hands…*

"It is a bit frightening," I admit modestly, and even as I say the words they feel alien in my mouth. I have never admitted to being frightened of anything. Ever.

"I think I'd be frightened too," says Ewan empathically.

We look at each other. I notice how tanned his face has become over the past few weeks and the slight reddish glow to the bridge of his nose, where his skin has burnt. His hair, too, has bleached in the sun, a few honey strands running through his chestnut locks. I feel my cheeks flush and look away.

"Anyway," I say quickly, "how have you ended up with a dog that keeps you awake all night?"

Realizing that the conversation has swiftly changed track, Ewan stands up and peers down at the dog.

"His owner was one of my clients, Mr. Gorzynski, an old guy who lived a couple of roads from here. He died last week. He always said he wanted me to have the dog, so here we are. A new team."

"Why did he want *you* to have the dog?" I ask, incredulous that anybody would entrust Ewan with permanent responsibility for a living creature.

"Let's just say he's got a special skill that comes in handy in my line of work," he says intriguingly.

"You mean he likes sitting on his backside drinking coffee?"

Ewan raises one eyebrow at me and pretends to be shocked.

"Why, Miss May, did you just make a joke?"

I bite my lip to stop myself from smiling.

"I'll have you know," he says, "that we've been out here since nine o'clock without so much as a cup of coffee and a slice of"—he peers over my shoulder at the cake that is sitting on the counter—"a slice of chocolate cake to keep us going."

"How tragic," I say mockingly, half startled and half amused by his audacity. "You'll just have to hope somebody takes pity on you and brings you some refreshments before you wither away."

Ewan smiles. "One can only hope."

I wait for him to go, but he remains on the patio, looking thoughtful.

"You know," he says, "I can make you a tincture for your nightmares if you like. Lemon balm, lavender, chamomile—"

"No, thank you," I say quickly, not wanting to get back on the topic. I already feel as if I have said too much.

"It can help in times of stress. I know things are hard with your mother—"

"I'm not stressed. I'm fine. Thank you. I'll bring your coffee down to you," I say to end our conversation.

Ewan gives me a brief nod before turning to head off back

down the garden. I lean my elbows on the kitchen counter and place my face in my hands, rubbing my tired eyes with the heels of my palms. I feel exhausted. And I have a terrible headache. Why did I tell him about my nightmares? I feel like I just stripped naked and ran up and down the garden in front of him.

"You know the best thing about Digger?"

I look up with a start, surprised to see Ewan still there. "What?"

"Digger. The dog. The best thing about him is he's a fantastic listener. If ever I've needed to talk about something, Digger's always been there. He's really quiet, never interrupts, and he's very discreet."

"I have nothing to talk about," I say conclusively.

I look at Digger sitting on the patio, panting, a thin line of drool hanging from his mouth.

"And even if I did, I certainly wouldn't waste my time talking to a mangy old dog."

Ewan shrugs. "Suit yourself. Maybe I'll just leave him here for the moment anyway. Just in case you change your mind."

"Why on earth would I want to talk to a dog? I'd have to be out of my…hey! Come back! Don't just leave him here!"

But Ewan is already halfway down the garden path, whistling as he goes.

The dog and I stare at each other. "You're not coming in."

It lets out a whining noise and lays its head on its paws. For a moment, I imagine I might have hurt its feelings and even feel a tiny bit guilty.

"Oh, don't be so soppy." I go to shut the kitchen door. "I'm not talking to you. I'm not as daft as your owner."

The dog looks at me accusingly.

"Your new owner, I mean," I say hastily. "Not Mr. Gorzynski. I'm sure he was perfectly sane and didn't waste his time talking to you."

Suddenly the dog lifts its head up and lets out a long, high-pitched wail.

"What on earth is the matter with you?" I ask, taken aback. "Stop being silly. What would Mr. Gorzynski think if he could see you?"

The dog lets out another loud, long wail.

"Why do you keep doing that whenever I say the name Mr. Gorzynski?"

Again the dog wails, and I cover my ears. I am about to shut the door when something occurs to me.

"Oh. You're missing Mr.—your old owner."

The dog lays its head back on its paws and looks depressed.

"Is that why you're howling all night? You miss him?"

I sit down on the back step and pick a leaf off the top of the dog's head cautiously in case it turns and bites me, but it just looks up at me with sad, dark eyes. Tentatively, I try stroking its ear. It is soft and warm. I stroke it some more. I peer down the garden to make sure Ewan is nowhere in sight and look around for any other people who might be lurking behind bushes just waiting for me to humiliate myself. When I am sure there is no one about to witness my foolishness, I speak to the dog in a quiet voice.

"Don't be sad. You have to remember the good times. The times you went for walks together, and sat cuddled up on the sofa, and lay in the garden in the sunshine side by side. You have to remember playing together in the park and dozing in front of the fire or just sitting in front of the TV together."

I lay my head on my knees, both of us in similar dejected poses, and continue to fondle the dog's ear.

"All those nice things you used to do with Mr.—with your old owner, no one can take those away from you. You'll always have those memories stored up here." I tap the top of the dog's head. "And when you feel sad, you can always snuggle up with one of his old sweaters, and, in a way, the person you've lost will be there with you."

The dog closes its eyes.

"It's sad, isn't it, to lose someone you love so much? But you have to be strong. You have to be a strong dog. Because you have the rest of your life ahead of you, and your old owner wouldn't want you to be sad. I know it's hard to imagine you will ever be as happy as you once were, but you have to carry on and try to make the best of your life."

The dog starts to snore softly. I see a tear splash onto the patio by my feet and realize it must be mine.

"You just have to be brave," I whisper.

"Bloody animal," curses Mark, dropping his bag in the hallway and brushing down his neat, cream-colored summer trousers.

"It's just a bit of mud," I tell him, closing the front door. "He was just excited to meet you."

"Meg," he says in that tone that tells me he is about to make an important point and that I should listen carefully. "I've just spent four hours in traffic. I don't expect to have a dirty hound lunge at me the moment I open my car door. These are dry-clean-only, you know. And the dry cleaners is only open until five o'clock during the week, so I'll have to leave work early and—"

He sneezes loudly.

"—and you know I'm allergic to animals and—"

Ah-choo!

"—and what's that damn gardener doing letting his dog run riot anyway?"

Ah-choo!

"It's really quite a nice dog," I say, trying to help Mark brush off his trousers.

"He's made holes all over your front garden, did you know that?" Mark asks, pushing my hand away.

"Yes, well, he's a digging dog, hence the name. Apparently he comes in very handy, but I think Ewan's having a bit of trouble taming his enthusiasm."

"Who on earth is Ewan?"

"The gardener."

"Oh, him. Well, that mutt is definitely not a pedigree, and he's probably riddled with disease. Dogs carry fleas, ticks, mites, tapeworms, roundworms…I can't imagine why anybody would want one. Unless you're a shepherd, owning a dog is completely unnecessary in this day and age."

"Well, some people like having animals for company," I say tentatively.

"Company is what other human beings are for."

"Perhaps some people find it easier to talk to animals rather than human beings. Perhaps when they're feeling down or lonely—"

"Meg," Mark says sternly, "only sad, desperate people talk to animals."

I fiddle with a strand of hair, embarrassed, and try to block from my mind the long conversation I had with Digger this morning. What on earth got into me? I had only meant to say a few gentle words to the sorry-looking animal, and an hour later I still found myself sitting there rambling on about my mother, my childhood, my dreams, my anxieties, my fears for the future...It's all Ewan's fault. I would never have done something so ridiculous if it hadn't been for him.

"People who talk to animals," says Mark, checking his trousers closely for any remaining flecks of dirt, "are the same people who talk to God. Or fairies. Or themselves. They are people who are unable to relate to other human beings. Or who are unable to manage their feelings any other way. People like your mother."

For a second I feel like I've been slapped in the face, but then I remind myself that of course Mark is absolutely right. I nod, silently chastising myself for my own behavior. I certainly won't be talking to that damn dog again.

"Yes," I agree, "it's just the sort of silly thing she would do."

"And look at you," he tuts, picking a few dog hairs from my blouse. "You're a complete mess as well. You must insist he leave that mutt at home."

I hastily examine myself for more offending hairs. I spent ages trying to make myself look nice, picking out clothes that Mark might like.

"You're right," I say, feeling annoyed now at both Ewan and Digger. "I will tell him."

"Anyway," says Mark, forcing a smile, "let's forget all that. I've brought you a little gift." He unzips his bag. "Close your eyes."

A gift? Mark doesn't buy gifts. He thinks they are "a gratuitous material substitute for affection." The only thing he has ever given me was a ballpoint pen, which he felt would help tame my slightly unruly capital letters. I close my eyes, feeling quite excited. Will it be flowers? Chocolates? A second later, I am bending over with the weight of a pile of books that have just been thrust into my arms.

"All the practical advice you need for the months ahead, so you don't have to worry about a thing."

I look through the titles: *The Complete Guide to Inheritance Tax*; *Financial Planning for the Under Thirties*; *So Someone Died and Left You Their Stuff...*

"I think that one might be a bit tongue-in-cheek," says Mark, "but there's still some excellent advice in it."

"Wow. Mark. I don't know what to say."

Mark smiles proudly. "The other two are lighter reading. For when you just want to put your feet up and relax. *One Thousand Things You Never Knew about Stem Cell Research* and *Monkey Man, Monkey Woman: Musings on Darwin's Origin of Species*. Plus, I thought this one might come in handy."

He pulls another book out of his bag and waves it eagerly at me. On the front is a picture of someone in a black balaclava. The title *TALK!* is printed in bold red letters.

"It's by some guy who used to be in the Special Air Services. It's all about interrogation techniques."

Mark plonks the book on top of the stack that I am already struggling to hold.

"Parts of that one might be a little extreme for domestic purposes, though, and I wouldn't recommend reading it right before going to bed."

I gaze at the scary-looking military man on the front cover and wonder what Mark is expecting me to do. Wire my mother's extremities to the microwave? Threaten her with an electric mixer? I know exactly what has brought this on, and in a way it's my own fault. I may have slightly deceived Mark by suggesting that, as agreed, I contacted the Camden council (when I didn't) and said I wanted to speak to someone about a Chinese takeout (which doesn't exist) and that I quoted the law that Mark told me to quote (which I can't even remember) and that after many, many attempts I hadn't gotten anywhere and was forced to give up. This resulted in much indignation on Mark's part about the state of local government offices and an adamant decision that if one method for obtaining the truth doesn't work, rather than wasting time, you simply find an alternative. I am assuming that donning a balaclava and threatening my mother into submission is the alternative.

He smiles at me, awaiting my response.

"What can I say?" I smile. "Thanks."

"I knew you'd be pleased. I thought long and hard about the kind of books that would be both practical and keep your spirits up."

He leans his face toward me, and I kiss him quickly on the lips while struggling under the weight of the books.

"It's a good job you know me so well," I say gratefully.

"Shall we take our dessert outside?" I ask after Mark and I have eaten a rather poor example of a vegetable lasagna, prepared all by myself in my mother's absence. Having been in rather good spirits all morning, she suddenly seemed to take a turn for the worse as soon as Mark arrived and immediately took to her bed, leaving me to put my recent cooking lessons into practice. I have to admit, I may not be a natural. Fortunately, when it came to transferring ice cream into two bowls, I fared much better.

"It's a little chilly outside," says Mark.

He's right. Today is the first of October. The long, hot days have gone, the evenings are drawing in, but I refuse to believe the summer has ended. I am determined that I will not let it go.

"No, look, it's still warm," I insist, flinging open the back door, a chill breeze immediately bringing out goose bumps on my skin. "We could snuggle up under a blanket on a sun lounger. It will be romantic."

"It's not good for the digestion, eating like that."

"Okay, we'll sit on the bench, then."

"You know I'm not keen on eating outside. All those little flies…"

"It's too late in the summer for flies."

"It looks like it might be starting to spit rain."

"What harm will that do?" I ask, suddenly feeling strangely impulsive. "It's just a little water. It will dry."

Mark looks at me as if I have gone mad, and for a moment I wonder if I have. I feel desperate to eat outside, just like my mother and I have done almost every day during the summer. French toast in the bright morning sunlight, bacon-and-avocado sandwiches in the midday heat, linguine with seafood as we watch the sunset.

"Let's make the most of the summer," I plead.

"The summer's over," says Mark, spooning into his ice cream at the kitchen table. "It's nearly dark."

I gaze outside and realize that I can't see the end of the garden. The apple trees are no more than murky silhouettes in the fading light. I pull my cardigan closer around me, shivering. My heart sinks.

I suddenly feel overwhelmed by a foreboding sense of change. I cannot recall having ever felt so powerless. I have always prided myself on being capable and strong and in control. But what good are these things to me now? I cannot stop the light from fading, nor the breeze from cooling; I cannot stop the flowers wilting, nor the leaves from falling from the trees. Autumn will come, followed by winter and spring, and when summer finally comes around again, I won't recognize it. There will be no scent of baking wafting out of the open windows of this house, no tubs of homemade ice cream stacking up on the freezer trays. There will be no berry picking as my mother and I chatter about our lives, no lazing in the garden side by side. There will be no nonsense stories about summers gone by, how July 1991 was so hot we baked a steak-and-Guinness pie on the windowsill and all the houseplants started sprouting pineapples and mangoes. There will be no one to ask me again and again, *Have you got enough sun lotion on?* or *Don't you think you should be wearing a hat?* Without all this, how will I even know it is summer at all?

"It's not that dark yet," I tell Mark hopefully, staring out into the garden. "There's still some light left."

Behind me, Mark noisily scrapes his spoon around his bowl. "Not for long."

Defeated, I close the kitchen door. "No, not for long."

chapter twelve

Fueled by a mouthful of my mother's mint cake, I crawled all the way from Tottenham High Road to Enfield Chase. Or so she says. Crawled in the sense that I was on all fours. In terms of my speed, I pretty much rocketed there.

For anyone who doesn't know, mint cake is comprised of boiled sugar with peppermint essence, formed into squares and dipped in melted chocolate. It should never be left within the reach of greedy little babies who will grab and consume anything they can lay their chubby hands on, and this was my mother's mistake.

"I was just so exhausted," she says. "Being a single mother can sometimes be extremely hard work, you know? So I made a batch of mint cake, like I often did in those days, to give me that extra boost of sugary energy I needed to get me through the day. I only let you out of my sight for a second, and the next thing I knew, the police were on the phone telling me that after a high-speed chase they had caught up with you in Enfield."

From piecing together reports from the police, local witnesses, the driver of the 192 bus, and an animal control officer, my mother ascertained that I had undergone quite an adventure for a one-year-old.

It seems that after helping myself to a square of mint cake, I must have acquired the energy and strength that it took to propel myself up to the front door handle and let myself out of the flat. I then rolled at high speed down three flights of stairs, tumbling past Mr. Ginsberg, who later said I was such a blur he had mistaken me for a football and shouted up the stairs at those "bloody kids from flat twenty-six" that the next time he caught them kicking a football around, he would confiscate it and never give it back. I had then crawled at what was later calculated to be approximately twenty miles per hour along the pavement of the busy main street, causing pedestrians to leap out of the way and a street sweeper to tumble into the gutter, before joining the traffic on the B154. At the Church Street intersection, I paid no attention to the traffic lights and cut straight across in front of the oncoming 192 bus, causing the driver to slam on his brakes and radio back to the bus station to say he had just narrowly avoided an accident with a high-speed baby and could someone possibly come and relieve him of his duty, as he was feeling shaken and unfit to drive. By the time he put the radio down, I was already long gone and somewhere in Enfield town center, where an RSPCA officer on patrol had spotted me and was after me in his van, leaning out the window and trying to catch me in a net. Meanwhile, the angry street sweeper had called the police, who came screeching around the corner in two patrol cars just as I eventually ran out of energy outside Enfield Chase railway station and skidded to a halt with steam coming out of my ears. As soon as one of the policemen gathered me up in his arms, I fell asleep, and I didn't wake up for three days.

"I was so embarrassed," my mother says, "when the officers

turned up on my doorstep with you. I hadn't even noticed you were gone! You were absolutely filthy and had squashed bugs stuck to your forehead. You smelled funny, as if something was burning, and the officer said you had obviously overheated, so I put you in the fridge while I made the nice policemen a cup of tea. At first they seemed quite angry with me, but when I explained about the mint cake and gave them a square to try, I could see they were impressed. They both said they got terribly tired on the job, especially doing the night shifts, and that if they had something like my mint cake to keep them going, they could catch twice as many criminals. So that's how I started providing mint cake to the Metropolitan Police force."

Ewan takes another bite of his hard mint cake and smiles at my mother.

"And did it work?" he asks. "Did they catch more criminals?"

"Oh, yes. There was a dramatic fall in crime that year, but of course nobody ever admitted it came down to the policemen having more energy."

"It came down to the major reforms that took place in the police force that year," I tell Ewan drily. "They introduced new legislation—"

"That's just a cover story, darling," interrupts my mother, waving her hand dismissively. "You mustn't believe everything people tell you. It was all because of my mint cake, you mark my word."

I shake my head and sigh. "If you say so, Mother."

"Well, it's definitely worked for me," says Ewan, finishing his mouthful and brushing his sticky hands on his scruffy jeans. "I'm ready to go again."

In a united effort, we three have spent the last two hours

gathering all the fruit in the garden in order to cook it, preserve it, freeze it, or give it away before the change of season. There is so much that the kitchen counters are already covered with strawberries, apples, plums, raspberries, lettuces, onions, peas, tomatoes...We have used every bit of equipment we can find to gather them in, from bowls and saucepans to plastic basins and even an old sunhat.

The sky is gray with dark clouds hanging overhead, and my back aches from all the crouching and carrying, but mainly I am just worried about my mother. She has persistently brushed aside Ewan's claims that he can manage alone and that it is, after all, his job. She insists that she wants to help, that she is perfectly capable of helping, and that although she has been a little under the weather lately, with her chest a little wheezy and her limbs a little achy, she is feeling absolutely fine now and wants to be of use. I know there is no point arguing with her.

"Let's go, then," I say, popping the last of my mint cake into my mouth.

My mother, who has been sitting on the bench beneath the kitchen window, tries to push herself up from her seat, but she is frail and weak, like an old lady instead of a woman who has yet to see her fortieth birthday. She has overdone it this morning and has no strength left. Her miraculous mint cake may well have energized an entire police force, but it has had little effect on her. She struggles and wheezes, looking embarrassed.

"Mother, look," I say. I am about to tell her how ridiculous this is, that she is far too ill to be doing physical work and should surely be resting in bed, but Ewan interrupts.

"You know what might be a really good idea?" he says hurriedly, placing his hand on my mother's shoulder to stop her from standing. "If you sort out the stuff we've already picked. We're running out of bowls and pans, and there's hardly any space left in the kitchen."

My mother smiles up at him, looking rather relieved at this suggestion.

"Well, I suppose there's no point picking more if we haven't anywhere to put it, is there? Are you sure you can do without me, though? I'm quite ready to keep going if you need me."

"I don't doubt it," says Ewan cheerfully. "You can out-pick me any day. You've already put me to shame this morning."

This, of course, is rubbish. My mother has, despite her best efforts, picked very little and has spent most of the morning wandering wearily in and out of bushes, chatting about all kinds of nonsense to whichever one of us happened to be nearest. Ewan's praise, however, makes her smile proudly.

"You might want a coat," Ewan calls to me as he heads off down the garden. "It's going to start raining in four minutes."

I look up at the sky, which actually seems a little brighter than it has all morning.

"I don't think so," I call.

He shrugs his shoulders without turning around. "Suit yourself."

There are cracks between the clouds, where gray-blue sky is showing through.

"Four minutes!" I scoff. "How on earth can he say it's going to rain in four minutes?"

I turn to my mother for her response, but she has already fallen asleep on the bench, dozing peacefully with her mouth hanging slightly open. I go inside and fetch a blanket.

"I told you not to overdo it," I chastise her gently as I tuck the blanket snugly around her. "But you are just so stubborn."

She moans softly in her sleep and mumbles something about cabbages.

"Why can't you ever listen to anyone else?" I whisper.

I tuck her cold, bony hands beneath the blanket, pick up my plastic bowl, and head down to the garden, just as it starts to rain.

Ewan and I work silently for a while, me crouching down in among the wet strawberry plants and Ewan picking plums from the trees nearby, placing them into a Tesco shopping bag. The best of the strawberries are gone, and the ones I can salvage will be pureed to make jam, ice cream, strawberry sauce...or at least they will if my mother is well enough.

She is still cooking, but not with the same frenzy as before, and my lessons seem to have fallen by the wayside. Instead, she lies on the couch and flips through books on French cuisine or watches Delia or Ainsley or Jamie, talking to them as if they can hear her through the TV screen, thanking them for their little tips or telling them off for leaving their hot oil unsupervised. The chance of her making use of all this fruit seems negligible, and I imagine opening the freezer a year from now and seeing it all still there, like a strange frozen shrine to her.

The idea of it makes my stomach lurch, and suddenly I wonder what the point is in any of this. I am kneeling on cold, wet ground, fiddling around among stodgy strawberries with the rain soaking through my sweater and what the hell for? So that all this fruit can go to waste inside the house rather than out here in the garden?

"Why are we doing this?" I suddenly shout, flinging a moldy strawberry across the garden. Digger, who has been lying obediently by Ewan's feet, leaps up and runs after it excitedly.

"What do you mean?" asks Ewan, examining a plum for maggot holes.

"What's going to happen to all this fruit? My mother hasn't got the energy to make use of all this. What are we freezing it for? She's not going to defrost it in a few months' time like she keeps saying she will. She's not even going to be here, for God's sake!"

Ewan looks at me, raindrops dripping from his hair. "Do you want to go and tell her that?"

"Well, someone should! This is madness. There's no point in it."

He gently places the plum in his bag. "There you go again," he sighs, "always needing everything to have a point."

"I just don't understand what she can be thinking. She's not going to be making strawberry ice cream with these strawberries next summer, or using those plums in the Christmas stuffing, or any of the other things she's been twittering on about all morning. Why is she pretending she is? And you're not helping, making out like she's champion fruit picker. I saw you earlier, adding blackberries to her basket when she wasn't looking."

"She's not pretending. Pretending means you're doing something on purpose. I don't think that's what your mother's doing. It's not a conscious decision. She's not deliberately lying to you.

I think she honestly believes she'll still be around to do all these things. She's convinced herself of it. Her mind is just trying to find a way of making her illness manageable."

"Thank you, Dr. Freud," I mutter, hurling another rotten strawberry across the garden for Digger to chase. "And since when do gardeners have degrees in psychology?"

"It's not rocket science," says Ewan, pulling the hood of his sweater up over his head as the rain begins to beat down harder. "People have been telling themselves stories ever since time began in order to make some sort of sense of the world they live in. Like those myths you think are so stupid. They're just another way of understanding the world. Remember your friend Prometheus, who gave fire to man and then was punished by having his liver eaten every night?"

"Both impossible and ridiculous."

"To you, maybe, but to people of the time, it explained the existence of fire. Other myths explain death, the seasons, how we came to be here..."

"Oh, don't tell me," I say, sighing irritably. "We're here because of something to do with a dragon and an apple."

Ewan smiles and shakes his head. "No, but why not? It could be anything that makes sense to you. In Egyptian mythology, man was fashioned out of clay. In Chinese mythology, Pangu grew out of an egg."

"Pang who?"

"Pangu."

Ewan gazes up at the sky, letting the rain fall against his face. He is the only person I have ever met who could possibly look so content picking plums in the rain on a gray, miserable day. I am cold and fed up and want to go indoors.

"In the beginning," he says, "there was nothing but darkness and chaos. But in the darkness formed an egg, and inside the egg grew the giant, Pangu. For millions of years Pangu grew and slept, until one day he stretched and his huge limbs broke out of the egg. The lighter parts of the egg floated upward to make the heavens, and the denser parts sank downward to make the earth. Pangu liked this new arrangement, but he was worried the earth and the sky might meld together again, so he placed himself between them with his feet on the earth and his head holding up the sky.

"When Pangu died, his breath formed the wind and the clouds, and his voice formed the thunder and lightning. His eyes became the sun and the moon, and his arms and legs became the four directions of the compass. His flesh became the soil, and his blood became the rivers, while stones and minerals were formed from his bones."

Ewan takes a bite from one of the plums. "Creation myths are just another way of trying to make sense of our world. Really, they're just trying to do the same thing science does, but in a different way."

I shake my head and am about to tell him he's talking rubbish and that the story of Pingu or Pongu or whatever his name is has nothing scientific about it. But as I turn a strawberry over in my fingers, I find myself pondering the way the cracking open of the egg bears some resemblance to the Big Bang theory and how the shape of the egg seems to have something in common with Einstein's theory of curved space.

"Even if you're right," I concede reluctantly, "and people do make up these silly tales to help make sense of the world, I can't see what that's got to do with my mother. She's not just trying to make sense of her illness. She's been making up ridiculous fantasies ever since I can remember, way before she got sick. All these ludicrous tales about my childhood, what are they possibly helping to make sense of, Dr. Freud?"

Ewan shrugs. "Perhaps that's the question," he says through a mouthful of plum.

I turn a squishy strawberry over and over in my fingers. *Perhaps that's the question.*

For someone who questions the purpose of everything, I am surprised to realize that there is one thing I never wondered about my mother's stories: what purpose do they serve? If Ewan is right, if stories help to make the world a more manageable place, then what is it that my mother is trying to manage?

I hear Ewan calling something to me, but I don't hear what he says, so lost am I in this new wave of thought.

Perhaps I have always been too caught up in the frustration, the anger, the battle to find out the truth, to ever ask the question that really counts: Why?

I am vaguely aware of the rain beating harder and harder on the strawberry plants, hitting the wet soil around me.

What purpose do these stories serve?

Perhaps that's the question.

Suddenly my mind is whirring.

What if there is a purpose to all these lies, and what if I never find out what it is? How will I ever make sense of my own life? How will

I ever find a meaning to all this? What happens when you don't know the truth but you can't believe the lies, when you can't find a way—through fact or fiction—to give meaning to your own existence? Without a narrative for your own life, do you ever really exist at all?

Do you go mad without meaning? Is that what will happen to me? Will I go madder than my mother? After all, her life has a story to it. It might be crazy and ridiculous and a lie, but it's something, at least, to provide explanations and reasons and meaning. Whereas what do I have? Nothing. I have no explanation for anything, nothing I can cling to, nothing that makes sense.

Is that enough to drive someone crazy?

"Meg!" Ewan shouts, trying to get my attention.

I look up at him, a strand of wet hair plastered to my face.

"Go inside," he says, raindrops dripping from his hood. "You're getting soaked."

What day is it today? Friday. And what's the date? The twenty-eighth.

The last Friday of the month.

I stand up quickly, my joints clicking, pins and needles shooting up my legs.

"I'm going to London," I suddenly announce.

Ewan frowns at me as I quickly make my way out of the strawberry patch, hopping over rows of bedraggled-looking plants.

"Now?" I hear him ask.

But I am already jogging up the garden path, my feet squelching inside my trainers, and don't stop to turn back.

"I've just remembered," I call over my shoulder. "I have a gig to go to!"

chapter thirteen

When I burst through the door of the Frog and Whistle, dripping wet and out of breath from my sprint down Euston Road in the middle of a thunderstorm, for a second I think I must have the wrong pub. This evening there are people leaning on the bar, slouching at the tables, hovering around the ancient slot machines, standing in little huddles nursing their pints, all enjoying the rowdy, high-spirited atmosphere. If it weren't for the familiar stench of stale beer and urinals, and the sight of Hot Stuff shrieking with laughter and spilling lager all over herself, I could easily think I was in the wrong place. I am surprised to realize that the aging rock band Chlorine is obviously quite a crowd puller. And when I hear them play, this surprises me even more.

As I linger uncertainly in the doorway, from the back of the pub a noise suddenly erupts that sounds like a car being mangled and someone screaming in pain. It is some time before I can make out a tune, but eventually I recognize the banging and wailing as a horrendous rendition of "Satisfaction" by the Rolling Stones. The customers, however, seem to love it. A group of shaven-headed men start shouting the words and punching their fists in the air while Hot Stuff gyrates her large, tracksuit-clad bottom for their entertainment. I stand on tiptoes, trying to see the band, but all I get is the odd glimpse of a guitar, then the sleeve of a leather jacket, then a microphone stand being waved in the air.

What if one of them looks like me? I wonder, my heart starting to thump nervously. What if I recognize my own face in one of theirs? Will our eyes instantly connect across the crowded room? Will the music suddenly stop, one of them gazing at me in awe and amazement, recognizing his long-lost daughter?

I work my way through the groups of people, narrowly avoiding being elbowed by one of the singing men, trying not to stare at Hot Stuff's distasteful dancing, until I reach the front of the pub. Standing before the band, I watch them—four men in their mid-forties with receding hairlines, haggard faces, too-tight jeans, out-of-tune voices—and can't help feeling slightly disappointed. Just like my first surreal encounter with the infamous Dr. Bloomberg, I somehow expected that this band, who might have some tenuous but genuine connection to my mother's past, would seem different, special, in some way magical. But instead they just look like four men in a state of midlife crisis.

Each of them catches my eye at some point, but none of them lingers there for more than a second. If one of them spies something familiar in my face, a memory from long ago, a ghost from his past, then it doesn't show. Not one of them looks like me, and it suddenly seems ridiculous that I ever wanted, or expected, them to.

Not knowing what else to do, and suddenly feeling rather self-conscious standing on my own, I find a stool at the corner of the bar and order a bottle of orange juice from the same flabby, lethargic barman I met before. I have no intention of drinking it for fear of catching something, but at least I don't feel so conspicuous with a glass in my hand. All I can do now is wait for the band to take a break.

After almost two hours of listening to Chlorine wailing and groaning with no break in sight, I am starting to get frustrated. My ears feel like they have suffered irreparable damage, and from the other side of the pub a man with a mermaid tattoo on his forearm keeps winking at me. Each time the music stops, I get ready to collar one of the band, but they only ever pause to swig their beer and exchange banter with the customers, who after the first thirty minutes started to dwindle considerably in number. The ones who remain seem to be on first-name terms with the band, and I imagine these are the faithful followers—friends, relatives, and a handful of loyal, tone-deaf fans. The lead singer—I guess this must be Wizz—is so drunk that he keeps forgetting the lyrics, and the lyrics he does remember are increasingly out of tune. Hot Stuff is even drunker than he is, and at various points in the evening she has flashed her breasts at the band, tried to start a fight with the barman, and attempted to commandeer the microphone for a karaoke-style sing-along.

And then, finally, I hear the sound I have been longing for…

"Ladies and gentlemen, you have been wondervul," Wizz drawls drunkenly into the microphone, "a wondervul crowd of… of ladies and…and of gentlemen. And we apprece it…appreciate it. We will be back next week. No, next month."

"Don't bother!" someone shouts.

During a mixture of booing, halfhearted clapping, whistling, and some screaming from Hot Stuff, I tentatively make my way forward. The list of questions I so carefully prepared on the train suddenly vanishes from my mind, and when I find myself standing in front of the tall, skinny drummer, who is the first to start making a beeline for the bar, I don't quite know what to say.

"Hello. Erm...can I talk to you? I have some questions. I... sorry, this probably sounds a bit strange, but I was wondering—"

"I love you!"

Hot Stuff suddenly pushes me out of the way and throws her arms around the shocked-looking drummer.

"Take me into the back alley and pretend I'm a groupie!" she shouts, licking her lips and pulling at the poor man's clothes.

"Can't we just go home?" asks the drummer, looking disgruntled. "I've got to work tomorrow. And it's probably still raining anyway."

"Oh, you're meant to be wild and crazy!" moans Hot Stuff, shoving the drummer angrily so that he almost loses his balance. "It's part of your job!"

"I work at B&Q," he says meekly, straightening his T-shirt, which she has half pulled off his bony shoulder. "You didn't marry Noel Gallagher, you know. I can't go doing my back in by getting up to no good in a back alley. I've got eighteen boxes of ceiling tiles to move tomorrow."

As Hot Stuff stomps off, ranting about how what a catch she is and how she could have married anyone she wanted, the drummer follows her, leaving me staring after them.

"All right, sweetheart?" someone drawls in my ear.

I turn around to find the drunken bass guitarist swigging from a bottle of beer and staring at me in a way that makes me pray he doesn't turn out to be my father.

"What d'ya think, then?" he asks, gesturing to the pile of instruments that have been discarded on the floor. "Good, eh? I played the bass guitar."

"Yes, I know," I say, forcing a smile. "I saw."

"It's the hardest part," he boasts, swaying slightly, "because there are so many strings and...and notes and stuff."

"It was very good," I lie. "Actually, I was wondering if you could help me."

In the background, a slot machine suddenly toots its winning tune, and loud cheering accompanies the clatter of coins falling down its shoot. Music starts up on a sound system.

"What?" he says, leaning toward me and cupping his ear. The smell of stale alcohol in my face makes me want to retch.

"I said I was wondering if you could help me," I shout. "I'm trying to find out if any of you once knew my mother."

The bass guitarist takes an unsteady step back and eyes me warily.

"Is this about child support?"

"No. I found this flier in my mother's house," I say, pulling the crumpled paper out of my pocket and showing him, "and it has this address on the back. See? And I understand from Tony the landlord that you once lived at that address. And I need to know why my mother had your address written down and—"

"Wizz!" the bass guitarist suddenly shouts excitedly over his shoulder. "Come here!"

Wizz, who is struggling to get his arm inside the wrong sleeve of his leather jacket, chucks the jacket on top of a speaker, picks up his beer bottle, and weaves a very wonky line over in our direction.

"Look at this!" grins the bass guitarist, waving the flier at him. "This is, like, really old! From when we were old!"

"Young," I say, correcting him.

"From when we were young!"

Wizz examines the flier closely with bloodshot eyes. His face is scrawny, his stubble shot through with gray. He might once have been good-looking, but twenty-odd years of living the rock-and-roll lifestyle have definitely taken their toll.

"It's hers!" exclaims the bass guitarist, pointing at me with a straight arm, even though I'm right in front of him.

"Hey, Rocket!" Wizz shouts over at the keyboard player. "Look what Beasty has found!"

Rocket, a chubby man with a receding hairline and an earring who has been helping a group of people celebrate their win at the slot machine, shuffles over.

"Wow," says Rocket, taking the flier, "that's old!"

"It's hers!" exclaims Beasty again, pointing at me.

"It's my mother's," I explain to them all. "It was inside an old suitcase of hers. I came here because I'm trying to find out if any of you ever knew my mother."

Wizz and Rocket immediately look worried.

"It's nothing to do with child support," I say, and immediately they relax. "I just need to know why my mother has your old address. That was your address, wasn't it?"

They all stare at the flier. "No, that's not our address," says Wizz, shaking his head. "That's the address of a pub."

"That's the address of *this* pub," says Beasty, "the one you're standing in."

"No, on the other side," I say impatiently, taking the flier and turning it over. "Fifteen Gray's Inn Road."

"Oh, there. Yes, we lived there." Rocket nods.

"Did we?" asks Beasty.

"Yeah. You remember. That place we had when we were just starting out. The place with mold on the walls and the hole in the bath."

Beasty shakes his head, looking confused. "That could be anywhere," he says. "That could be where I live now."

"The place where you broke a door by driving a motorbike through it. The one where Wizz set fire to his own pants and I had to spray him with lemonade to put him out. The place where Bomber threw a TV set out the window and it nearly killed a tramp."

Beasty continues shaking his head.

"The place where we used to watch that girl getting undressed in the window opposite," says Wizz.

"Oh, that place!" says Beasty, his face lighting up. "I remember that place!"

They all laugh and slap each other playfully, and I no longer know what I hope to achieve this evening, but it definitely isn't to discover that one of them is my real father.

"Apparently there were two girls who lived with you for a while," I say, trying to make myself heard now that they are all laughing about their wild past.

"Oh, there were lots of girls!" Wizz says with a grin, attempting a drunken wink, and they all start laughing again.

"Those were the days!"

"Do you remember the twins?"

"Oh, the twins! Suzy and Sarah."

"How could anyone forget them."

"Now, that's why you join a band!"

"One of the girls had a baby," I say over the laughter.

They all stop laughing and look at each other.

"Really?" asks Beasty. "When?"

"Wasn't me," says Wizz.

"Wasn't me," says Rocket.

"Which one was it?" asks Beasty. "Suzy or Sarah?"

"No," I say with a sigh, shaking my head and wishing they were all a lot more sober. "There was a baby who lived with you at the time. That's what Tony said. Two girls lived with you, and one of them had a baby."

"Oh!" says Rocket. "Yes. There was a baby."

"I don't remember a baby," says Wizz. "I remember a cat. I think we had a cat."

"What did it look like?" asks Beasty.

"It was ginger and white…"

"Not the cat, the baby!"

"What do you mean, what diz it look like?" says Rocket, slurring his words. "It looked like a baby. It was very small."

"All babies are small."

"No, but it was *really* small. You remember. Too small. That's what I remember about it. She thought there was something wong…wrong with it."

"Who did?"

"The mum. What was her name again?"

Too small? My heart starts pounding in my chest as I wait for them to tell me the name. It couldn't be. Could it?

"I remember!" Wizz suddenly cries. "Little baby. Cried a lot. Ahh, she was a cute little thing. You remember, Beasty."

"No, I don't. Are you sure? Why would a baby have been living with us? Are you sure you weren't hallucinating? Because you did used to hallucinate a lot, when you were, you know..."

Wizz hiccups loudly. "No, we both remember it, don't we, Rocket? You *must* remember, Beasty!"

"What was her name?" I ask impatiently.

"It was small, Beasty," insists Wizz, leaning heavily on Beasty's shoulder, "and noisy. I used to sing to it, but I don't think it liked it much."

"But what was the name?" I almost shout.

"The mum or the baby?" asks Rocket.

"Either."

"No idea. Hey, what was the name?" he asks, tugging on Wizz's T-shirt.

"Oh, now zat's a diffcul...difficult question," says Wizz, wagging a finger at me, "and you should ask someone who hasn't drunk so much."

"Was it Val?" I ask, my heart in my mouth.

They all shake their heads.

"Val. No. Not Val," says Rocket. "That wouldn't suit a little baby."

"Babies are called things like...like Emily and Lucy," drawls Wizz.

"And Thomas," adds Beasty.

Wizz slaps Beasty heartily on the back. "Thomas is an ess… excellent name for a baby."

"Thank you, mate," says Beasty, slapping him back.

"No, not the baby," I insist, "the mother. Was the mother's name Val?"

"Gwennie!" Beasty suddenly shouts. "The girl was Gwennie!"

"No, no, no, no," says Rocket, "not Gwennie. Gwennie was Bomber's girl."

"His wife!" shouts Wizz, raising his bottle in the air as if celebrating the couple's union.

"Yes, later she became his wive…wife," confirms Rocket, "but at the time she lived with us she was just his girl. It was her best mate who also lived with us; she was the one who had the baby."

"Val?" I ask again hopefully. "Was she called Val?"

They all shake their heads.

"No, not Val…"

"Valerie!" shouts Rocket.

"Valerie!" Wizz and Beasty agree loudly, nodding their heads.

"Oh, the lovely Valerie!"

"Beautiful Valerie!"

"Valerie with the baby! The little pink baby!"

My heart is suddenly beating so fast in my chest that I can barely breathe.

"And the baby," I say, not even attempting to mask the urgency in my voice now. "Was the baby called Meg?"

"Meg!" they all shout at once.

"Little baby Meg!"

"Little Meggy!"

"That's me!" I suddenly shout excitedly. "I'm Meg. I'm the baby! Valerie's my mother!"

They all stop shouting and look me up and down, confused.

"You look vevy...very different," says Rocket.

"I'm older now!" I am so overcome with emotion that I don't even care how ridiculous this comment is. This is it! I've done it! I've found a link to my mother's past. To *my* past!

"You're the baby?" asks Wizz.

"Yes! I have no idea why I was living with you, but I have this flier with your address on it," I say, snatching the flier from Rocket and waving it at them. "And this is the year of my birth, and my mother is called Valerie, and I'm Meg, and—"

Before I can even finish my sentence, Wizz throws his arms around me.

"Meg!" he yells in my ear. "Little baby Meggy!"

"Little Meggy!" the other two shout, joining in. "Baby Meg!"

I am squashed in a three-sided hug that smells of beer, cigarettes, and body odor, my mind whirring. What does all of this mean? Why were we living with these people? How did my mother know them? Who was my mother's friend Gwennie?

They all step back and examine me with wonder, as if they never knew a baby could grow up and turn into an adult.

"Ahh, little baby Meggy," drones Wizz, patting me clumsily on the head.

"How's Valerie?"

"How old are you now?"

"Why did you leave us? You should have stayed and lizzed... lived with us forever."

They pat me and stroke my hair, squeeze my cheeks, and ask me several questions all at once.

"How did you know my mother?" I ask, desperate to get to the bottom of all this.

"She lived with us," declares Rocket.

"Yes, but why? How did she—did we—end up living with you?"

They all look thoughtful.

"She came with her friend Gwennie," says Beasty. "I think they just, sort of, turned up one day."

"I do remember she didn't stay that long," says Wizz, pointing a finger in the air to indicate a thought. "It didn't really work, I don't think, having a baby there."

"She came to us," says Rocket, swaying slightly, "because she was thrown out of her home."

The others nod their heads in agreement, recalling this piece of information.

"Sad, sad," mutters Rocket.

Thrown out of her home? My mother was never thrown out of her home. My heart sinks as I begin to wonder whether we really are all talking about the same person.

"They didn't like the fact she'd had a baby, did they?" asks Wizz, turning to the other two.

Rocket and Beasty mutter confirmations of this, hazy memories coming back to them, while I rub my forehead, wondering what they are talking about. Perhaps it's the drink. Perhaps they're confusing her with someone else. My grandparents loved me. They helped raise me. For the first six months of my life, we lived as one big, warm extended family.

"So Valerie followed us here from Cambridge," Wizz continues. "I don't think she had anywhere else to go."

"You're from Cambridge?" I ask.

They all nod. Perhaps they *are* talking about the right person after all. They must be. But my grandparents never threw us out.

Did they?

"Where did we go after we left?" I ask. "My mother and I?"

"That's what *I* was asking *you*," drawls Wizz, leaning on me and grinning. "Where did you go? You left us."

"You should have stayed!" says Beasty, stroking my face. "You should have stayed forever and we would have raised you."

"We should all move back in together!" says Rocket, his face lighting up.

The three of them raise their bottles in the air and clink glasses to celebrate this fantastic idea, excitedly discussing the logistics of this new arrangement.

"What else can you tell me?" I ask, trying to keep them on track. "What else do you know about my mother?"

They all shake their heads and shrug.

"She had long hair," offers Beasty.

"We didn't really know her that well," says Wizz. "She only stayed a few weeks."

"And it was a very long time ago," says Beasty.

"And we're all quite drunk," adds Rocket.

"What about Gwennie?" I ask. "You said she was my mother's friend. Do you know what happened to her?"

They all shake their heads.

"Haven't seen her in years," says Wizz.

"You said she married someone..."

"Bomber," says Rocket. "Our drummer."

My mouth drops as I struggle to process this information. Hot Stuff? My mother used to be best friends with Hot Stuff!

"Your drummer? You mean the tall man who just left with—"

"No, no, no," says Rocket, "that's Wonky. That's not the drummer we had when we started. Bomber was our original drummer. He later married Gwennie. But it didn't last long."

I rack my brain trying to work out where to go from here.

"I think I need to get in touch with Gwennie," I tell them.

"Yes, we *do* need to find Gwennie," agrees Rocket, "so we can tell her we're all moving back in together!"

They all cheer and clink beer bottles again.

"Okay," I say, thinking it might just be easier to go along with this ridiculous idea. "So how do we find her?"

Rocket and Beasty look thoughtful, and then Beasty raises a finger in the air, having come up with the solution.

"We could call—"

"Bomber!" shouts Wizz into his cell phone before Beasty can even finish his sentence. "How are you? Guess what! We're all moving back in together! Me and you and Beasty and Gwennie and—"

"Bomber, guess what?" yells Rocket, grabbing the phone out of Wizz's hand. "We have a surprise for you! It's the baby! Here she is!"

He holds the phone out to me, and I take it hesitantly.

"Hello?"

"Who's that?" a tired voice asks. He sounds like he has just been woken up.

"My name's Meg May," I say, placing my hand over my free ear to block out the noise of the band drunkenly discussing our new communal living arrangements. "My mother is Valerie May. We lived with you for a short while on Gray's Inn Road when I was a baby. My mother was friends with your ex-wife, Gwennie."

There's silence at the end of the line before the voice says, "Yes, I remember. Gosh. That was a long time ago. Wow. How are you?"

"I'm…I'm fine," I fumble, slightly taken aback by his sensible tone and smart accent. From the sleep in his voice, I suddenly realize it must be very late and Bomber has clearly left the rock-and-roll lifestyle well behind him. "I'm sorry about this, Bomber. We're not really all moving back in together—"

He laughs quietly. "Too right we're not. And, please, it's Timothy. People don't really want a lawyer called Bomber. It gives the wrong impression. Anyway, I really should learn not to answer the phone on a Friday night. I expect they're all slaughtered, aren't they?"

I glance at the three men hugging each other and singing something about being reunited forever.

"They are a little drunk, yes."

I take the phone over to the corner of the pub so that I can hear better. "I know this must all seem very strange, but I'm trying to get hold of Gwennie."

"Ok-ay," he says slowly, as if thinking this through. "Has your mother decided to get back in touch with her?"

"Erm…sort of."

"Gosh. That will be a surprise for Gwennie. She was absolutely devastated when your mother broke off contact with her, although she understood Val's reasons."

I don't say anything, wondering what on earth he can mean.

"To be honest," he continues, "I was always grateful your mother did what she did. Your father was...well, I'm sure I don't need to tell you. Sorry, your stepfather, I mean."

"My stepfather?"

"Yes. Robert."

"Robert?"

There is a long pause, during which time we listen to the remaining members of Chlorine singing. I only realize I have been holding my breath when I start running out of air.

"Was my mother married?" I ask, shocked.

"Gosh, I'm sorry," Timothy says hesitantly. "Maybe I shouldn't have said...I just...I thought you would know. I mean, I thought you would remember."

My mind is completely blank. I can't think what to say. He thought I would remember? Suddenly nothing seems to make sense.

"Look, perhaps I should just give you Gwennie's number."

"No, please! I need to know. My mother has hardly told me anything about my childhood. I had a *stepfather*? My mother was *married*?"

"Gosh. I'm sorry, it really would be better if you spoke to Gwennie," says Timothy apologetically. "She'll be able to tell you anything you want to know. After all, she was the one who—"

"Time, please, people!" yells the flabby barman, banging a spoon against a pint glass. "Time, please!"

"I'm sorry, I didn't hear that," I say, clamping my hand over my free ear. "What did you say?"

The music is switched off. Outside I hear the thunder still rumbling.

"I said," repeats Timothy, "she was the one who found you."

chapter fourteen

I am desperate to dial Gwennie's number, dying to question her, itching to hear everything she has to tell me, longing to finally hear the truth about my life.

And I will, once I have helped my mother defrost the freezer. And tidied the kitchen. And made that phone call to Dr. Coldman. And popped over to the shops for some bread.

A day passes. And then another. And another.

All too soon a week has passed, and I simply cannot understand it.

This is what I have waited for my entire life: a flashing arrow pointing straight to the truth. I have pleaded and begged, argued and insisted, struggled and searched, and now here I am, hesitating. The beer coaster with Gwennie's phone number on it sits patiently in my bedside drawer, waiting for me to come to my senses, pull myself together, and do what needs to be done. It's like finding the Holy Grail and tucking it away in a shoe box for a rainy day. It just isn't the way it's meant to be.

What is it that's holding me back? I wonder as I watch my mother crumbling some old pastry onto the bird feeder, cheerfully telling me about the day we scattered pastry crumbs in Hyde Park and thousands of birds suddenly swooped down from above, surrounding us in a cloud of beating wings before trying to carry me off into the sky.

"You were such a tiny thing that they mistook you for a pastry crumb," she chuckles, her breath catching in her chest and making her cough.

What is it that makes it so hard to pick up the phone? I think as my mother hands me the whisk and a bowl of egg whites, telling me not to overdo it like she once did.

"I filled the entire kitchen with bubbles of egg white," she laughs, her face tired and pale, "and I had to burst one of the bubbles in order to get you out."

What is it that makes me hesitate? I ask myself as she tells me how I once stuck my nose in a sachet of curry powder and sneezed nonstop for seven days and seven nights.

"The neighbors complained about the noise," she chortles as she rubs her aching back, "but there was nothing I could do. I just had to wait until all the sneezes were out."

What is making me find excuses, day after day, for why I can't dial Gwennie's number? Is it the way my mother smiles, the way she laughs, the way her face lights up when she remembers when, and recalls the time, and recollects the day? Is it the way her pain seems to vanish when she tells a story of our past?

Is it the way mine does, too?

It never occurred to me that one day I would find myself standing at the cliff edge, wondering whether to jump. It never occurred to me that when the key to the universe was offered up to me, I wouldn't know whether to take it. It never occurred to me that this life—this stupid, humiliating, ridiculous life—could mean more to me than I had ever imagined.

It never occurred to me that once she is gone, it will be all I have left of her.

I hate myself for being weak, for being anything other than rational and strong, logical and brave. I hate my indecision and my procrastination. "Stop being so pathetic!" I tell myself. "Stop being such a baby!"

But I need to hear that I am weak, otherwise I will never pick up the phone. I need to feel that I am pathetic in order to spur me on. I need someone to tell me this has nothing to do with feelings and emotions, and everything to do with logic and reason, and that it is perfectly clear-cut, and perfectly simple, and that all I have to do is pick up the phone, because there is only one objective in all this, and that is to find out the truth.

And so I call Mark, because I need to hear that life is not about shifting patterns and shades of gray. It is about black and white, and that is all.

I don't tell him that I lied about the house on Gray's Inn Road having been converted into a takeout restaurant, or about the council offices refusing to help me, or about having reached a dead end weeks ago in my search for another clue. He would never understand my need. Instead, I tell him that I happened to stumble across a poster for one of Chlorine's gigs on a recent trip to the British Library, went along to watch them play, and from that point on I tell him the truth. He is impressed by both my determination to seek out the band and my dedication to academic study in this difficult time. Other than that, thankfully, Mark is as harsh and critical as I hoped he would be.

"Meg, why on earth have you not called this woman? What's the matter with you? This is it. This is your chance to find out the truth!"

"I know. And I need to do it now, don't I?" I ask, willing him to tell me what I need to hear.

"Of course you need to do it now! You want to be able to verify things with your mother, to clarify facts. Once you know the truth, there will be questions you'll need to ask her. The first one being: why did she feel the need to keep things from you all these years. And you don't have time to waste. She'll be dead soon!"

There is a silence on the line while I struggle with these last words, taking a deep breath and trying to control my emotions. He's right, I remind myself, he's only telling the truth. Mark, more than anyone else in my life, always tells me the truth. And that's a good thing. It's what I need to hear.

"I'm not sure why I've been putting it off," I tell him, embarrassed by my own lack of fortitude. I feel vulnerable admitting my confusion. I feel weak. And I hate myself for being weak in front of Mark, but I don't know what else to do. There is clearly something wrong with the way my brain is functioning right now, and Mark is the smartest person I know. If anybody can tell me why I am failing to think and behave in a rational manner, surely it is him.

"I have no idea why you're putting it off either," he says bluntly. "There's no reason for it. It's not like you at all."

This isn't quite the response I wanted, but it *is* the response I need. When Mark says, *It's not like you at all*, I know exactly what he means. He means: *This isn't the girl I fell in love with.* He means: *I thought you were better than this.* He means: *Show me you're as strong and as logical as you have always been, because a weak, irrational girl just isn't for me.*

By the time I get off the phone with Mark, my mind feels eased of its burden and things seem straightforward again. I know where I need to go, I know what I have to do, and I know there is only one way forward.

I look down on my mother from the bedroom window as she putters around the garden talking to plants, and as I dial Gwennie's number, I chastise myself for having wasted so much valuable time.

"I can't believe it's really you," says Gwennie, quite emotional. "You sound so grown up."

Unlike my first encounter with Chlorine, this time I don't excitedly point out that I've grown older since I was a baby. The excitement has gone now, replaced by something far more uncomfortable. Trepidation? Anxiety? Dread?

"The last time I saw you was the day before your fifth birthday. I gave you a princess dolly. You probably don't have that anymore, though, do you? I suppose you might not have even taken it with you when you left. I know you didn't take much."

"Left where?" I ask.

"Your home. Your home in Brighton."

My home in Brighton? I never lived in Brighton. We were living in our flat in Tottenham when I was five.

Except obviously we weren't. And that's exactly the point. Why do I keep thinking that I know anything about my life?

"I've thought about your mother—about both of you—so much over the years," continues Gwennie, "and several times I thought about trying to find you. I almost tried a couple of years ago, after my father said he thought he passed Val in Tottenham on his way to a football game, but he wasn't sure if it was her, and I didn't quite know where to start, and I suppose, in all honesty, I was never sure if she would want to see me again. She wanted to leave the past behind, and I can understand that. I just always wished I'd had the chance to say good-bye, that's all. I understand why she couldn't tell me where she was going, though, when she left. She was trying to protect me. I understand that."

Protect you? Leave the past behind? What on earth is going on? I rub my forehead, not knowing where to start.

"I know this must be strange for you," I say, "my phoning you out of the blue like this. It's just, my mother hasn't told me very much about my life around that time. And what she has told me, well, let's just say it's very unlikely to be the truth. And now I've started to find things out from other people, bits of information that simply don't make sense to me, and I didn't even know until last week that I had a stepfather, someone called Robert, and now you're telling me I lived in Brighton, which I never knew…and… and someone else said my grandparents had thrown us out…and then it turns out we lived with a rock band and…and to be honest, I'm just really confused."

There is a long silence, during which time I notice my hands are shaking. I clench my fists, trying to stop them, telling myself to get a grip.

"You mean Val hasn't told you anything?" Gwennie says, astonished.

I shake my head, which is not much use on the phone, but I am afraid that if I speak, my voice will crack with emotion. And the last thing I need is some stranger thinking I'm a complete basket case.

"Can't you ask her?" Gwennie asks.

I feel anger rising in my chest, and I have to suppress the urge to shout, *Now, why didn't I think of that!*

"She's not exactly forthcoming," I say as calmly as possible.

"Gosh," Gwennie says, and for a moment I can tell that she was married to Bomber, or Timothy, or whatever he calls himself. "Gosh, Meg, look, I'm not sure it's my place to go interfering. I'm sure Val—I mean, your mother—has her reasons for keeping certain things from you—"

"I'm twenty-one!" I suddenly cry, and then, ashamed of myself for letting my emotions get out of control, I repeat more quietly, "I'm twenty-one. And I have a big gap in my life that no one seems able, or willing, to tell me about. Please, if you can help me, then please…"

I can hear Gwennie's jagged breathing through the phone, and I can tell I am not the only one shaking. I have startled her, phoning her out of the blue like this, putting this pressure on her.

"Your ex-husband said you were the one who found me," I tell her calmly. "What did he mean by that?"

I can almost hear Gwennie's mind entering into a state of panic, wondering what she should and should not say.

"Meg, I don't think it's my place...you need to speak to your mother about—"

"Then just tell me this," I ask quickly, a lump suddenly rising in my throat. "Am I hers?"

The question is out before I know it, and for a moment I have no idea where it came from, but as I hear my voice trembling I realize that this, this question, this is one of the many reasons why I have been unable to make this phone call. *She was the one who found you.* Ever since Timothy said those words, a thought has been playing at the back of my mind that I have not allowed myself to acknowledge, that I have not even allowed myself to entertain. But it has been there, I see that now. I feel it in the shaking of my hands and the lump in my throat. *She was the one who found you.* What else could it mean?

Am I even her daughter?

Gwennie gives a short, shocked laugh. "Of course you're hers! Gosh...of course you are!"

Every muscle in my body relaxes slightly, but for some reason, the lump in my throat just lodges itself harder, and I feel even more like crying than I did a second ago. *Pull yourself together, Meg May!* I tell myself, pinching my arm. *Stop being such a fool!*

"My mother's sick," I tell Gwennie. "She's very sick."

There is a long pause before Gwennie asks, "How sick?"

I can't say it. I just can't. I open my mouth, but the words won't come out. I hear my own shaky breathing down the telephone line.

"How long does she have?" asks Gwennie, doing the work for me.

"Not that long," I tell her, rubbing at the ache that rises beneath my rib cage. Is that the first time I have ever said it? Is that the first time I have let myself speak those words? It might be. Or it might not. How would I know? However many times I said it, it would always hurt the same.

"Oh," breathes Gwennie, the air going out of her. "Oh, I see. Gosh."

"I'm worried I'm never going to know the truth," I tell her, "and that nothing will ever be reconciled between us. It shouldn't be like this; it shouldn't have to end in a pack of lies. Whatever happened, I need to know, because she's not just my mother, she's my best friend, and if it weren't for this…this gap, these lies, then the time we've had together would be perfect. And that's how it should end. Perfectly. Not like this. Not without any understanding or any closure. Not all in a mess."

There is a long silence, during which time I think I can hear Gwennie crying quietly.

"She was my best friend, too," she says, her voice thick with emotion.

I don't know what to say. I've never known my mother to have any friends. None other than me, that is.

"She's a wonderful mother," I tell her sadly, as if this information sums up everything Gwennie has missed in the last sixteen years.

"I know she is," sniffs Gwennie. "I always knew she would be."

It is silent for a long time. I look down from my bedroom window, holding the phone to my ear, watching my mother picking flowers from the garden border, assuming she is gathering a little bouquet for the kitchen table. But instead, she carries the flowers over to the compost heap. They are no good. It is too late for flowers now. From up here I can see that the array of colors that filled the garden has dwindled and faded without my ever noticing, and the flowers that remain are wilting, clinging to their last breath of life.

"Please, help me," I beg Gwennie.

Gwennie lets out a heavy sigh, clearly burdened by this decision. "Where are you living now?"

She is surprised to hear my mother is back where she started, in the house where she grew up, and even more surprised to realize that all this time the three of us have been so close.

"I'm just outside Cambridge," she says. "Isn't it funny how people go back to their roots?"

"I wouldn't know," I say flatly, reminding her that without her help, I am, and might always be, rootless.

"I would love to see your mother one last time," muses Gwennie. "We were so close. This isn't how I wanted things to end either."

"Then let's help each other," I say eagerly. "Maybe seeing you is just what my mother needs. I'm sure she would love to see you again, whatever happened in the past, and maybe it will help bring some closure to all this."

"But I don't know," Gwennie says, seemingly torn. "Maybe it's not the right thing to do. Maybe it's better to just let things be. Although I really would love to see her one last time, and I think she would like to see me, but maybe I'm wrong, maybe she wouldn't. Oh, I don't know."

I can see what a difficult position I have put her in, and I know that my phone call must be quite a shock, but part of me wishes I could just reach down the telephone line, grab her by the neck, and shake her until she understands what this means to me. I don't have time for indecision. I don't have time for ifs and buts. Where can I go from here if she won't help me? There's no one else I can turn to. This feels like my last chance.

"I don't think I can help you, Meg," says Gwennie after a while, her voice full of sadness and regret. "I'm so sorry, but I really don't. It's not my place to tell you things your mother might not want you to know. It's not for me to interfere. I've already said far too much. And I don't think I should come and see her, even though I would love to. If there's even the slightest chance that seeing me would upset her, then I don't think it would be right. Not now. Not now that..."

Her voice trails off, fading along with any hope I had of knowing the truth about my past.

"I'm so sorry," she says again.

I don't respond. I don't know how to. I feel this is my cue to make her feel better by saying something like "don't worry" or "it doesn't matter." But it does. It matters more than she can ever imagine.

I hang up the phone, not because I want to be rude or hurt her or express my anger, but because I can't think of a single word that could make this situation better for either of us.

I spend the rest of the day lying on my bed, staring at the ceiling, looking at the little star-shaped stickers that my mother carefully peeled off the ceiling of my bedroom in Tottenham and brought with her when she moved. They didn't stick once she got them here, so she went to the painstaking effort of gluing each one back into its original constellation. I thought it was sweet, at first. Sweet but strange. Why would she still think I wanted glow-in-the-dark star stickers when I was eighteen years old and not even living here? It's like she can't let go of the little girl I once was, like she wants to keep that child forever wrapped in a wonderful bubble of fairy-tale goodness. And she can't even see the harm she's doing me. She can't even see that inside her tight embrace I am struggling to be free, unable to breathe, unable to find myself.

So that's it, I think. That's the end. Chlorine can't help me anymore, Timothy won't help me anymore, and Gwennie already thinks she's said too much. Maybe one day they will change their minds, maybe one day, somehow, the truth will come out. But by then it will be too late. My mother will be gone, along with any chance for questions, or discussion, or mutual understanding. I will never know it all. Not now. I will never hear it from her side.

And my mother will die in a state of delusion, her mind muddled and fogged by images of things that never happened, images of Christmas turkeys running wild and her baby daughter floating around the kitchen in an egg-white bubble. Nobody wants that. Nobody wants to leave this life without being able to remember, in those final moments, what it was all about. What it was *really* all about.

I wanted to bring her back down to earth before the end. I wanted her to think clearly, to remember who she is and where she came from and what she has done with her life. I wanted her to have peace and clarity, coherence and understanding. But there's no chance of that. Not for either of us.

I wonder who my mother is when she's stripped of all the lies. I wonder who really exists underneath that layer of make-believe. It makes me sad that we will never be able to communicate at the same level. Not fully, anyway. I will never know her adult-to-adult. We will never talk woman-to-woman.

I look up at the stars and almost laugh.

As if she could ever think of me as anything other than a little girl.

By half past five, the light from the bedroom window is starting to fade, and I remember the days, not so long ago, when it was still light at nine in the evening, and my mother and I would sit on the patio in just shorts and T-shirts, eating ice cream and doing the crossword. Where did it go, I wonder, that summer that was meant to last forever? How did I ever let it slip away?

I hear my mother's bedroom door close as she goes to take a rest. Later she will deny ever lying down on the bed, her limbs aching, her breathing a struggle, and she will tell me that she was spring cleaning or trying on some old clothes.

Shortly after, I hear the squeak of the back gate as Ewan enters the garden, his tools clattering on the ground. After a while he turns his radio on, and I can hear the faint sound of music playing. Sometime after that, Digger starts barking.

And barking.

And growling.

And then there is a squeal, like an animal is being stabbed with a pitchfork.

I jump up and look out the window. There is Digger down by the open gate, tumbling over and over with a little white ball of fur—a rabbit? a cat?—while Ewan sprints across the garden shouting at him.

I rush downstairs, tugging my shoes on as I go, and fly out the back door, skidding on the muddy grass as I run through the garden. I'm not sure what worries me more: the idea that my mother might be woken from her nap or the idea that our gardener's dog is trying to kill our neighbor's cat. As I get closer, I can see that Digger is caught in a tussle with a small white terrier, the pair of them rolling over and over in a ball, emitting bloodcurdling yelps and squeals, while Ewan tries to pry them apart and a woman in a green anorak flaps her arms and screams, "Byron! My little Byron! Oh God, he's going to die!"

By the time I reach them, Ewan has Digger by the collar and the little white dog (which is now muddy brown) is cowering in the arms of the irate woman.

"You should keep him under control!" the woman screams.

"You should keep your dog out of other people's gardens!" Ewan snaps back.

Digger is straining to get away from him, barking angrily at the little dog, who he clearly sees as an intruder. The little dog, in turn, is baring his teeth and snarling. Both of them are muddy and bedraggled.

"He could have killed my poor Byron!" shouts the woman, clutching the dog protectively to her bosom.

"Maybe poor Byron should stay on a lead," Ewan suggests, clearly trying to contain his anger.

"Well, if you're going to leave your back gate open—"

"That's no excuse for just letting him wander in here."

"I was trying to get your attention, but your radio was on—"

"Digger, quiet!" snaps Ewan, yanking the barking dog's collar.

"Oh, Byron, stop struggling!" complains the woman, clutching the wriggling terrier tighter.

"Sorry, who are you?" I ask, sounding ridiculously polite amid all the chaos.

The woman looks up, aware of me for the first time, but instead of meeting my eye, she gazes over my right shoulder, the anger suddenly draining from her face.

Ewan and I both turn to see my mother standing behind us, her arms wrapped tightly around her frail body, shivering. She looks pale and startled, staring at the woman as if she were a ghost.

"Val," the woman whispers, her eyes locked with my mother's in mutual disbelief. "Gosh."

And suddenly I realize who this woman is.

"Hello, Val," Gwennie says, smiling cautiously.

My mother just stares at her, frozen.

"Mother, it's Gwennie," I say, gently touching her arm, "your friend. Do you remember?"

My mother shakes her head almost imperceptibly.

"No," she whispers quietly, "no, I don't remember."

"Val," Gwennie smiles, taking a step forward, "it's me, Gwennie. You must remember—"

"No," says my mother, taking a step back, "I don't remember. I don't remember anything. I—"

Before I even notice she is about to fall, Ewan rushes to my mother's side and catches her as she collapses.

"Mother!" I gasp, running to her side and supporting her lolling head. Her eyes roll, and she groans quietly.

I lean in close, trying to hear what she is saying, but all I hear her murmur are the words *I don't remember.*

chapter fifteen

"What do you want to know?" Gwennie asks.

Like a child in a sweet shop, I want to gorge myself, to grab hold of every fact, every piece of information that's on offer. I am starving for truth.

"Everything," I say greedily. "Tell me everything you know."

There is no hesitation now, no putting it off until another day, no wondering whether this is the right thing to do. I know what it feels like to have the truth offered up like a delicious treat, only to have it snatched away at the last moment. And I don't intend to go through that again.

We sit at the kitchen table facing each other, steaming mugs of tea in front of us, the rain pitter-pattering against the windowpane. Outside, the sky is gloomy and gray, but inside the kitchen it is bright and warm, with Gwennie's wet raincoat hanging by the back door and our shoes drying on the mat. I sense that Gwennie could flee at any moment. She is hesitant, still undecided on some level, fiddling nervously with Byron's ears as he snores softly in her lap, exhausted by his tussle with Digger.

I try to remain calm and still, waiting patiently for her to speak, sensing that one false move could scare her away. I don't want to pressure her. But if she thinks I won't barricade the door and slash the tires of her car to stop her from leaving, she is making a big mistake.

After laying my mother on the couch, Ewan left, quiet and confused, and I sat with her, stroking her hand, watching her eyes race back and forth behind their papery lids, while Gwennie hovered anxiously in the doorway, chewing her fingernails and asking how she could help. Finally, once my mother's nightmares had subsided, giving way to dreams that made her smile and mutter quietly about butterbeans, I felt able to leave her side.

"If you really want to help," I tell Gwennie matter-of-factly, hardened by shock and exhaustion, "then tell me the truth about my life."

As she gazes at my mother lying listlessly on the couch, her pale, thin body tucked beneath a blanket, perhaps she finally understands that she really is my only chance.

"All right," she says, "all right, I'll tell you."

"Your mother and I had been best friends for many years," Gwennie says, her hands wrapped tightly around her mug of tea. "Since we were eight or nine, I suppose, when I joined her school. I lived a couple of roads from here, and we were always running around together, getting into mischief. We both loved being outdoors, and we used to take milk bottles and go fairy hunting in Coley Woods, even though we weren't allowed to go in there.

We had such wild imaginations. I think that's why we got along so well. A hole in a tree could instantaneously become the portal into the fairy kingdom, and a glint of sunlight through the leaves could suddenly turn into two fairies dancing. We would always come home covered in dirt, and our parents would get ever so angry, but we didn't really care. Our games were all such good fun. One minute we would be American Indians looking out for cowboys, and the next we would be elegant princesses waiting to be rescued from our tower. We lived in a wonderful, magical world of make-believe, just like little girls should. Not a care in the world. We would laugh and laugh until our bellies ached and tears streamed down our cheeks, the kind of laughter you forget as an adult. It was a fantastical, carefree, happy time. The best years of my life in many ways.

"We grew out of it, of course. That kind of innocence doesn't last long. By the time we were teenagers, we had all the usual pressures of exams, nagging parents, and homework to contend with. We still went out and had fun, just in a different way, I suppose. Your mother was always such a vivacious, bubbly girl, very lively and outgoing, and extremely pretty with long auburn hair and big, sparkling blue eyes. She used to love going dancing on a Saturday evening down at the Forum, and all the boys had an eye on her. But she wasn't interested. She was a true romantic, waiting for Mr. Right, and until he arrived and swept her off her feet, she wasn't going to waste her time on any of the boys from town. Besides, she had so many other things to accomplish that for a long time boys just didn't come into the picture. She was expected to do well in her exams and planned to go to university and study English literature before spending a couple of years traveling to remote places around the world and coming back, falling in love, getting married, and having children.

"'There's just so many things to do, Gwennie,' she used to tell me, 'so many places to see, so many people to meet.'

"She was full of life, so full of energy and enthusiasm. The world was out there waiting for her, and she was straining at the leash, dying to embrace it all."

I try to imagine my mother eager to get out into the world, desperate to meet people and see things and go places. It's hard to do, when the farthest I have known her to travel is from London to Cambridge, and she only did that the once, when she finally moved to a new house.

"My mother doesn't really like people," I tell Gwennie, finding it hard to imagine the picture she is painting.

Gwennie nods slowly, as if this makes sense. "You can learn not to," she tells me sadly, fiddling with Byron's little white ear. I notice a red line of dried blood on the soft, pink inside, where he must have been scratched in the fight.

"At fifteen, she fell in love for the first time," Gwennie says, "and it was like she was walking on air. He was an American, I think, in the army, if I remember correctly. It was all part of a pen pal scheme that our youth group initiated. She loved writing and the idea of travel, so writing to someone in the armed forces appealed to her tremendously. She got to hear all about the places he had been stationed, and within a couple of months she was really quite besotted. She believed she had found the love of her life. He wrote her long, gushing letters full of adoration and told her they would marry as soon as she turned eighteen. She was desperate to tell me everything about him, each little thing he had said or done, but I really didn't want to hear. I was jealous, you see. My pen pal was a German girl called Nadine with a hairy upper lip and an obsession with ant farms.

"I was angry with your mother for falling in love. I wanted to fall in love too, and letting Wally Waters squeeze my left breast in the back row of the cinema just seemed so shallow and pointless compared to the romance your mother had found. So I wouldn't listen to all the things they had said to each other or the plans they had made for the future. I would change the subject, or turn the record player up, or tell her to stop going on about him all the time, anything so that I didn't have to hear how wonderful he was. That's why, I'm afraid, I don't know very much about him. But I do remember his name, if you would like to know it."

I shrug, wondering whether Gwennie is going to take me on a journey through every single relationship my mother might have ever had.

"Only if it's relevant," I say, eager to get to the crux of all this.

"Well, I suppose it's relevant," says Gwennie. "After all, he was your father."

I stare at her, shocked, and for a moment I don't believe her. She's confused. She must be. My father was a French pastry chef, not some American pen pal from the armed forces. But then I remember that I'm the one who is confused, as always, and I wonder why I keep forgetting this. So I nod, holding my breath.

"His name was Don," says Gwennie.

"Don," I whisper, seeing how the name feels on my tongue. "Don."

I don't know what I expected to feel when this moment finally came, but what I didn't expect to feel was nothing. I search my soul, seeking out some little spark of fulfillment, some sense that I have suddenly become whole, that my identity is now complete. But there's nothing there. This name means nothing to me.

Gwennie eyes me cautiously, as if waiting for some sudden and startling reaction. But I just look at her blankly.

"Go on," I say, as if nothing has happened, as if my world has not just changed forever.

"One day," continues Gwennie, "your mother didn't want to go dancing anymore. She didn't want to listen to her favorite records, or go cycling down by the river, or go to the shops, or do anything at all. It was as if someone had pricked her with a pin and taken all the air out of her. She slept all the time, which aggravated her parents, and when she was awake all she wanted to do was bury her head in books, and not even the schoolbooks we were meant to be reading. We were weeks away from taking our finals, but she was devouring romantic fiction and fantasy novels like they were going out of fashion. She seemed withdrawn and spaced out, lost in her own little world.

"'Gwennie,' she said to me one day, in an unusual burst of enthusiasm, 'why don't we go fairy hunting? You know, like we used to?'

"Well, I looked at her as if she were mad. 'We're not children anymore, Valerie,' I told her.

"'So what?' she said. 'Why can't we still do those things? It was such fun, wasn't it? Things were so good back then.'

"'Val,' I complained, 'I've got studying to do. And a Saturday job. I don't have time for playing around anymore.'

"Her eyes became wide and tear-filled, like a child who had been chastised.

"'No,' she said, apologetically, 'of course not.'

"But then, that weekend, I caught her. I was in the woods with Wally Waters when we stumbled across her in the bushes, milk bottle in hand.

"'What are you doing creeping about in the bushes, you weirdo?' Wally asked her, a cigarette dangling from his lips. 'Are you spying on us?'

"Your mother looked at me, red-faced and guilty, and I just stared at her, wondering why she had suddenly taken up fairy hunting again when she had just turned sixteen.

"'I reckon she's spying on us, Gwennie,' Wally said. 'Perhaps she's jealous. Perhaps she fancies me. Do you fancy me, Valerie?' he asked teasingly, reaching out to touch her chin.

"Your mother, who had always thought Wally was a lovable idiot, suddenly went white as a sheet and ran off as fast as her legs would carry her.

"'Your best pal's a complete nutter,' said Wally.

"Well, that was the end of Wally and me. Needless to say, your mother did very poorly in her O-levels. Sitting in that exam hall, I watched her, one day after the next, staring blankly at the wall, barely writing a thing. Nobody knew what was wrong with her, and talking to her was like talking to a brick wall. She would insist that she was perfectly fine, but it was as if the lights were on but nobody was home. At the same time, you could see her mind was whirring away, lost in thought, but about what, who could tell? Nobody imagined for one second that she was pregnant; she managed to hide it so well. I think she even managed to hide it from herself."

"So when did she meet up with my…with Don?" I ask, feeling we have skipped an enormous chunk of the story. I can't bring myself to use the word "father." There is no meaning in it for me, no association I can make with this unknown man. It's ridiculous, but I realize the only person I feel comfortable calling father is an imaginary pastry chef from Paris.

"I don't know," says Gwennie, shaking her head. "I was never entirely sure when they met up. It wasn't until later that…well, it's complicated. Shall I just—?"

"I'm sorry," I say, realizing I have interrupted her flow of thought. "Please, carry on."

Gwennie takes a sip of tea and clears her throat. "I found you in the shed," she says, "which is an unusual place to find a baby. I knew what had happened from the moment your mother opened the front door. There was blood on her clothes, and she was clearly in shock. I suppose there could have been other explanations, but they never crossed my mind. I just knew she had given birth. I don't know how, but I just knew.

"I kept asking where the baby was, but she couldn't answer me. She just stared at the floor and hugged her arms around her body. So I started to search for you all throughout the house, and then it occurred to me that if you weren't in the house, you must be in the garden. And there you were. Tucked up in a blanket, nestled between a bag of compost and a watering can.

"'I have to cook dinner,' was all your mother would say when I brought you inside. 'Mother and Father will be home soon, so I must get the dinner on.'

"She was crazy, of course. Temporarily insane. She had managed to convince herself that none of it was real—the conception, the pregnancy, the birth—she had blocked it all out, and her brain clearly couldn't make sense of your arrival. And I was no help, really. I didn't know what to do. I was scared. I'd never even held a baby before, and I remember wondering how long you would live without food.

"'You have to feed it,' I said, holding you out to your mother.

"'Okay, okay,' she said, flustered, flinging open the oven door. 'Put it straight in then.'

"'No,' I shouted at her, 'feed it, not cook it!'

"But your mother just looked at me blankly and started pulling pots and pans out of the cupboards. And then your grandparents walked in, looking rather startled, to say the least.

"'What is that?' your grandfather demanded, pointing at you.

"Your mother didn't answer, so I said, 'It's a baby.'

"'I can see it's a bloody baby!' he snapped. 'What's it doing here?'

"But even as he asked the question, I could see him looking at the blood on your mother's clothes and piecing two and two together. Your grandmother, one step ahead of him, had already burst into tears and was wringing her hands and asking the Lord's forgiveness."

"So they weren't there when I was born?" I ask, finding it surprisingly hard to let go of the "truth" as I have always known it. "They didn't help her through the labor?"

"Gosh, no! I don't think they could have coped with that. They both went into a state of shock as it was. I can't tell you exactly what happened next, because it was all such a blur. I remember your grandmother becoming quite hysterical and your mother calmly asking her what was wrong, which made your grandmother wail even louder, because she thought her daughter had gone mad, which effectively she had. Then the gasman arrived at the back door asking to look at some pipes, and your grandfather, who was all worked up and in a temper, grabbed him by the collar so that the poor gasman had to defend himself with a nearby frying pan. And the next thing I knew your grandfather had snatched you out of my arms.

"'There's no way you can keep it,' he said. 'It'll have to go up for adoption.'

"And that was the moment your mother suddenly came to life again.

"'No!' she screamed, charging toward your grandfather and grabbing you from him. She clutched you so tight I thought she might kill you. I'm not sure she knew herself at that point what she was doing or who you were. I think you could have been a frozen chicken, for all she knew, but she was clear about one thing, and that was that you belonged to her and she was not letting anyone take you away.

"'Fine,' your grandfather said, 'you keep it. But you're on your own. You can stay two months, and then I want you gone. You've disgraced me.'

"He never spoke to her again. Even for the months you were living under the same roof, he completely ignored the pair of you.

And your grandmother wasn't much better, although I think she was mainly scared of getting into trouble with your grandfather. He was a severe man. Very religious, very concerned with what other people thought."

"So it's true, then," I interrupt, feeling disgusted by my grandparents' behavior. "They did throw us out. I thought we lived with them. I thought—"

"Gosh, no," says Gwennie. "They didn't lift one finger to help your mother out, not emotionally, not practically, not financially. She struggled terribly, as you can imagine. It took some time for her to fully accept that you were even her baby—I honestly don't think she remembered giving birth to you—but once she did accept you were hers, she adored you from your little head down to your tiny little toes. I kept asking who the father was, because she had never once mentioned meeting up with her pen pal—with Don, I mean—but whenever I brought the topic up, she just looked confused and started to mumble rubbish. She seemed to think you were a miracle conception."

Gwennie takes a sip of tea while I watch her impatiently, wondering how on earth she can pause to drink tea when I have just been born.

"As far as all the practicalities of motherhood were concerned," Gwennie continues, "she was a disaster zone. With no one to help her, she was completely clueless as to what to do with you. I tried to help her, but it was like the blind leading the blind. We were like two little girls playing with a doll that had lots of working parts but no instructions. And the fact that your mother seemed to keep zoning out, going off somewhere in her mind, losing concentration, really didn't help. I used to come around and find you in the strangest of places. She'd put you down and forget where she left you. I once found you in the water heater closet. And another time I found you on the windowsill. But whatever else was going on inside your mother's head, the one thing she never lost was her spirit and determination, and she was going to build a life for you both, whatever it took, even if she had to do every step of it alone. But as it turned out, she didn't have to be alone."

"But I don't understand," I say, getting restless. "How do you know he was my father, then? How do you know they ever met up if—"

"I'm getting there," says Gwennie, holding up a hand to stop me from talking. "After my exams, I decided I had to get away from home. I wasn't getting on with my parents either, and one evening, after a blazing row, I decided I just had to get out. Your mother's two months were almost up, and she was soon going to be homeless, so we decided to leave together. And there was only one place we could think to go.

"A band called Chlorine had played a few times at the Forum, and on a couple of occasions your mother and I had gotten to chatting with the boys in the band. To be honest, I think we were just a couple of silly schoolgirls to them, but your mother and I thought we were the height of cool, knowing a real live rock band. Anyway, the boys were moving to London to seek fortune and fame, and they gave us their address, saying that if we were ever in London and needed a place to stay, we should call on them. So off to London we went. Except obviously when Wizz—the lead singer, who you met—obviously when he made that offer, he hadn't expected us to turn up with a baby. He was good to his word and let us stay, but it was a nightmare. Everybody moaned about your crying, the place was filthy, the band was always practicing and making noise. Most nights they'd be drunk, or worse."

"And that's when you got together with Bomb—I mean, Timothy?"

"That's right. Within days we were an item, which made the situation even more awkward, because I was trying to help Val look after you, but what I really wanted to do was spend all my time with Timothy. We started to bicker, Val and I, which didn't help anyone, and then your mother decided it wasn't going to work and that she had to move out.

"She was so full of determination that within a month she had gotten herself a job as a waitress and moved out into a tiny studio. It was a miserable, dark, cold little place, but it was all she could afford. The landlord was always banging on her door demanding rent, the neighbors upstairs fought all night long, the babysitter was always letting her down, and when she couldn't work she didn't get paid…it was a hopeless situation. You were often sick. You'd been born slightly prematurely and you didn't seem to be growing very quickly. Your mother was starting to look ill herself. It was all a dreadful mess, but your mother soldiered on, insisting she was fine and that she wanted to earn her own money and manage alone. Until one night when it all got too much, and she finally broke down in tears. And that's when she told me what had happened with Don."

I lean across the table, hanging on Gwennie's every word. We look at each other for what feels like a very long time, her eyes wide and suddenly anxious, mine glaring and impatient.

"And?" I almost shout.

Gwennie swallows hard. "He had been on a visit to Portsmouth—which makes me think now that perhaps he was in the navy, not the army—and he had asked your mother to go and meet him. She hadn't told anyone, because she knew perfectly well her parents would never had let her go, and it was just bad timing that I was on a family holiday in Devon. If I hadn't been on holiday, then I expect she would have told me and perhaps asked me to go with her, and then maybe things would never have happened the way they did…"

Gwennie stares off into the distance, lost in thought.

"What would never have happened?" I ask urgently.

Gwennie tuts and looks pained. "He wasn't what she imagined, Meg. He wasn't the gentleman he made himself out to be. She was young and naïve…so, so naïve. She just didn't have a clue."

I feel a sense of panic rising in my chest. "What happened?"

Gwennie shakes her head despairingly. "They went somewhere, I don't know where it was, just to be alone. Your mother was so innocent; all she wanted to do was talk and perhaps have her first-ever kiss, a romantic moment to remember forever, her first embrace with the man of her dreams. But what happened between them… she never wanted that. She never, ever wanted that. And she told him so, but he didn't listen, or didn't care." Gwennie looks up and sighs. "She trusted him, Meg. He said he loved her, that he wanted to marry her, and she trusted him implicitly." She shakes her head regretfully. "She was such a silly girl. Such a very silly girl."

I suddenly feel like I am going to be sick. "You're lying," I hear myself say angrily.

Gwennie touches my arm gently.

"You're lying, aren't you?" I accuse, snatching my arm away.

She just looks at me sadly.

Of course she's not lying. I know that. But I wish so much that she was. I have never wanted someone to lie to me so much in my life.

"She only spoke about it that one time, and the next day it was as if nothing had happened. She went back to acting as if everything was just hunky-dory, even though she was clearly sinking. I told her to go home, to ask your grandparents to take her back, to explain that it wasn't her fault she got pregnant, but she was too ashamed to tell them, and she had too much pride to go back. They knew where she was, because my parents told them. They even sent her some money and a letter expressing their concern. But she had been far too deeply wounded by their rejection and refused to make contact. If they thought she had disgraced them, if they wanted her gone, then that's what they could have, she said. She would make something of her life and show them. All the kids back home who called her names when they found out she had had a baby, all the neighbors who had whispered when they found out what happened, she would show them all. She struggled on for a year, but there was no way she could cope. At that point she may well have married anybody who offered. Unfortunately, the person who offered was Robert Scott."

"My stepfather," I whisper.

"Yes. Your stepfather. She met him in the café where she

worked. He was a butcher by trade, up from Brighton for a few days visiting a friend in London. They struck up a conversation about the quality of the sausages, and six months later they were married. I should have stopped her. I knew there was something not right about him, but your mother couldn't see it. Desperation made her blind. He offered her a home for you both, and he was attentive and kind to her, at least to start with. He was an awkward man with pockmarked skin and a stutter, and I think your mother mistook his shyness for gentleness. I don't think she was attracted to him, but she was grateful, and that was enough.

"They had a cheap wedding in a registry office in Brighton, just the two of them, and myself as witness. After that they moved into Robert's little terraced house in the center of town. Your mother did her best to make it a home and did everything from the DIY to growing a vegetable patch, but things were bad right from the start. As I understand it, the beatings started within weeks of the marriage. Robert would fly into terrible rages, hitting your mother about the head, pushing her against walls and furniture, once even fracturing her wrist. She never told me any of this, of course. I had to piece it all together from snippets the neighbors gave away. By this point Timothy had split from the band, and we had moved to Oxford so that Timothy could pursue a master's degree in law. We were penniless, and I only got to see your mother every so often, whenever I could afford the train fare to Brighton. Whenever I did see her, she seemed to have sunk deeper and deeper into denial, insisting that everything was fine when that was clearly not the case. She started cooking all the time, always having to be busy. I think it was her way of coping."

"Why didn't she leave him?" I ask, unable to comprehend how she could have stayed in such a miserable situation. "Why did she let him treat her like that?"

"I begged your mother to leave him, but she wouldn't. In the end, I gave my telephone number to one of the neighbors and asked them to call me if anything happened. I was honestly scared for her life. The neighbor told me she had heard Robert threaten to track your mother down and kill you both if she ever left him. Your mother must have been terrified, although she completely denied that Robert ever said such a thing, of course. She denied everything. She was always telling me that she had fallen down the stairs or walked into doors. I think she even managed to convince herself. It was ludicrous."

"But surely the police—"

"There was nothing they could do unless your mother made an official complaint."

I place my head in my hands. This is so much worse than I ever expected. Never in a million years could I have been prepared for this.

"Although your mother seemed to spend half her time in a daze," Gwennie continues, "she was always one step ahead of Robert where you were concerned. She tried to keep you well out of his way, and if ever he got angry because you were crying or had knocked something over, she would make sure she was the one to bear the brunt of his fury, not you. Generally, he just ignored you. You were no more than an annoyance to him. The tragic thing was that you so wanted him to love you. You tried desperately to get his attention, but it never worked, which was probably just as well. You used to call him Daddy."

I clutch my stomach, feeling sick at the thought of it. *Daddy*. I always wanted to say that word to someone. I just can't believe I used to say it to such a monster.

"Your mother finally summoned the courage to leave on the day of your fifth birthday," says Gwennie. "The day he tried to strangle you."

I look up at her, my face expressionless, my heart numb. Her words are like waves washing over me, barely disturbing the surface. Nothing could shock me anymore. Nothing could be any worse that what I have already heard.

"You had spilled paint all over something or other, and he had blown his top. He grabbed you by the neck and hit your head against a coffee table. Your mother tried to pry him off you, and when he didn't let go, she pulled a knife out of the kitchen drawer and charged at him with it. She would have killed him, I'm sure of it, but he let go of you and grabbed the knife from her. I'm not sure what happened next, because your mother really wasn't making much sense when she phoned me, but obviously it was enough to shock her into action."

I stare at the table, trying to imagine this scene: my mother charging at someone with a knife, clearly intending to kill him. My mother who won't swat a fly and who apologizes to vegetables before chopping them up, who thanks each piece of meat for the life it has sacrificed and who has started talking to trees to help them grow. She would have murdered him. She would have plunged a knife in his heart.

"She left everything behind but the clothes on your backs. Robert called me, demanding to know where you had gone, and when I hung up on him, he drove all the way to Oxford and started banging on our door in a terrible rage. For a moment I knew what it must have felt like to be your mother. It was absolutely terrifying. To this day I thank heaven that Timothy was there; otherwise, who knows what he might have done? But the thing is, I couldn't have told Robert anything even if I had wanted to. Your mother honestly hadn't told me about her plans. She knew, I think, that if Robert suspected I had any information, he would have stopped at nothing to get that information out of me. It was too much of a risk. She was trying to protect me."

"So that was it?" I ask. "That was the last time you ever saw her?"

"Yes. Until today. I waited and waited for news to come, but it never did. I even visited Val's parents, but they didn't know anything either. It was as if the pair of you had just vanished into the night, breaking all contact with anything and anyone from the past."

I stare into my mug of cold, untouched tea, my mind blank, my heart empty. I feel as if all the life has been drained out of me.

"Was I..." Gwennie begins uncertainly. "Was I right to tell you?"

I shiver, even though the kitchen is so warm that condensation mists the windows. I don't know the answer to this question.

"You did what I asked you to do," I say flatly.

There is a long and painful silence between us. I'm sure I should have more questions to ask, but I feel dead inside. My head aches and my stomach feels sick.

"Why did you change your mind," I ask, "about coming here?"

Gwennie sighs and gives a listless shrug. "I suppose I needed to know the truth as well. For all those years I tried to believe that you had started again, that you were safe and well and happy. I liked to think that maybe your mother had fallen in love, become a cook, and traveled to all the places she dreamed about visiting. And that you had grown to a healthy size, were doing well in school, and enjoying a new family life. But I never knew. Not for sure. I suppose I had my own gap to fill."

She picks up her teaspoon and rubs it between her fingers as if wishing a genie would appear and with a click of his fingers make this horrible situation go away.

"Plus, I have a daughter," she adds. "She's younger than you, just thirteen. Her father and I might not be together, but she knows where she came from, who she is. I think that's her right. I wouldn't ever want her to be without that knowledge."

I trace my finger around the rim of my mug, over and over again, gazing at the cold film of milk on the surface of my tea.

"Do you get along?" I ask, for no particular reason.

Gwennie gives a little, quiet laugh. "She rather hates me right now. But I'm hoping she'll grow out of it."

I nod and muster a small, appreciative smile. "She will," I tell her. "I promise."

Gwennie examines my face closely, staring into my sad, tired eyes. "You're so like your mother," she says, and I almost laugh at the irony of it.

I have strived all my life to be nothing like my mother. I have clung desperately to the principles of truth, logic, and rationality, while my mother has indulged in fantasy and denial. I have wrung my hands, stamped my feet, and wept tears of frustration in the face of her delusions. And yet I wonder now how different I have really been.

I recall Dr. Bloomberg's words when I visited his office that day. *It's amazing what we can forget.*

I touch the scar on my forehead, the scar I now know came from having my head banged against a coffee table, not from being attacked by a crab cake. I have forgotten everything, not because I have wanted to, but because I have needed to. And yet I am filled with the horrible certainty that deep down some part of me still remembers. The White Giant who haunts my dreams is no giant at all, but a man in a butcher's coat. Those calloused hands around my neck are no figment of my imagination, but the shadow of my past. His name, his face, his pockmarked skin. That house, the fear, the violence…it is all still there, lurking in the deepest recesses of my mind. The memories that I so desperately wanted to recall have been there all this time, and now, like a sleeping beast that has been prodded with a stick, they have begun to stir. Vague recollections are now teetering on the edge of my consciousness, and I have a sense that it would all come flooding back to me if only I let myself remember.

The question is: do I want to?

chapter sixteen

I sometimes think that Mark should wear a spandex leotard, a mask, and a cape with an enormous *R* printed on the back. Rationality Man to the rescue, applying logic in the midst of chaos. I called him late last night, after Gwennie had left, like a damsel in distress. "Help!" I wanted to scream down the line. "I've just discovered the truth about my past! My mind is in turmoil, my thoughts are confused, and my feelings are threatening to overwhelm me! Save me, Rationality Man!" Of course, what I actually said was, "Mark, I've just been told the truth about my past. It's all been rather a lot to take on board. I was wondering whether you might be able to come down tomorrow instead of Sunday so that we can go over it? I mean, if not, don't worry. I'm absolutely fine."

Mark arrives, not in spandex, but in well-shined shoes, freshly pressed jeans, and a sensible waterproof jacket, which would be my second choice of outfit for Rationality Man. Just seeing him is like a drug for me. Watching him stride confidently up the front path, full of composure and self-assurance, I already feel my confusion and anxiety starting to subside. By the time he has cleared the kitchen table of baskets of fruit, sat me down, and said, "Right, let's start at the beginning," I am ready to abandon myself to his powers of orderliness.

By the time I have finished telling Mark everything I have found out, he already has a list of facts and questions written out neatly on a piece of paper.

"So," he says, rubbing his chin and examining his notes, "this has certainly filled in a lot of the gaps. But there are now several questions that arise as a result of this newfound knowledge. For example, question one, where is your biological father now? You have a right to know."

"I told you," I say, "it was just a fling. She probably can't even remember his name."

Okay. So perhaps I haven't told Mark *everything*. I may have glossed over the circumstances of my conception. I know that what happened to my mother is not a reflection on me, but I can't help wondering if Mark would see me differently. Tainted. Impure. Guilty…all these things that keep popping into my head and I keep trying to push out because I know they are illogical. I don't want Mark to see me as any less than perfect.

"I don't think I want to think about my real father just yet," I say swiftly.

"Okay," says Mark, as if he's chairing a meeting. "We can come back to that. Let's move on to question two. Is your mother still married?"

This hadn't even occurred to me. The thought that she could still be legally tied to that man makes my stomach turn. I could still legally be his stepdaughter.

"Now, on the one hand," says Mark, "we know that your

mother uses her maiden name. This is fairly standard practice when a woman divorces her husband. However, this evidence is somewhat counteracted by the fact that your mother would have needed to maintain some sort of contact with Robert Scott, even if only via a lawyer, in order for a divorce to go ahead, and we don't think this is likely. Now—"

"Mark," I interrupt, "I'm not really sure I want to talk about Robert Scott right now either."

"If your mother is still married, Meg, it could have legal and financial implications when your mother dies. Have you thought about that?"

I shake my head.

"Well, you need to. Now, I'm not a lawyer, as you know, but I imagine this Robert Scott fellow may still be entitled to some of your mother's money. Perhaps we should brainstorm possible routes to pursue depending on what your mother's answer is."

I nod, starting to feel rather overwhelmed again. "Okay," I agree. "Answer to what?"

Mark looks a little exasperated. He likes to work faster and more efficiently than this. "Her answer to whether she's still legally married or not."

"Oh, right, sorry. How will we know that?"

Mark's fingers tighten against his pencil, turning them white at the tips. "Because you're going to ask her."

"What? I…am I?"

This morning my mother had dragged herself downstairs in her dressing gown, pale and weary, but forcing her usual smile. "Good morning, darling," she had said, as if nothing had changed. She had examined some eggs, some cereal, some bread, and some milk as if it were all contaminated before declaring she was not hungry.

"Are you still feeling faint?" I had asked, watching her shuffle unsteadily around the kitchen.

"Was I feeling faint?" she asked, confused.

"Well, yes. You fainted," I told her, "yesterday afternoon. When you saw Gwennie."

My mother shook her head, baffled. "Who's Gwennie?"

"I don't see how I can question my mother about any of this," I tell Mark, "when she doesn't even remember Gwennie being here."

Mark raises one eyebrow skeptically. "So she says. Look, Meg, your mother's a wonderful liar, you know that."

"I'm not sure she's lying. I honestly don't think she remembers anything in between picking fruit yesterday and waking up this morning." Then, remembering Ewan's words yesterday, I add, "There's a difference between pretending and believing."

Mark shakes his head and looks at me in the way one might look at a mistreated puppy. "Meg," he says, taking my hand, "doesn't that seem rather convenient? This way your mother doesn't have to answer any awkward questions, she can deny all knowledge of Gwennie, and she can carry on just as things were before, telling you silly stories, denying you the truth. I suspect the reason she fainted yesterday was sheer panic, panic that her lies were all about to be revealed. Or, even more likely, she pretended to faint, just like last time. She used exactly the same transparent strategy. She pretended to faint as a distraction. She hoped that in the chaos Gwennie would just go away. But what she still doesn't know is that Gwennie didn't go away. She sat here and told you what really happened when you were little, and so now you are the one holding all the balls. You're in the perfect position to catch your mother out, to take her by surprise and make her own up to the truth."

I rub my eyes, feeling exhausted. I didn't sleep a wink last night and this is all too much. Catch my mother out? Take her by surprise? My mother's not the enemy. This isn't about tactics. I hope this isn't the bit where Mark expects me to whip out my copy of *TALK!* and wire her up to the food processor, because I simply am not going to do it. But Mark seems so confident in what he's saying, and his line of reasoning sounds so logical. And he has a pencil and a piece of paper with points listed on it...

"My mother's very weak," I tell Mark. "What if all this is too much for her?"

"If what's too much for her? Her only daughter wanting to fill in the missing pieces of her life? Her only daughter wanting to know the truth so that she doesn't keep making a fool of herself by repeating silly stories about getting nipped by crab cakes and having her fingers dipped in sugar?"

"Toes."

"Whatever. The point is that you have a right to this information. And you said it yourself, soon it will be too late."

I shake my head, more confused than ever. I wanted Mark to make me feel in control again. I wanted him to help me sort my thoughts into piles and my feelings into compartments. I wanted him to do what he does best: take what's there and give it structure, tidy it up, make it neat, rid it of any emotion, and reduce it down to hard, cold facts that can't be felt, only known.

But I forgot that there's another side to what he does, and that's the research. He not only processes facts that are already known, but he also builds on them, searching for answers, prodding and probing until he gets to the bottom of every single question. That's what a good scientist does; he never stops questioning. Out of nowhere a memory comes back to me of a science lesson in secondary school when we had to dissect a daffodil. We pulled it apart bit by bit, locating the stamen, the receptacle, the stigma, the sepal…By the time we had finished, we knew what was beneath those pretty yellow petals, but of course all the beauty had gone, and all that was left was a tattered, ruined mess.

"Maybe I don't need to know anymore," I say wearily. "Maybe I don't want to."

Mark lets go of my hand. "You mean you would rather not know the truth because it's easier that way," he says disapprovingly.

"I would rather spend the final days with my mother some way other than confronting her, and fighting her, and trying to wheedle things out of her that she clearly doesn't want to remember and I might not want to know."

"That's what this is about really, isn't it?" says Mark, rather harshly. "The fact that you don't want to know. This isn't all about your mother. It's about the fact that after going on and on about how you wanted to know the truth, you don't like what you've heard and you suddenly don't want to know anymore."

"Is that really so wrong?" I snap, suddenly annoyed by his lack of understanding.

"It is when you've been saying for months, and quite rightly so, that your mother needs to face facts."

"Well, perhaps I was wrong!" I shout, jumping out of my seat. "Maybe she doesn't want to face facts!"

"You mean maybe *you* don't want to!" snaps Mark, standing up.

"Okay, maybe I don't want to! Maybe the childhood I knew was just a pack of lies, but at least it was a happy one, and at least it felt like mine. I threw it away, and in return I got a miserable childhood that doesn't feel like it has any connection to me at all!"

"So you would have preferred not to know the truth? You would have preferred to carry on living a life of ridiculous stories and silly lies?"

"Yes!" I startle myself with my response. Yes, yes, I would have preferred it. If only I'd known what was to come. "I want to have been bitten by a crab cake!" I shout, my voice trembling with emotion. "I want to have dipped my toes in the neighbors' tea! I want to have been involved in a high-speed chase from Tottenham High Road to Enfield Chase!"

"Then you are just as delusional as your crazy mother!"

"Maybe I am! So what? What does it matter?"

Mark shakes his head in despair. "I thought you were better than that. I thought you were a paragon of truth and reason and logic, but it seems that was just when it was convenient for you. I'm disappointed in you, Meg."

Disappointed in me! I clench my fists by my sides, swallow down the lump in my throat, and look the admirable Mark Daly squarely in the eye.

"If that's the case," I say, "then I guess this particular experiment has reached its conclusion."

Lying on my bed, I close my eyes, trying to go back to the day the spaghetti plant sprouted in our window box. If I concentrate hard, I can see it there, stringy pieces of spaghetti hanging between green leaves.

"Well, I never!" my mother had exclaimed. "I bet that came from Mrs. Trivelli in the flat above. She's always leaving bits and bobs on her kitchen windowsill for the birds. I bet she went to put a piece of spaghetti out and it fell down into our window box and sprouted." My mother licked her finger and held it out the kitchen window. "Yes," she said, nodding, "I thought as much. A westerly wind. That will make a spaghetti plant sprout before you can say 'Bob's your uncle.' You know the problem with spaghetti plants, don't you?"

I looked up at her and shook my head. Being only four years old, I had no idea about the problems with spaghetti plants.

"They grow and grow and grow, and before you know it they're as big as a house. In South America there's a vast jungle of spaghetti plants so dense and thick that nobody who has ever gone in there has found their way out alive. In 1953, an explorer by the name of George Wallis Boo Cooper entered the spaghetti jungle, and they say he's still in there now, wandering around and around in circles, eating spaghetti all day long. Do you know what the moral of that story is?"

I thought carefully. "Don't go into a spaghetti jungle?"

"No, don't throw food out your window when you live in a flat. You never know what might grow from it. Now, the only way to stop a spaghetti plant from growing and spreading is to pick the spaghetti as quickly as possible. So I think the best idea is if I dangle you out of the window by your legs and you start picking."

I thought about the number of stairs we had to climb to get to the fourth floor and about all the traffic going by on the main road below. "It's a long, long way down," I said, curling my hair anxiously around my finger and chewing my lip.

"We all have to do things we don't like in life, darling," said my mother, picking me up by the ankles and swinging me out of the window. I felt my dress fall over my head and the wind whipping around my bare legs.

"Nobody's looking at you," said my mother in the way that mothers do when their children are clearly exposed to all and sundry. "Now, if the spaghetti is ripe, it will feel warm and soft with still a little bit of bite. If it's hard and brittle, it's not ready for picking. Do you understand?"

"Yes," I called from underneath the skirt of my dress. All the blood was rushing to my head, and I felt pleased I couldn't see the traffic whizzing by below. I started picking as quickly as possible, going by feel alone, as I couldn't see a thing. And after my initial fear had subsided, I started to quite enjoy myself. "Look how much I'm picking!" I shouted to my mother as I dangled from her grasp.

"You're doing wonderfully, darling!" she called. "You'll be a champion spaghetti picker when you grow up. The best in the world!"

And so that was what I wanted to be when I grew up. I planned to travel to South America and earn my fortune picking my way through the spaghetti jungles. I wasn't scared of getting lost like George Wallis Boo Cooper, who clearly didn't have the natural knack for feeling his way around spaghetti plants like I did. I was going to pick enough spaghetti in six months to feed the whole of Italy, and then I'd buy a big house for my mother to live in so that she wouldn't have to put up with Mrs. Trivelli throwing old bits of dinner into her window box.

I open my eyes and look up at the ceiling, somehow surprised to find myself still lying on my bed. A faint smile comes to my lips, and for the first time in days I feel calm.

Ewan has picked the last of the fruit due for harvesting and left it in three Tesco bags outside the kitchen door. I can't see him, but every so often I catch a glimpse of Digger crossing the far end of the garden, so I know he must be down there somewhere. I put the kettle on and make two mugs of strong black coffee before shrugging on the baggy green sweater that my mother keeps by the back door for gardening purposes and then heading outside.

The sky is gray and overcast, promising rain again. Ewan is sitting on an upturned wooden crate with his back to me, eating a handful of blackberries.

"I could charge you for those, you know," I say as I approach.

He turns with a start and then smiles. I walk toward him across a patch of soil that previously bore rows of lettuce but that today lies bare, the soil freshly dug over. I look around me and see that several patches are in the same state. Naked, stripped of their summer plants, they wait in limbo between one season and the next. I hold out one of the mugs to Ewan, and he looks slightly surprised but takes it.

"How's your mother?" he asks, looking up at me, his face full of concern.

"She's okay. Tired. She's been in bed most of the day. She doesn't remember anything about yesterday. About Gwennie arriving, I mean, and fainting."

Ewan nods. I wonder if he's going to ask me about Gwennie, about who she was, why my mother was so shocked to see her, what happened after he left, but he doesn't.

Instead he just says, "I hope everything's okay."

I smile, grateful for this simple, nonintrusive gesture of support. "Thanks."

Digger trots over to see me and I fondle his ear.

"We saw Mark leaving earlier," says Ewan. "Unfortunately, I couldn't stop Digger from rushing over to say hello to his old friend. I think Mark will be spending the evening washing muddy paw prints out of his clothes."

"Well, don't worry," I say. "You won't be seeing Mark around here again."

Ewan raises his eyebrows, surprised. "I'm sorry."

I give him a knowing look. "No, you're not."

"No, honestly, I am. I mean, if you're upset, then I'm sorry."

I shake my head. "Actually, it's strange. I'm not nearly as upset as I thought I would be."

"In that case, I couldn't care less."

I turn to him, shocked by his bluntness. He flashes me a cheeky half smile, and I almost laugh.

We sip our coffee in silence until Ewan catches me looking around for somewhere to sit and quickly shifts sideways along the wooden crate. I can feel him watching me curiously as I settle myself next to him. He is not used to my being in his presence voluntarily, let alone deliberately sitting down with him. I feel slightly awkward and wonder if he does too, but my mother is in bed asleep, and I don't want to be on my own right now. The crate is small for the two of us, and I try to hold my body at an angle so that there is a little gap between us. We sit looking around us, gazing at the sky, at the orchard, at the barren vegetable patches. I count the holes in the ground that Digger has made. Only five. He's definitely getting better.

"I'm going to fill them in later," says Ewan, reading my mind.

"I should hope so," I tell him.

Out of the corner of my eye, I watch his hands, covered in grime, clasped around his coffee cup, and his sinewy forearms, tanned and covered with golden-brown hairs. I look at the rip in his grubby jeans, just over the knee, where the skin of his leg just shows through, and at his tatty boots, covered in mud, with laces that don't match.

"Will you tell me a story?" I ask him.

He strokes the top of Digger's head, long, hard strokes that pull the dog's skin back, revealing the white at the top of his eyes. It is some time before he speaks, and in that silence I realize how confused Ewan must be. After the way I have mocked his legends and ridiculed his myths, accused him of having his head in the clouds and scolded him for being a fantasist. And now I have the gall to ask this of him.

"What sort of a story?" he asks finally.

I shake my head. "I don't mind. Anything." *Anything*, I think, *to take me away from here for a while.*

Digger lies down by Ewan's feet and settles his head on one of his master's boots as if waiting for him to begin. Ewan gazes thoughtfully at the garden.

"After Zeus had punished Prometheus for giving fire to man," he begins, "he decided that all humans should be punished for their lack of respect. So he came up with a very cunning plan. He created a woman from clay. The goddess Athena breathed life into the clay, Aphrodite made her very beautiful, and Hermes taught her how to be charming and deceitful. Zeus called her Pandora, and he sent her as a gift to Prometheus's brother, Epimetheus.

"'Don't trust any gift from Zeus,' Prometheus warned his brother. 'He is cruel. Think about what he did to me.'

"But Epimetheus had already fallen head over heels in love with Pandora, and so he decided to marry her.

"Zeus was pleased. His trap was working. He gave Pandora a wedding gift of a beautiful box.

"'But I give you this gift on one condition,' he told her. 'You must never, ever open the box.'

"Well, every day Pandora wondered what was in that box. She couldn't for the life of her understand why Zeus would keep it a secret. It seemed to make no sense. It drove her crazy, to the point where she couldn't think of anything else except finding out what was inside.

"Finally, Pandora could no longer bear the agony of not knowing. One day, she took the key off the shelf, crept up to the box, carefully fit the key into the lock, and turned it. Slowly, she lifted the lid of the box, holding her breath. 'What will I find?' she wondered. 'Perhaps some fine silks, some gold bracelets, or even a large sum of money?'

"But there was no golden treasure. There were no shining bracelets and no fine silks. Pandora's excitement quickly turned to disappointment, and then to horror. Inside were all the evils she could think of. Out of the box poured terrible misery, sadness, anger, and pain, all shaped like tiny buzzing moths. The creatures stung Pandora over and over again, and she slammed the lid shut. Epimetheus ran into the room to find her crying in pain.

"'Pandora,' he said to her, tending to her stings. 'Zeus tried to warn you. Why did you have to find out what lay inside that box? Well, now you know. You should never have opened it.'"

Ewan stops and sips his coffee.

I don't know what to say. I feel like I've been slapped in the face. The message of the story is clear: pursue the truth and you might not like what you find. Either way, on your head be it.

Ewan knows what has happened without my saying a word. And this is his message to me? That I have to suffer the consequences of my actions? That I made my bed and now I must lie in it? This isn't the story I wanted. This isn't what I wanted to hear. I feel a lump rise in my throat and prepare to leave.

"But that wasn't the end," Ewan suddenly begins again, "because Pandora could still hear a voice calling to her from the box, pleading with her to be let out. Epimetheus agreed that nothing inside the box could be worse than the horrors that had already been released, so together they opened the lid once more. And inside they found that something had been left behind."

Ewan pauses. I turn, watching his profile expectantly. The clouds overhead have parted slightly, bathing us in comforting rays of warm afternoon sunshine. I study the way the golden light illuminates Ewan's eyelashes, the stubble on his chin, his eyebrows, highlighting the contours of his face.

"What was inside?" I ask quietly.

He turns to face me, flecks of amber twinkling in his warm brown eyes. One side of his mouth raises slightly into a smile.

"Hope," he says.

chapter seventeen

A day comes, all too soon, when my mother can't get out of bed.

"I'll get up in a minute and make us both some breakfast," she murmurs, pulling the covers closer around her. "What would you like? Perhaps some cinnamon toast? Or some stewed apples?"

"Mother," I say, about to tell her that it is already two o'clock in the afternoon and that she has missed both breakfast and lunch, but she is already asleep again.

Later, when she still hasn't risen, I offer her soup, toast, fruit, ice cream, tea, juice, but she doesn't want anything.

"I might get up and make myself something in a while," she says, but she never does.

That night she doesn't sleep at all, complaining of an ache in her bones that she puts down to too much exertion recently.

"Perhaps I've overdone it this summer," she wonders out loud, wincing as she shifts under the covers, trying to get comfortable.

Her breathing is labored and wheezy, and she complains that it feels like an elephant is sitting on her chest.

"Do you remember the time that elephant broke through the railings," she asks, looking up at me with heavy eyes as I adjust her pillow, "in a bid to get to our delicious iced buns?"

"Shhh," I whisper, gently placing my hand on hers. "Don't."

Dr. Bloomberg comes. He gives her pink pills to stop the pain and blue pills to stop the nausea caused by the pink pills.

"Would you like to stay for dinner, Doctor?" my mother asks, smiling up at him from her bed. Her face is white and her skin has taken on a certain transparency. "There's some lovely stroganoff in the freezer."

She struggles to push herself up from the pillow, ready to start playing hostess.

"I'm afraid I've just eaten, Valerie," the doctor says, laying a large hand on her shoulder so that she sinks back down. "Otherwise I wouldn't miss your stroganoff for the world."

"You need to start preparing yourself, Meg," Dr. Bloomberg tells me gently as we stand in the hallway.

I know what he is saying, but it feels unreal, as if this is a play and we are all actors. Any minute now, I expect the curtain to fall, and when it rises again my mother will run down the stairs and we will all link hands and take a bow amid a flourish of applause.

"As things progress," says Dr. Bloomberg, lowering his head and peering at me over the top of his spectacles, "there are various options. The hospice is one, although at this stage a hospital might be—"

"She's staying here," I blurt out immediately.

My mother has always hated hospitals, and it had never even occurred to me that she would die anywhere else but at home, or that anyone else should take care of her other than me.

"It may be hard," says Dr. Bloomberg, "as she gets worse—"

"She's staying here," I repeat forcibly.

Dr. Bloomberg frowns, his bushy white eyebrows meeting in the middle. "Meg," he says slowly and clearly, "if things get bad…"

I hold my hand up to stop him. Okay, okay, I understand. Just don't say it. Don't say that she will be in pain. Don't say that it will be too much to bear.

"I will call as soon as I need someone," I say quickly to cut him off. "I promise."

"What's the weather like?"

Every time my mother wakes, she asks me this same question.

"It's raining," I tell her.

"I can't hear the rain," she says, twisting and straining to try to get a glimpse out of the window.

"It's raining very quietly," I say.

In fact, it hasn't rained all day, but my mother is such a lover of the great outdoors that I am convinced it would only pain her to know that the sun is shining while she is confined to her bed.

"I've always rather liked the rain," muses my mother, somewhat undermining my plan. "It's so refreshing on your skin."

"I can sprinkle you with the watering can if you like," I suggest.

She laughs, a wheezy, painful laugh, and I laugh too at the very idea of it.

But then she starts to cough, taking in great gulps of air, and within seconds I am holding her as she gasps for breath, her chest rattling like a pinball machine, her body shaking as she hunches over and I rub her back.

"It's okay," I whisper. "It's okay."

Ewan comes and brings her a tangled, unruly spray of wildflowers with odd names such as toadflax and sneezewort, which my mother finds very amusing.

"They're absolutely beautiful." She smiles, her eyes lighting up for the first time in ages. "I miss being outdoors in my garden. Have you brought in the last of the tomatoes?"

"Yes, and I've hung them by the kitchen window to ripen," says Ewan.

"And the basil will need bringing in, won't it?"

"It's good for a few weeks yet."

"And the onion sets will need planting."

"Give me a chance, boss!" he laughs. "Anyway, who's the gardener here, you or me?"

"You are, but I'm still in charge. I'll be out there tomorrow checking to see if you've done it all properly," my mother teases.

Ewan smiles tactfully, knowing just from looking at her that she won't be going anywhere. Simply getting to the bathroom across the hall now requires all the strength and stamina she can muster.

"What's the weather like this evening?" my mother asks him.

"Not bad. Fairly warm," says Ewan.

She nods, looking sad. I feel my heart aching for her, cooped up here inside.

"This is no good at all," Ewan says, standing up purposefully and slapping his thigh. "Meg, help me shift that dressing table."

Ten minutes later, after a lot of pushing and pulling and Ewan repeatedly demanding that I put some muscle into it, the furniture has all been moved and my mother's bed turned a hundred and eighty degrees so that she can now see out of the window, which Ewan has flung wide open despite my protestations about my mother's breathing. Nothing is accessible. The wardrobe doors cannot be opened, the dresser has been abandoned in the middle of the floor, and the chest of drawers now sits out on the landing, but my mother is delighted. She lies with her head propped up on two pillows, her eyes glistening with wonder as she stares out at the sky.

"Now, that's what I call a sunset," she says with a sigh.

I sit next to her on the bed while Ewan stands nearby with Digger quietly at his side, all four of us gazing in awe at the pink and orange glow that seems to have lit up the world.

"Never forget how beautiful life can be, darling," says my

mother, taking my hand in hers. I give her bony fingers a gentle squeeze and show her my bravest smile.

"I won't, I promise."

The evening we watch the sunset, Digger refuses to leave with Ewan. Instead the scruffy dog sits by the side of my mother's bed, cocking his head to one side and looking baffled as Ewan whispers to him from the doorway, "Come on, boy. Come along."

My mother has fallen asleep, her hand hanging out from underneath the covers. Digger sniffs her fingers and gives them a gentle lick, letting out a small whine before settling himself down on the carpet. He has made himself perfectly clear: he is here for the long haul.

For the next week he stays, only reluctantly leaving my mother's side when I insist on dragging him out for a walk tied to piece of string. The rest of the time he lies quietly on her bed, allowing her to brush him gently with an old hairbrush. After three days, he looks like a completely different dog. His matted, straggly fur is now smooth and shiny, and with all the dust having been brushed out, it looks at least a couple of shades lighter. My mother claims that next year she will enter him into a dog show under the name Horatio, which she thinks is far more fitting for such a handsome dog.

On Fridays and Wednesdays Ewan comes as usual, letting himself in the back gate and getting straight down to a couple hours' work in the garden. When he is done, he comes to the house and knocks quietly on the back door in case my mother is asleep. He hands me tins of dog food from his van and removes his muddy boots before padding up the stairs in threadbare socks to see Digger, who wags his tail furiously against the mattress but never leaves my mother's side.

From downstairs I can hear Ewan's voice, slow and deep, and I know that he is telling my mother tales of gods and goddesses, heroes and heroines, as he sits by her side. He moves the TV from the kitchen into her bedroom, spending nearly an hour fiddling with electric cables and antennas, so she can watch all her favorite cooking programs. He makes her herbal teas that fill the house with the scent of sage, peppermint, dandelion, and chamomile and that ease her pain better than the pink and blue pills combined. He hands me a flier for half-price pizza, on the back of which he has scrawled the preparation instructions for various concoctions. He also hands me a large bag of leaves, which I spend ages identifying with the aid of a gardening book rather than calling him to admit that I don't know my milk thistle from my rosehip.

As usual, whenever Ewan is working in the garden, I take him his mug of coffee. There are no homemade delicacies to accompany it now, no apple strudel or fudge cake, just a plate of cookies if he's lucky and I've remembered to pick some up from Tesco. The day

I approach him empty-handed and announce that the kettle has just boiled, he looks quizzically at my empty hands.

"Well, I don't see why I should keep trudging down here to serve you," I say. "You've got legs; you can come to the house and have it."

Ewan stares at me as if I am someone he doesn't quite recognize while I turn and walk back up the path, my face strangely hot, my stomach knotted, wondering if he will follow me. When I hear the clatter of his spade being dropped on the ground and then the sound of his boots on the grass, I smile to myself, feeling relieved.

"You look dreadful," says Ewan as I sit opposite him at the kitchen table.

"Thanks. You're such a flatterer."

"Sorry." He smiles. "That came out wrong. I just meant you look really tired."

I rub my eyes, feeling like I could fall asleep right here and now. "I'm fine," I tell him.

Ewan stuffs a whole cookie in his mouth and shakes his head.

"Liar," he mumbles, crumbs stuck to his lips.

He's right, of course, I'm not fine at all. I'm not eating. I'm not sleeping. I am desperately trying not to think about the past, telling myself that now is not the time, that I have to concentrate on caring for my mother, but every time I look at her gaunt face, Gwennie's words come flooding back, filling me with all kinds of conflicting thoughts and questions and feelings. One moment

I want to track down the people who wronged my mother and tear them limb from limb, and the next I just want to curl into a ball and pretend none of it is real. One minute I want to tell my mother that it's okay, that I know the truth, that she doesn't have to pretend anymore, and the next I want to shake her and tell her that this isn't fair, that she can't just leave me, not now, not on my own. I want to scream, but I need to be composed; I want to weep, but I need to be strong. I am so tired and so confused, and there is only one thing I am sure of: I need to keep it together, because I am all she has.

"I just don't know what to do to make things better," I tell Ewan. "I feel so useless."

Even as the words tumble out of my mouth, I want to grab them and stuff them back in, to say that I'm actually fine, I know what I'm doing, everything's under control. But I am just so tired that I don't have the energy to pretend.

"You're doing great," Ewan says encouragingly.

"But sometimes I just don't know what to say to her," I admit sadly. "When I see her sick and in pain…what can I say to help make that better?"

Ewan shrugs and stares into his coffee. "Maybe you just have to be with her. Perhaps there's nothing you can say."

I don't tell him that every time I open my mouth to speak I am terrified of what might come spilling out, how a million questions are now constantly on the tip of my tongue, how I hush my mother each time she starts to tell a story of the past, acutely aware of the painful truth that lurks behind the lies. I don't tell him about how everything has changed, about how it now takes all my effort to see my mother as the same vibrant, positive, and slightly eccentric woman I have always known instead of someone who is bruised and broken. I don't tell him that now, when I finally know her better than I ever have before, she sometimes feels like a stranger. I don't tell him, because it is too hard to admit these things even to myself, let alone to somebody else.

"If you can't think of anything to say, perhaps try telling her a story. I know she loves that. I think it takes her away from it all."

"I couldn't," I say adamantly. "I wouldn't know where to begin."

"It doesn't matter where you begin. It's where you go that's important."

I shake my head, although he's probably right. I know how much my mother loves it when Ewan tells her tales of dragons and gods and whatever else he babbles on about, and in the middle of the night when she can't sleep, I sometimes long for something to soothe her. But telling stories, that's just not me.

"I can't. I'm no good at things like that. I couldn't do all that imaginary make-believe stuff. Fairies and magic kingdoms and romance. I just can't."

"Sure you can. Look, I'll give you an opening line and you just say whatever comes into your head. A long time ago, in a galaxy far, far away…"

Ewan pauses and looks at me expectantly. I feel like an awkward teenager who has just been shoved in front of a room full of relatives and ordered to dance for everyone's amusement. I just know I'm going to mess it up and make a fool of myself, but if it might help my mother, I am willing to give it a go. I open my mouth to speak, but my mind is completely blank.

"I don't know," I say. "That's a silly beginning. What could come after that?"

"Oh, come on!" exclaims Ewan. "It's the opening of *Star Wars*!"

"I've never seen *Star Wars*."

"You've never…you are kidding me, right?"

"In case you hadn't realized, I'm not really into films about flying saucers or aliens or whatever it's about."

"Okay, forget *Star Wars*. Let's try again. A long time ago, in a far and distant land, there was a…"

I try to think, looking around me for inspiration. This really shouldn't be so hard.

"An oven," I say, blurting out the first thing I see.

Ewan raises an eyebrow. "An oven? Well, that's different. Okay, and what did this oven do?"

"What do you mean 'what did it do'?"

"Well, an oven just sitting there in a faraway land isn't much of a story. Something has to happen."

"I don't know. Come to think of it, a long time ago in a distant land, they might not have even had ovens. Is this set in Europe? How long ago are we talking?"

Ewan shakes his head, looking perplexed. "I don't know. I think we're getting sidetracked. The exact date isn't really that important."

"It is if the story is going to have an oven in it."

"It doesn't have to be realistic," he says, looking at me as if I'm from another planet. "That's not the point of a story."

"Well, I don't know!" I snap, feeling foolish. "I told you I'm no good at these kinds of things!"

"But you're not trying."

"I am trying!"

"Then perhaps you're trying too hard. If you just let yourself go—"

"I can't!" I snap at him, feeling useless.

Ewan holds his hands up in the air. "Okay," he says in a pacifying tone, "okay."

We sip our coffee in silence for a few minutes. I tell myself it doesn't matter, that stories are for daydreamers and fools, that my inability to fantasize is a strength, not something I should feel bad about. But I feel frustrated that Ewan can lift my mother's spirits in a way I can't. How does he do it? How does he just let his mind go off on some crazy path to who knows where?

"I don't know how you ended up with such a wild imagination anyway," I say grumpily, struggling to keep the resentment out of my voice. "Your father's a scientist. I would have thought he might have steered you away from such nonsense."

Ewan cups his grimy hands around his mug and shrugs.

"Well, my dad is a scientist. But he's also a philosopher. And a poet. And a historian. He's an avid reader, and he got me interested in mythology. And he loves crosswords. He's also a rally driver—"

I frown.

"You said your father was a geologist. That night at dinner."

"No, you said that. And you were right, he is. It's not how he earns his living, though."

"So what *does* he do for a living?"

Ewan stuffs another cookie in his mouth.

"He has a job as an administrator for the council," he mumbles.

I feel irritated and confused. I don't understand why people can't just talk in plain facts these days.

"He's never really liked it," Ewan adds. "It just pays the bills. But it's not who he is, it's just what he does. He doesn't let it get to him, but he always wanted us kids to follow our hearts, do something we enjoyed."

"And what does your mother do, then? *Is* she an actress?"

"Yeah. She's been in loads of plays. She lives for her acting. She doesn't earn anything from it, though."

"So what does she do? I mean, what's her *job*?"

"Well, she doesn't have a paid job, if that's what you mean. She raised five kids, and now she looks after my sister, who has learning difficulties and some physical problems."

I raise an eyebrow, surprised, and realize I never imagined Ewan having any real issues in his life. He always seems so positive, so upbeat. But then I have never really imagined Ewan having a life outside our garden.

"I'm sorry to hear that about your sister," I offer.

"Oh, Belle's the happiest person I know!" Ewan says, laughing. "But it's a lot of work for my mum. We all pitch in as much as we can, but my mum's life is pretty much dedicated to Belle. So in terms of a job, I guess you could say she's a nurse-slash-actress-slash-cook-slash-cleaner..."

He smiles at me.

"Does that help you categorize my parents? And me?"

"No, I wasn't...I just...if someone asks what your parents do—"

"They didn't."

"Well, no, maybe not, but if someone asks about your parents, they generally want to know what they do...as in, do for a living."

Ewan frowns.

"Really? You think what matters about someone is what they do from nine to five to earn a few quid rather than what their passions are, what gets them up in the morning, what makes them smile?"

"I'm not saying that."

Although I'm not entirely sure what I *am* trying to say.

"So who are you, then, Meg May?" he asks, his eyes twinkling with interest. "A scientist? Is that what defines you?"

"Yes," I say proudly. "Absolutely."

"But you don't get paid for what you do."

"Well, no," I mumble, "but…but one day soon. Hopefully."

"Hopefully?"

"Well, funding is always a problem."

"And if you don't get paid work as a scientist? Will that mean you're no longer a scientist?"

"No, I'll be…I…I'll be…"

Nothing.

Absolutely nothing.

I feel a surge of fear rise in my chest at this sudden realization. Have I spent so long trying to become a series of labels—Scientist. Rational. Sensible. Logical—that labels are all I am now? Is there anything else left? Because if there is, I can't see it.

"And what about me?" asks Ewan. "Am I a gardener? Is that who I am?"

I feel my face flush as I remember what I used to call Ewan. The Gardener. I never knew Ewan had siblings. For some reason, even after finding out he had a niece, it never occurred to me that he must have brothers or sisters. He knows my home, my family (what little there is)…and what do I know about him? Nothing. Because he's a gardener. And I thought that was all I needed to know.

"I don't think that's all I am," says Ewan in response to his own question. He leans forward slightly, trying to meet my eye. "And I know that 'scientist' is not all you are."

I fumble with the cookies, trying to stuff them back into the box. I swallow down the lump that has inexplicably risen in my throat. I want to scream at him, *Well, who am I, then? If you know, then tell me, because I sure as hell don't!* Instead, I stand up and start to clear the mugs away.

"I have to go and check on my mother," I say quietly.

"What's the weather like?" asks my mother, her voice no more than a whisper.

"It's a little chilly," I tell her, "and rather gray."

"It was gray the day you were born, but as soon as I held you in my arms the sun came out, as if from nowhere."

I smile, wondering if this could be true. At what point might the sun have suddenly emerged from behind the clouds on the day I was born? At the point when she tucked me in between the bag of compost and the watering can in the old, rickety shed? At the point when Gwennie handed me to her and she, in her state of delirium, tried to put me in the oven? At the point when she grabbed me from my grandfather's arms, declaring she would never give me up for adoption?

"It was at that moment when the gasman scooped you out of

the frying pan and handed you to me," smiles my mother. "All of a sudden, the sun shone in through the window and lit up the room."

Sitting on the little wooden chair next to her bed, I gaze around me, trying to imagine the scene twenty-one years ago when I came into the world and supposedly lit up this room in a blaze of sunshine. My mother always said I was born at two in the afternoon, three hours after the gasman coughed out that fateful morsel of cake that hit the timer off the fridge and triggered her labor, but I realize now that the sunlight never hits this room in the afternoon, even on a midsummer's day.

"I think it was the happiest moment of my life," muses my mother.

"Shhh," I tell her. "You must rest."

As she drifts asleep, I listen to the rattle deep inside her chest and watch her eyes flitting slowly back and forth beneath their white, papery lids, wondering how much longer it will be now.

When she wakes sometime later, I am still by her side. She turns her head toward me, opening her eyes ever so slightly, and whispers something I cannot hear. I lean in closer.

"I can smell date-and-almond cake," she says.

I shake my head sadly. "No," I tell her. "There's no date-and-almond cake."

She smiles faintly and nods. "Yes. And cherry pastries."

I reach underneath the covers and take her hand.

"Is he waiting?" she asks quietly. "He waits in the evenings, you know, outside the window."

I shake my head, confused. "Who does?"

She licks her dry lips and closes her eyes. "Do you remember the time...?" she whispers.

I wait, leaning in, listening carefully, but there is nothing more, just the rasping sound her breath makes as she inhales and Digger's soft snoring coming from where he lies curled up at the foot of her bed.

"Wait!"

I run out into the garden just as Ewan is closing the back gate behind him. On seeing me coming he stops, watching me curiously as I stand in front of him, speechless, catching my breath.

I have no idea what I'm doing or what I want to say. All I know is the sound of him throwing equipment into the back of his van, preparing to leave, filled me with panic, sending me flying from my mother's room and down the stairs.

Don't leave me! I think it's time! Don't leave me to do this alone! I don't know what I'm doing! But then what if it's not time? What if it's not today, but the day after, or the day after that, or even a week from now? I can't expect him to stay with me. I have to pull myself together. I have to get a grip.

"I just wanted to see if you needed any help," I say, thinking on my feet.

Ewan frowns. "With what?"

I make a vague gesture toward the van, wishing I had come up with something better. "With packing your stuff away."

Ewan looks at his van, which is parked in the lane on the other side of the garden fence. "No, I'm okay, thanks."

"Great," I say with a smile, already backing away. "Well, just thought I'd check. See you later, then."

"Meg, is everything okay?" he asks just as I am about to turn and run back inside. "I mean, do you need me for anything? Because I can hang around if you want me to."

For a moment, I think how easy it would be just to say yes, please don't go, please wait with me. Please help me decide whether to call the doctor, whether to phone for an ambulance, or whether to just wait and see what happens, because it's a lot of responsibility and I don't want to do it all alone and I'm scared.

"No, I'm fine," I say.

Ewan lowers his head, trying to look me in the eye, but I turn and start striding back toward the house.

"Thanks," I call back to him. "I can manage."

My mother drifts in and out of sleep for the rest of the day, occasionally opening her eyes to gaze blankly at the TV, where her favorite cooking programs repeat on loop, her only reason for ever investing in cable. She mumbles something about Gordon's foul language or Jamie's new restaurant, which, in her confusion, she insists is being run by fifteen Chinese immigrants, but it is hard to understand exactly what she is saying. I place a straw between her lips, encouraging her to take a bit of the herbal tea I have prepared, but a couple of feeble sips are all she can manage. As it grows dark outside, I switch on the small lamp, which casts a soft orange glow over the room, and I settle down on the wooden chair to watch Marco Pierre White preparing a cheese-and-caramelized-onion tart. The next thing I know, I am being woken by Digger whining gently at the foot of my mother's bed.

"What is it?" I ask him, rubbing my eyes.

He lays his head on my mother's feet and looks unhappy. The clock on the wall reads nine o'clock, and I check my watch, wondering if that can be right. The TV plays quietly, Marco Pierre White having been replaced by Delia, who is showing viewers the splendid Tuscan casserole dish that she bought on holiday last year.

My mother's breathing is shallow and difficult. I ease my aching body from the hard wooden chair, which I am convinced has crippled me for life, and kneel on the rug by the side of her bed.

"Mother?" I whisper, brushing a strand of hair away from her face.

Slowly, she opens her eyes, just a little bit, and looks at me. "Hello, you," she whispers.

I force a smile, trying to ignore the butterflies that have risen from nowhere in my stomach and the way my heart has suddenly started thumping in my chest. "Hello," I say back.

Her brow furrows as she takes a sharp breath.

"Are you all right?" I ask. "Should I call the doctor?"

My mother shakes her head almost imperceptibly and mouths "no," but I am starting to get scared. Maybe I should call the doctor anyway; after all, she's never known what's best for her. I need to make a decision. Perhaps she should go to the hospital. Perhaps I should call Dr. Bloomberg. I rub my forehead, trying to think straight.

"What will it be like," whispers my mother, "where I'm going?"

Nestled against the pillows, she suddenly looks so small and vulnerable, like a child waiting to hear a bedtime story, longing to be comforted. I feel my throat burning, and I have to swallow once, twice, to feel that I can breathe.

I shake my head, tears rising and misting my vision.

I am about to tell her that I don't know, that no one knows the answer to that, but when I open my mouth, those aren't the words that come out.

"Close your eyes," I whisper, "and I will tell you."

Her eyes drift shut, and I reach out and stroke her hair, just as she stroked mine when I was a little girl.

"It's the most wonderful place you can possibly imagine," I hear myself say softly. "There are clouds made of marshmallow and rivers of wine. Baked apples grow in the fields, and the air is scented with spice. The ground under your feet is soft and bouncy like sponge cake, and your favorite lemon bonbons grow from the trees, lightly dusted in icing sugar, which drifts down in a powdery haze when you pull the bonbons off the branch. Beautiful white swans lay chocolate eggs while bees buzz among the flowers, making the sweetest honey. In the meadows grow the most delicious delicacies—apricot turnovers, strawberry tarts, raspberry meringues—all just waiting to be picked. The grass is made of licorice, and the rain upon your tongue tastes like elderberry cordial. Flowers grow in abundance all year-round, and in the summer they smell like picnics on a warm beach, while in the winter they smell like mince pies by the fireplace. On Christmas Day, snowflakes made of sugar drift down from the sky, and in spring the cows grazing in the meadows produce banana milkshakes. There are little bridges made of gingerbread and picket fences made of pastry…"

I gently touch my mother's shoulder, whispering, "Mother?"

She is still and silent. The wheezing from her chest has stopped, her eyes no longer flickering beneath their lids. She looks peaceful in the warm glow of the lamplight, a faint smile resting on her lips. Digger crawls up the bed on his belly, his ears back, and lays his head on my mother's thighs, letting out a small, sad whimper. I lean forward and kiss her cold cheek, trying to inhale the scent of her skin, of her hair, expecting the familiar aroma of baking and sunshine, but there is nothing there.

She has gone.

My head is empty, my body numb. I get slowly to my feet and walk over to the window. Outside it has grown dark, and I reach out to draw the curtains, just as I do every evening around this time. I notice Ewan's van is still in the lane below, parked under a streetlight. He is asleep, his head resting against the driver's window. I reach out and switch off the TV, just as Delia is saying good-bye for another season.

chapter eighteen

Pots, pans, and casserole dishes. Birds, trees, and vegetable patches. Books, TV, and BBC Radio 4. These were my mother's friends, and now I understand why. None of these things hurt you in the way that people do.

It seems odd that such a kindhearted, bubbly, vivacious woman should shy away from the world, but that's exactly what she did, ducking behind nearby bushes whenever she saw neighbors in the street, turning down every invitation, leaving the shelter of her home only when necessary, and then scurrying back for cover. It breaks my heart to think that my mother's avoidance of others was not, as I had always thought, due to an inherent personality trait that made her an eccentric loner, but due to a mistrust of others that resulted from being burned one too many times.

I am dreading the funeral for so many reasons, but mainly I am dreading the emptiness and the silence. Gwennie, Ewan, Dr. Bloomberg, and I can only fill so much space in the parish church, and the rows upon rows of empty pews will be a sad testimony to my mother's lack of connection with the real world, a depressing reminder of the relationships that she was too afraid to make.

When I think about how there will be so few people to send her on her way, it makes me want to weep. It shouldn't have been that way. Not for someone like her.

It seems ironic, then, that on a gray day in mid-October, I somehow manage to turn up at the wrong funeral, the funeral of someone who must have had hordes of friends and family, judging by the swarm of people milling around. As Gwennie and I crunch our way up the little gravel path that leads to the church, I curse the stupid vicar for timing two funerals so closely together. The fact that there are so many of them and so few of us only serves to make my mother's situation all the more tragic.

But cars appear to be pulling up, not leaving, and people in dark suits and dresses seem to be heading inside the church rather than coming out. I glance at my watch, making sure I have the right time, and mentally check the date.

"Who are all these people?" I ask Gwennie as we pick our way through the crowd of unfamiliar faces.

"I wouldn't know. Those two gentleman there look rather bookish. Was your mother a member of a reading group at all?"

Sometimes I forget that Gwennie knows nothing about the past sixteen years of my mother's life. Over the past week, I have tried to fill her in, but how do you sum up sixteen years in a nutshell? She talks about my mother as if no time has lapsed at all, as if it were only yesterday that they were listening to records together or going dancing at the Forum. Her affection for my mother has not waned in spite of their estrangement, and her loyalty has not dimmed. She understands why my mother cut her off and doesn't feel an ounce of bitterness. She seems to have taken me under her wing, believing it's what my mother would have wanted. After all, she keeps reminding me, she was the one who found me.

"Excuse me, dearie, are you Valerie's daughter?"

I turn to face an elderly woman with scraggy cheeks, bright blue eye shadow, and lipstick that looks as if it has been applied in the dark. To my horror, she is wearing what appears to be a dead weasel around her neck and a little black hat with some straggly feathers sticking out the top. I think I recognize her.

"Yes, I'm Meg," I say, confused. "I'm sorry, do I know you?"

The old lady reaches out and shakes my hand as best she can. Her fingers are all stiff and gnarled. "My name's Beryl Lampard. I live at number seventy-four. I was so sorry to hear about your mother, dearie. I didn't even know she was ill."

"You knew her?" I ask, more than a little surprised.

"No, I didn't know her at all, dearie. I'm ashamed to say I didn't even know her name until a couple of weeks ago, and I only managed to find that out because I asked my neighbor, William, and he only knew because he asked the postman. I had tried to find out her name before, but she never stopped to talk, you see, dearie, so it was rather difficult. And then I wondered if maybe she had told me at some point and I had forgotten, because I do tend to forget a lot of things these days, but I don't think she ever did. And when William told me, I rushed inside—well, I say rushed, but I don't really rush anywhere these days—and wrote it down so that I would remember. But then I forgot where I wrote it down, so I had to go and ask William again."

She smiles at me, displaying lipstick-stained dentures, while I wonder why she is here. Perhaps she just wanted a little outing, or maybe she came hoping to get a free plate of sandwiches afterward.

"I did start to wonder if something was wrong a couple of weeks back, dearie, when I hadn't seen her around, but then I thought she could have gone on holiday, or to visit family, or on one of those mini breaks you can win from entering the *Woman's Weekly* crossword competition. Those are very popular these days, aren't they, dearie? But then I spoke to William, and he said she had passed away, although he only knew because he heard it from Dave, who heard it from Alice, who heard it from the postman. And William was able to tell me when the funeral was being held, and I decided there and then I would definitely go and pay my respects because your mother was such a wonderful woman, but then I forgot what day he said, and I had to go and ask him again. And William said that he wanted to come too and that he would take me in his car, so we arranged that he would call for me at eleven on the dot, but I forgot we had arranged that. It was all right, though, because I came with Dave."

Not only am I baffled as to why this old lady has come to my mother's funeral, but now I'm also baffled as to why William and Dave have come.

"It's very kind of you to want to pay your respects," I say quickly, before she starts talking again, "but I don't really understand. I mean, if you didn't know my mother—"

"Because of the stews, of course, dearie! Every Monday and

Thursday without fail. I can barely lift a milk bottle with my arthritic hands, let alone cook a meal, but your mother kept me going. I really don't know what I'm going to do without her. She was like a mysterious guardian angel, one who left beef stew on your doorstep and then vanished without a trace. By the way, I still have a ceramic dish of hers. It's a lovely blue one with little flowers on it. I wrote a note to remind myself to bring it with me, and then I lost the note. I did write another one, but I forgot where I put it."

"Major William Jefferson Reece. I live at number seventy-two. Pleasure to make your acquaintance, young lady. What a shame it needs to be on such a solemn occasion. Your mother really was one damn fine woman, you know, an absolute trooper. Let me tell you, I've been shot twice in the leg, almost run over by a tank, and had a bomb go off so near to my head that I'm deaf in one ear. What? Yes, completely deaf. After surviving all that, I thought I was pretty much invincible, but nothing prepared me for being told I was diabetic. Nothing at all. Didn't fit with my view of myself, you see. I was in totally unfamiliar territory. A good soldier is always prepared, but I couldn't have prepared myself for this. I've always been a stiff-upper-lip sort of chap; after all, it's what makes us Brits great. But I sunk into a bit of a low mood there for a while, I'm afraid to say. What? Yes, a low mood.

"Anyhow, one day I said to myself, 'Come on William, old chap, snap out of it! No one ever won the war by sitting around feeling glum! Life goes on.' So I contacted this special shop that sells diabetic food, and I was amazed to find you could buy chocolate, cookies, sweets, all kinds of things, so I ordered a whole hamper. Bloody revolting it was! Worse than army rations. But then your mother saved the day, swooping in just in time like the best of allies. Don't have a bloody clue how she knew about my predicament, but all these wonderful little cakes and sweets started appearing on my doorstep, with a little note to say they were suitable for people such as myself. Well, I hadn't been so surprised since Corporal James Matterson declared he wanted to be a lady and started calling himself Gloria! I marched straight over to her living quarters and knocked to say thank you, but there was no reply, and every time I tried, it was always the same. I thought maybe your mother wasn't keen on strangers infiltrating her territory but hoped I might manage to meet her on neutral terrain, such as in the street one day. She kept a very low profile, though. What? Low profile, yes. In the end, I wrote a note and dropped it through the letterbox, inviting her for tea at fifteen hundred hours the next day. She didn't come, but she kept on leaving the cakes for me all the same. Such generosity of spirit is what makes this country great! I salute you, young lady. Your mother made me proud to be British!"

"Dave Brown. Live at number seventy, love. I wasn't sure whether to come, 'cause I didn't really know yer mum, but old Beryl said she was comin', so I thought it would be all right. I'll tell yer something', your mum, absolutely flippin' fantastic, she was. I dunno whether old Colonel Mustard there filled you in, but last year me old lady left me. Three kids I've got. Three flippin' kids! Kevin, he's four and a little terror. You've probably seen him tearin' about the street on his bike. Lee, he's nine and thinks he's bloody David Beckham, and Stacey, she's thirteen going on thirty, if yer know what I mean. And Paula just buggered off and left me with the whole herd of 'em! Ran off with me best mate, Steve, she did.

"Well, I didn't know whether I was comin' or goin' for a while there. We spent the first three weeks eatin' Pot Noodles and beans on toast. I can't cook for turkey, and I 'aven't got time anyway. I work as a plumber, always on the go. God knows how your mum got wind of all this—I thought old Beryl there must have opened her trap, but she swears she didn't—but anyhow, your mum started leavin' all this food on our step. Potato wedges and chicken wraps and homemade burgers and little pork balls on sticks…bloody 'ell, the kids thought they'd died and gone to 'eaven! They love all that. Anyway, I had no idea where all this food was comin' from till old Beryl told me your mum was cookin' for her too. I didn't know what to make of it at first. I mean, I never even met your mum. But she seriously saved my bacon, love, 'cause at last the kids were goin' to bed on full bellies, and not only that but their behavior bucked up too. Once they stopped eatin' all those additives and stuff, they were like different kids. Nice ones. The sort I always wanted. Still cheeky and always givin' me lip, but much better than they were. Anyways, we was all gutted to hear what had happened to yer mum, 'specially 'cause I never managed to thank her properly. Proper hard to get hold of she was, but amazin' all the same. Even restored my faith in women. Now, if I could meet a good woman like yer mum, I'd make sure I never introduced her to any of me mates."

"Alice Boyle."

"And Margaret Evans."

"We're nurses at St. Mary's Cancer Hospice, aren't we, Margaret?"

"Indeed we are. And we were so terribly sorry to hear about Val, weren't we, Alice?"

"Oh, goodness, yes! We didn't even know she was ill."

"No idea at all. She used to come on the first of each month with a cake."

"A cake or some scones."

"And it cheered our patients up no end, didn't it, Alice?"

"Absolutely! A little treat can make all the difference, can't it, Margaret?"

"All the difference."

"She never stopped for a chat, did she?"

"No, never stopped. Always rushing off somewhere, wasn't she, Alice?"

"Yes, rushing, all the time. But a wonderful woman who will be very much missed."

"Very much. We're going to dedicate a bench to her, aren't we, Alice?"

"Yes, Margaret, a bench in the rose garden. *In memory of Valerie May, who filled our hearts and stomachs.*"

"I am Tanek Kuklinksi. I am happy to meet you. I am in this country three month. I look for job, but I am told no job for you. I have no money for pay rent, so I live one month in door of shop. People give me money, but is not enough for buying food, just chips, and I get tired and sick. Then I am too sick to look for job. Then woman come and give me food. Good food. Hot food that she make for me. I get well and I look for job. I find job and now I live in room of old man. I am rent boy. I pay him rent for room. I send money to my family. This I can do because of woman who gave me food. I thank her very much, and I am very sad she die."

"Hello, my name's Frankie Jack. Frankie's my first name and Jack's my second name. Some people get confused because they can both be first names, but with me they're not. I got the bus here today, which was frightening because I've never been on a bus on my own and I didn't know where I was going. But I was able to do it, because I just asked the driver for the church and he told me it was two pounds ten and I gave him the money and then asked him to tell me when we were at the church so I could get off and he did. I wanted to come because Valerie was nice and she helped me by cooking good meals with all the right nutrients so that I could be fit and healthy and not get sick and die, which is what would happen if you ate food that had no nutrients in it. Cooking was one of the things I found hard about living on my own, but

I wanted to live on my own and not in what they call the 'community scheme,' because my gran always said I could do the same as most people if I tried hard, and most people don't live in the community scheme, they live on their own. It can be hard living on your own, because there are lots of things you have to do like cleaning and making the bed and taking the bin out on a Tuesday, and sometimes there are so many things to think about that I start to feel worried. But I haven't had to worry about getting sick and dying from no nutrients, and that's because Valerie helped me."

One after the other, people push forward to meet me, eager to tell me what a wonderful woman my mother was. They come from all walks of life. Whether they are old or young, rich or poor, they all have tales to tell of how, when they found themselves most in need, my mother swooped in like an angel from heaven, easing their burden with a chicken pie or a sponge cake. Several times the vicar tries to usher the crowd into the church, nervously checking his wristwatch, until finally, with the help of the verger, they resort to physically rounding us up and steering us through the door, as if shepherding a flock of sheep. As I stand in the front pew, I barely hear a word of the dry, monotonous speech the vicar delivers. I am too busy gazing over my shoulder at the rows upon rows of people who have come to say their good-byes to my mother.

Afterward, outside the church, Dr. Bloomberg takes my hands in his, peering over his spectacles at me with concern.

"How are you, Meg?"

I'm worried he's about to whip out one of his leaflets for the counseling service again, one of those ones with a scary pair of eyes inviting me to see things from a new perspective.

"I'm okay," I say with a smile.

Dr. Bloomberg looks pityingly at me, as if he thinks I'm lying for his benefit, but nothing could be further from the truth. Yes, I admit that I have a tendency to put on a brave face at times. Yes, it's true that I always want to be seen as calm, confident, and in control, but I actually do feel a hundred times better than I thought I would. Honestly. My ability to just get on with things over the past few days has surprised even me. Ironically, I think Mark would be rather proud of me. Of course I feel sad. But I also feel unexpectedly relieved that my mother's suffering is over and that it wasn't nearly as acute or as prolonged as might have been expected. Besides, she wouldn't want me to be sad.

Obviously I have shed a few tears here and there, standing in the silence of her empty bedroom or bagging up her clothes for the charity shop—well, there's no point in hanging on to these things, and it's got to be done at some point—but really I've been so busy that I haven't had time to wallow in self-pity. I am rather impressed by my own fortitude, and I would prefer it if Dr. Bloomberg was too, rather than looking at me in the way one might look at a blind, three-legged, abandoned puppy. People die all the time. He should know that.

"You know, just after you were born," says Dr. Bloomberg,

"I came to the house to see you. You were a tiny little thing, and your mother was so very young. She looked confused and scared, and I remember thinking to myself how on earth is this child going to manage with a child of her own? She was in quite a panic, your mother, worrying that you were so small she might break you. Do you know what I told her?"

You told her to spin on her head next time she found out she was pregnant and that she should feed me bicarbonate of soda and place me in the water heater closet to rise.

"No," I say, "I have no idea."

Dr. Bloomberg smooths down his big white mustache. "I told her that it takes the mighty oak tree no less than twenty years to produce an acorn."

I stare at him, astonished. He actually said that? He really said those immortal words? So not everything my mother told me was a lie.

"I meant to imply that your mother was too young to care for you, but I was wrong. She may not have had the physical strength or age of a mighty oak tree, but she had the spirit of one. And that's something you've inherited. Her strength of spirit. But you know, Meg, even the mighty oak tree can be damaged by strong winds."

As he shakes my hand, I smile at him and thank him for coming. What on earth is he talking about? Why would I be interested in what happens to an oak tree in the wind? Honestly, I think Dr. Bloomberg's going a bit funny in his old age.

"Hi."

Just as I thought the last of the mourners had left, I turn to find yet another stranger in front of me, no doubt waiting to tell me how my mother used to leave cherry tarts and spicy chicken wings on his front porch. Don't get me wrong, I am delighted by the endless stories of her good deeds, but I am also utterly exhausted. The stream of people waiting to talk to me has been constant, and two hours after the service finished I am ready to go home. It takes me a moment before I recognize that the person in front of me is not a stranger at all.

"Ewan, hi," I say, sounding surprised.

He is wearing a smart black suit and tie, his hair has been slicked back, and he is clean-shaven. He looks like a completely different person. Really, he scrubs up rather well. It must be the embarrassment of failing to recognize him that's making my cheeks flush and my palms all sweaty.

The last time I saw Ewan was four days ago, when I walked calmly down the stairs and out of the back gate, knocked on the window of his van, and told him that my mother had just died. He called an ambulance while I angrily insisted that doing so was a waste of National Health Service resources because she was definitely dead, and he showed the paramedics up to my mother's bedroom while I walked around and around the garden in the dark humming the tune to *Ready Steady Cook* before falling over a tree stump and scraping the skin off my arm. Looking back, I suspect that I was in a state of shock, but after Ewan sat me down and made me drink a large mug of herbal tea that smelled of old socks, I fell asleep on the sofa and didn't wake up until the morning.

I vaguely recall finding Ewan the next day, slumped over the kitchen table, asleep, and then ushering him out the back door, insisting that I had several things to get on with, while he repeatedly asked if I was okay and told me to call if I needed anything. Since then, we have spoken only once, briefly, when I called to explain the funeral arrangements, telling him after two minutes that I had to go because I was rearranging the bookshelf in alphabetical order and it was a task that required urgent attention. Half an hour later, I noticed his number come up on the call monitor, but I couldn't answer, because by that time I was busy organizing buttons into piles according to their shape and texture.

"I've been waiting to say hello," Ewan says, "but there was quite a queue. I didn't realize your mother knew so many people."

"It came as a surprise to me too."

"It was a nice service. I thought your mother would have liked the bit when the vicar tripped over his lectern."

"Yes, and the bit when he talked about a 'fleet of socks' instead of a 'flock of sheep.'"

"Yeah, that was unfortunate. Poor guy. I think he was nervous."

"He's probably not used to seeing that many people in church."

Ewan nods and we fall silent for a moment, both waiting for the other one to speak. Ewan pushes his hands deep into his trouser pockets, and I fiddle with my bracelet.

"How's Digger?" I ask.

"Good. I think he was depressed for a few days after…you know, after I took him home. He had all the signs of depression, anyway. Wasn't eating, wasn't interested in exercising, started listening to Radiohead, that kind of thing."

We smile at each other.

"How are you?" he asks.

"I'm fine," I say brightly, then realizing I might sound rather heartless, I add, "Under the circumstances, I mean." I'm actually beginning to feel a little guilty for coping so well.

"Is there anything I can do?"

"Thanks, but everything's under control. In fact, my feet haven't really touched the ground this past week. There's been so much to do. I've been sorting through my mother's belongings and signing all the paperwork for the house and finances, and then there's been lawyers and funeral directors to see. Plus, I suddenly noticed that the house was looking a bit shabby, so I painted the banisters, varnished the windowsills, washed all the windows, cleaned out all the cupboards, polished all the silverware..."

"Wow. Sounds like you've been busy."

"Rushed off my feet! But I thought I might as well get on with it all. No point hanging about."

Ewan eyes me carefully. "No, I guess not. Well, listen, you have my number, so if you need anything—"

"Oh," I say, taken aback, "you mean you're not coming to do the garden anymore?"

It had never occurred to me that Ewan would stop doing the garden twice a week. I had assumed, for some reason, that things would just carry on as normal. He runs a finger inside his shirt collar, clearly uncomfortable in a suit and tie.

"I guess I just wasn't sure what the arrangement would be now that...well, you know."

"Now my mother's dead," I say, matter-of-factly. "Well, I

haven't got a clue about gardens, so somebody's going to have to look after it. I don't see why things shouldn't just carry on as before. Plants don't just stop growing when somebody dies, do they? There's still work to be done."

Ewan looks rather astonished by my no-nonsense approach. "Meg," he says, falteringly, "you don't think maybe..."

"What?" I ask.

He studies my face closely and then shakes his head. "Nothing. I'll see you Wednesday, then. Just...just look after yourself." Ewan turns and starts crunching his way along the gravel path, but after a few steps he stops. "You're not going to be alone when you get home, are you?"

"Yes, but I'll be fine." I smile. "To be honest, I'd quite like to just have some time alone."

"Are you sure?" he asks, looking concerned.

I nod. "Yes. Quite sure. Besides, I really should defrost the freezer and scrub the patio."

In fact, I probably would have liked some company, but my choices are somewhat limited. I have no family now. It might have been nice to have brothers or sisters, aunts and uncles, even distant cousins to support me at this time, but the fact is that I'm alone. Gwennie did offer to return home with me after the funeral, and I was almost tempted to agree, but she has her own family to care for—three teenage kids and a disabled husband, as it transpires—and I really don't want her to feel sorry for me. No, I'm just going to have to manage alone; it's as simple as that. And that's fine, because despite the pitying looks I have been receiving all day long, frankly I think I'm coping rather well. In fact, as I say good-bye to Ewan, waving the funeral program that I am still clutching in my hand, I am already thinking about getting home and bagging up some of my mother's cookbooks to give to the charity shop. Really, she always did have far too many of them.

chapter nineteen

In my dream, I am running.

I can't see what's behind me, but I have a sense that it is a huge, dark, shadowy creature and that if it catches up with me I will be swallowed whole, gulped down into the black pit of its stomach from where I will never return. I run and run, willing myself to go faster, panting, sweating, my heart pounding, but all the time I am barely moving and the shadowy beast is gaining on me. I can hear its footsteps at my back, its breath upon my neck, telling me I can't escape, telling me that however hard I try I will never outrun it, and then its huge mouth opens wide like a cave, engulfing me, sucking me in, and I am being swallowed down.

Down, down into the abyss.

I wake with a start to find myself lying on my mother's bed, my heart thumping in my chest. The curtains are open, and I can see the moon hanging in the sky, casting a ghostly bluish glow across the room. I quickly tug my sweater off, throwing it onto the floor, and flap the bottom of my T-shirt, a chill running up my spine as the hot sweat on my skin immediately starts to cool. I look around for the clock before realizing I have packed it away in one of the several cardboard boxes that lie scattered across the floor. The house is silent and still. There is nobody here except me, all alone, surrounded by my mother's packaged belongings.

I gaze around at my mother's empty room: the bare dressing table, the naked shelves, the wardrobe with its doors flung open and nothing inside but a few lonely hangers. There is only one thing I seem to have missed, and I spy it now from where I sit on the bed. On the windowsill, half concealed behind the curtain, is something square and white.

I stand up and walk over to the window, picking up the little white book, slowly turning it over in my hands. Carefully I trace the title on the front cover, printed in large blue letters: *The Tale of the Jiggly-Wop*. How is it, I wonder, that this book keeps finding its way back to me? My mother must have taken this out of my wastepaper bin when I threw it away all those weeks ago, the day I arrived home from university. This story that she read to me over and over again when I was a little girl may have no longer had a place in my life, but it still had a place in hers. I open the front cover tentatively, my heart thumping anxiously, as if all the memories of my mother are kept inside and I am afraid to look at them.

"In a land far away, there lived a creature that didn't know quite what it was..."

I bring the book up to my face and breathe in the scent of its pages. I'm sure I can still smell the rosewater that my mother wore when I was a little girl, the scent of the hot chocolate I drank at bedtime, the laundry detergent she used that left my duvet smelling of peaches. I close my eyes and see us there, me tucked up cozily in my bed, my mother sitting on the mattress beside me, stroking my hair as I listen to the soft tones of her voice.

"It had huge ears like an elephant, a flowing mane like a lion, webbed feet like a duck, a stripy body like a tiger, and its face was all covered in feathers that made it sneeze."

In my mind's eye I see myself, a little girl with fine brown hair, giggling, finding something funny about the idea of the Jiggly-Wop sneezing because of its own feathers. I am small and warm, nestled against the pillows, sucking my thumb, and gazing at my mother's beautiful face in wonder, thinking how clever she is to be reading this book with so many big words. There is Blue Bear sitting on the bedside table and my coloring book on the floor. I am in a room that I have never before remembered that suddenly floods back to me with absolute clarity. This must be my room at our house in Brighton, I realize, the house we shared with that man that I called Daddy. This is the first time I have ever remembered anything from before I was five, but there it is, a perfectly clear picture in my mind, as if it were only yesterday.

"And so the Jiggly-Wop saw that the old baboon was right, and off he went on his merry way, back to the place where he belonged."

"Read it again," I beg my mother as she shuts the book.

"No, darling, it's time to sleep now."

She leans over and kisses me gently on the forehead. Her hair, hanging in long auburn locks, tickles my face and smells of spice and roses.

"Good night, Mummy," I say sleepily as she tucks Blue Bear under the duvet with me. "I love you."

"Sweet dreams, Meg May," she whispers, switching out the light. "I love you more."

I open my eyes to find my reflection staring back at me from the blackness of the window, the little book clutched to my chest, fat tears rolling down my cheeks. The pain is so bad that I can barely breathe, my body shuddering with the great sobs that catch in my throat and make me gasp for air. I double over with agony. It feels like someone has reached inside me and grabbed my insides, twisting them mercilessly into a tighter and tighter knot. My legs give way and I collapse onto my knees, tears streaming down my face and falling onto the pages of the book, running over the beautiful lettering, soaking the colorful illustrations.

I don't know how long I have been lying on the floor, worrying the fringe of my mother's bedroom rug between my fingers, lost in thoughts of despair, when I hear a noise from downstairs. One hour? Two, maybe? Who knows? Time has lost its meaning now, just as everything has. I lift my head slowly, my temples pounding from all the crying, and listen for a moment. There it is again. A small, scratching noise. It could be an intruder, I think, breaking in to murder me. I lay my head back on the carpet. I really don't care. Why would it matter anyway?

But the noise continues, getting louder and louder, and added to the scratching there is a high-pitched whining. After a couple of minutes, I slowly haul myself to my feet, supposing that if it is an intruder, I probably should make some attempt to find out. I stagger down the stairs, my head heavy and painful, flicking on light switches as I go, throwing the house into a brightness that stings my red, swollen eyes. The noise is coming from outside in the garden. Once I would have been anxious, terrified even, wondering who was lurking out there in the darkness so late in the evening, but right now I am too dead inside to care. I carelessly throw open the kitchen door, and there on the patio, illuminated by a square of light from the kitchen window, sits Digger, looking at me with his head cocked to one side.

"What do you want?" I ask, confused, my voice groggy.

Cautiously, Digger comes toward me with his head lowered and his ears back, his tail wagging submissively. I crouch down and put my arms around his neck, burying my face in his fur.

"You miss her too, don't you?" I whisper.

He snuffles around my ear, licking my face.

"Me too," I say.

"He was worried about you."

I look up to see Ewan stepping forward out of the shadows.

"We both were."

I stare at him, feeling dazed and numb. He has changed out of his smart suit and back into jeans, more like the Ewan I recognize.

I have never seen him wearing a jacket before, though, and there is something about the way he buries his chin deep inside his collar and pushes his hands into his pockets that makes me sad. Why can't things be just as they were a few weeks ago when the sun was warm, the vegetable patches still overflowing, and my mother still here beside me?

"I know it's late," says Ewan, "but I tried calling and there was no answer. I just wanted to make sure you were okay." He studies me, an expression of concern on his face. "*Are* you okay?" he asks when I don't reply.

I am so exhausted, so defeated, that it doesn't even occur to me to lie. "No," I tell him wearily, fresh tears springing to my eyes. "I don't think I am."

"I put all her stuff in boxes," I tell Ewan forlornly as we stand in the doorway of my mother's bedroom.

In the full-length mirror on the wall opposite, the only thing I have not been able to pack away, I see us both, Ewan gazing around the room in dismay, and me shivering in my funeral dress with tousled hair and bright red eyes, chewing anxiously on my thumbnail. I look a state, but I am past caring.

"Do you really want all her stuff in boxes?" Ewan asks gently, as if I am a dotty old woman who has done something incredibly foolish.

"No," I croak, my voice hoarse from sobbing. "No, I want it all back exactly as it was."

Slowly he opens the nearest box, watching me carefully as if he's not sure quite what I'll do next.

"Okay, then," he says, cautiously, "let's put it all back."

I am stressing Ewan out; I know I am. When he makes me a chamomile tea to calm my nerves, he makes himself one too, something I have never seen him do before. Every time he takes an item from one of the boxes and places it somewhere in my mother's room, I tell him to move it an inch to the left, no, an inch to the right, slightly lower, a bit higher. Somewhere deep inside I know this is only temporary, that sometime soon, not very far in the future, I will have to pack her things away again, but for now everything must be exactly as she left it. For now it must feel, even if only for a little while, that she is still here with me.

As we unpack, I tell Ewan how my mother got that vase at a garage sale in exchange for a treacle tart, how she painted that picture herself one warm summer's day, how she gathered those pinecones for potpourri, how she found that shell on Brighton Beach. I tell him all this because someone other than me should know. And all the time he listens patiently, working quietly beside me, not saying a word.

It takes us over two hours to put everything back where it belongs, and as I finally place my mother's clock back on her dressing table, I see that it is nearly midnight. I am so exhausted that I can barely stand, and the room seems to keep moving around me. Ewan switches on the TV to make sure it is working, having just reconnected the wires that I had pulled out and packed away in a box neatly labeled "Electrical Equipment." On the screen appears an American woman with a pearly smile demonstrating the new five-way vegetable chopper. Her co-presenter, a man with teeth so white I think Ewan must have accidentally altered the color, is helpfully handing her one carrot after another.

"How long would it normally take someone to chop all those carrots, Jessica?"

"Well, Brad, I'd say at least an hour, but look at how quickly you can do it with the new five-way vegetable chopper. You just slide them in—"

"Wow! That's incredible! Look how quickly they come out!"

"My mother used to love watching all the kitchen gadgets on the shopping channels," I say wearily, sitting down on the edge of her bed. "It kept her entertained whenever she couldn't sleep. She would have bought everything on the show if she'd had the money."

Ewan sits down on the little wooden chair next to the bed and gazes sleepily at Jessica and Brad demonstrating the different ways in which a cucumber can be sliced with various blade attachments.

I stretch out on the bed, exhausted. Digger jumps up beside me, snuggling next to me for warmth, and I put my arms around him.

"She was some woman, your mother," murmurs Ewan.

I breathe in the reassuring scent of Digger's fur. He smells of mud and rain, reminding me of the garden, of my mother's love of nature. "She was my best friend," I say sadly.

We both stare blindly at the TV screen.

"I don't know what I'm going to do without her," I confess. "I don't know how I'll cope. This house, the garden. I could never consider selling it, but it all seems too much."

On the screen, Jessica and Brad suddenly burst into laughter, as if cruelly mocking my feelings of inadequacy and incompetence.

"You don't have to do it all alone," says Ewan. "It's okay to ask for help."

"I'm not very good at asking for help. I can be stubborn at times."

"Really?"

His sarcasm makes me smile to myself. How is it that he knows things about me I am only just realizing myself?

"You always try to carry the weight of the world on your shoulders."

"Like Atlas," I say, yawning.

"Just like Atlas. And you don't have to carry all that weight alone."

"But look at what happened to Atlas," I say sleepily. "He placed his trust in Hercules to help him carry the weight of the world, and Hercules made a fool out of him. He tricked him and ran off laughing, leaving Atlas just looking stupid."

"Maybe, but Atlas couldn't let that one bad experience tarnish his view of the world forever. He had a choice. He could choose never to really trust anyone ever again, or he could take a chance on someone new."

"So what's the catch, Jessica?" Brad is saying. "I mean, surely this offer is too good to be true."

"So what did he choose?" I ask, closing my eyes, my words sounding distant in my own head. Digger's body is warm next to mine, and his breathing is slow and deep. Even as I struggle to stay awake, waiting to hear Ewan's reply, I can feel myself drifting further and further away. The last thing I am aware of is a man's voice, perhaps Ewan's, perhaps Brad's, telling me I can trust him.

In the weeks that follow my mother's death, my world takes on a dreamy, surreal quality as I go through the motions of starting to build a new life without her. There are papers to sign and lawyers to see, bills to pay, letters to write, and people to notify. Throughout the day, as I go about my tasks, I switch the TV from one cooking program to another so that in the background there is always something to remind me of her. I try cooking steak-and-kidney pie the way she taught me, and when the pastry burns, I am overwhelmed with emotion and collapse on the floor sobbing. At night, in the silence of the empty house, I cry, sitting on her bed, clutching her sweaters to my face, breathing in her fast-disappearing scent. Each night I fall asleep with the image of her face in my mind, wondering how I will get through the next day without her.

But I always do. And slowly, without my even noticing, the agony turns to a pain that I can bear.

I receive letters from Gwennie, who is holidaying in the south of France. She tells me what a delight it has been to find me after all these years, and in page after page of scrawled notes she shares her fondest memories of her friendship with my mother. She offers up further snippets of information about my past, slowly and cautiously drip-feeding me the truth, some of which hurts and some of which helps. I learn, for example, that Robert Scott died some years ago, and this seems to help me lay the past to rest. Whether my mother knew of his death I can't be sure, but the fact that he died in a freak butchery accident involving a pork mincer makes me wonder.

I am grateful for Gwennie's honesty, but I don't ask her for information. There is always time, and besides, the truth doesn't seem so important as it once did. At the end of one of her letters, Gwennie invites me to stay with her for Christmas and to join her family at their home in Montpellier next summer. "Any daughter of Valerie's is a daughter of mine," she writes before signing off, making me smile and cry at the same time.

In fact, the strange and subtle ways in which my mother touched the lives of others means I rarely feel alone. Dave, the plumber whose wife left him and whose kids survived on frozen additives until my mother stepped in, invites himself over to fix a problem with the water tank after spying a problem with my overflow pipe.

"Get away with yer!" he scoffs when I ask how much I owe him. "After what yer mum did for me, you'll be getting free plumbing for the rest of yer life, love! Cuppa tea wouldn't go amiss, mind."

And so Dave becomes the first of our neighbors to ever be invited in for tea, followed by his cocky thirteen-going-on-thirty daughter, who I somehow end up agreeing to tutor in science on a Thursday after school. Underneath the makeup, bravado, and attitude, I see a girl who is insecure, lacking in confidence, and desperately trying to be someone she's not. There is definitely something about her that reminds me of myself, and oddly enough we strike up quite a friendship.

Beryl Lampard is my third guest, after she turns up on my doorstep with my mother's ceramic dish and a clump of knitting that she claims is a tea cozy.

"I made it for your mother, dearie," she says, "but as I said before, I never had a chance to catch her. There should be a hole in it where the spout goes through, but I forgot to make one, so you might have to cut a hole in it yourself. Or I suppose you could wear it as a hat."

I almost laugh, but it seems she is quite serious. Standing on my doorstep with her wig on back to front and earrings that don't match, she awaits my response to her suggestion.

"It seems a shame not to use it for its original purpose," I say politely. "If you'd like to come in for a cup of tea, we could try it out."

She beams at me, and I can't help but stare at her ill-fitting dentures, wondering if it would be too risky to offer her a biscuit.

It is through my conversation with Beryl that I learn Major William Jefferson Reece and I share a common interest in genetics, and so it is that the following week I find myself sitting in his front room surrounded by model tanks and airplanes while he shouts at me from his armchair and waves a newspaper article at me.

"A mouse with five legs! Bloody incredible! I want you to tell me how these scientists do it, young lady, because if there's something out there that can help me grow a new leg, I want some of it, I tell you! They gave me this metal one," he says, banging his leg with a walking stick, "but it's not like having the real thing. What? No, not like a real leg. Now, with a new leg I could ask Beryl Lampard to go to the tea dance with me, what do you think? Don't look so surprised, my girl, there's life in this old dog yet!"

Although Major William Jefferson Reece was disappointed to learn that he cannot be genetically modified to grow a new leg, he did follow my suggestion that he should ask Beryl to go to the tea dance anyway. After all, I told him, a woman who wears her wig back to front is hardly going to notice that he has a limp. It warms my heart when I see them one day, tottering off down the street arm in arm, all done up to the nines, the major's blazer lapels covered in medals and Beryl in a smart coat wearing what appears to be a tea cozy on her head.

Love also blossoms for Dave the plumber, after he kindly drives me to St. Mary's Hospice to see the bench that has been dedicated to my mother. It's made of redwood and sits in the little rose garden there. It's a windy day when we go, and all the roses are dead, of course, but I can imagine it in the summer, full of color, and I think my mother would have loved it.

"She was such a generous lady, wasn't she, Alice?" says Margaret. "Always bringing cakes for the patients. Or lovely cookies."

"Or little tarts, Margaret," says Alice. "Don't forget those little tarts she used to bring. They always went down well."

"The raspberry ones, were they?" pipes up Dave. "With crumbly pastry? They were bloody marvelous, they were. My favorite."

"They were my favorite, too!" agrees Alice enthusiastically.

Dave smiles at her and she smiles back, blushing. Their eyes linger on each other just long enough to make Margaret and me exchange a knowing glance. The next thing I hear, they've been on a couple of dates and have decided to enroll in a cooking course together.

"In honor of yer mum!" winks Dave.

It seems that love and friendship are blossoming all over the street. Several more neighbors who were not at the funeral turn up on my doorstep, offering their condolences and sharing their own stories of how my mother fed and watered them, offering them nourishment in times of hardship and skulking off like a thief in the night before they could thank her, never wanting anything in return. Through each other we share information, put people in touch with one another, and learn about the previously secret lives of those around us. The quiet little street takes on a new sense of solidarity and community, with people chatting on the pavement, offering each other a helping hand, waving good morning as they pass by. And it is all because of my mother, I think, all because her generosity gave us something in common. It seems incredible that a woman who kept herself so isolated could have engendered such warmth and community spirit.

I am so very, very proud of her.

Ewan comes and goes, sometimes when I am out, so I don't even realize he has been until I notice that the fence has been fixed or that he has harvested some pumpkins and left them on the back porch. I give him a key to let himself in the back door to make a cup of coffee if I am not there, and it makes me smile when one day I return from the supermarket to find a Post-it stuck to a packet of Custard Creams on which he has scrawled, *What were you thinking? Chocolate Hob-Nobs next time, please.* I take a fresh Post-it and write, *Only when you've eaten all of these, greedy guts*, before sticking it to the Custard Creams and placing them back in the cupboard. At the end of the month, I leave the money he is owed in an envelope on the kitchen table and am confused to find it still there later that day, even though he has clearly come and gone, leaving a trail of cookie crumbs in his wake. I turn the envelope over in my hand thoughtfully and make a mental note to tell him he is a scatterbrain.

One morning, I find myself watching him through the kitchen window as he rakes up the fallen leaves, gathering them up in his arms and dumping them in a pile on one of the barren vegetable patches. It is a cold, bright day, and he is wearing a T-shirt with a scarf wrapped tightly around his neck, the light glistening on his hair. His niece is with him, dressed in a pink scarf and sweater, and she is helping, clumsily gathering up leaves and transporting them from one place to another, dropping most of them as she goes. They are chatting and smiling, and I think of all the carefree autumn days I have ever spent with my mother, toasting marshmallows over a candle, baking hot apple pie, carving out pumpkins for Halloween. I grab a scarf and my mother's old oversized green sweater from a peg by the back door, and pulling them on, I rush outside to join in, eager to forget the sadness that weighs on my heart and to experience being carefree once again.

Digger rushes to greet me, wagging his tail, but the little girl stops what she is doing and looks terrified. The last time she saw me I was telling her off for playing so irresponsibly, ranting about the horrors of tornado damage and ridiculing her pretend wedding arrangements.

"Hello," I say to her with a smile. "It's nice to see you again." My voice sounds formal, as if I'm meeting a business acquaintance. I never have been very at ease with young children. "Do you want some help?" I ask her, trying to look friendly.

She stares at me, scared and resentful. Clearly the scary lady has spoiled the nice morning she was having with Uncle Ewan.

"Just grab some leaves," says Ewan, continuing his work, "and dump them on the pile. I'll sort them into pens later for rotting down to leaf mold."

Pens? Leaf mold? I have no idea what he's talking about, but I want to join in and be helpful, so I do as I'm told. The little girl, glancing warily at me out of the corner of her eye, goes back to gathering leaves in silence, and I suddenly feel like an unwanted intruder in my own garden.

"What's your name?" I ask the little girl, trying to make conversation.

"Lucy," she whispers shyly.

"That's a nice name. I'm Meg. I like the autumn, don't you? The leaves are so pretty."

She doesn't respond.

"It's nice of you to help your uncle. Are your mummy and daddy out today?"

She nods solemnly and inches away from me.

"When I was little," I say, "my mummy used to take me to the woods and we'd look for fairies among the fallen leaves. They love living in piles of leaves, because it's warm and no one can see them. If you're really careful and quiet, sometimes you can lift up a leaf and there will be a fairy sleeping underneath it."

I crouch down and very carefully lift a golden leaf, pretending to be looking for a fairy. Out of the corner of my eye, I can see Lucy looking over, straining to see what might be there.

"There's no such thing as fairies," she says suddenly.

"Oh, yes, there is."

"I've never seen one."

"Really?" I ask, feigning surprise. "I've seen several. Maybe you're not being quiet enough. They fly away at the slightest noise."

Lucy frowns at me, trying to decide if I'm telling the truth. She glances over her shoulder at Ewan for guidance, but he's busy trying to pry the handle of his rake out of Digger's jaws.

"Oh, there goes one!" I exclaim, pointing into the air. "Did you see it?"

"No," says Lucy, her eyes darting around. "Where?"

"I've lost it," I say, searching the sky. "Oh, there! See, there she is!"

"I can't see her!" says Lucy, suddenly desperate to see the fairy. "Where is she?"

"She just ducked into the pile of leaves!" I say excitedly.

Lucy and I run over to the leaf pile and examine it. Her cheeks are rosy red, and her eyes are bright with anticipation and excitement.

"Is there really one in there?" she says.

"Yes, but you must be very quiet," I whisper to her.

"What's in there?" asks Ewan, appearing beside us with a bent rake. "A frog?"

"No, a fairy," whispers Lucy. "Be quiet or you'll scare her."

Ewan smiles at me and raises his eyebrows questioningly. In the sunlight, I notice the chip in his front tooth and wonder what I ever found so annoying about it. In fact, this imperfection is rather endearing and somehow suits his cheeky smile. I loosen the scarf around my neck, feeling my face getting rather warm.

"Well, you know how to get the fairy to come out, don't you, Luce?" asks Ewan.

Lucy shakes her head and gazes up at him, adoring and intrigued.

"You have to take it by surprise!" he shouts, suddenly grabbing an armful of leaves and throwing them up in the air.

Lucy squeals with shock and excitement, covering her head as the leaves fall down over her, and then she suddenly delves into the pile, grabbing one armful of leaves after the other, throwing them into the air and searching for the fairy. Ewan and I both join her, throwing red and yellow leaves up into the sky, which Digger tries to catch in his snapping jaws as they flutter down around him. Then we are all throwing leaves at each other and laughing, Ewan lobbing fistfuls at Lucy and me with gusto, and the two of us mounting a counterattack against him as best we can, grabbing at his arms and trying to stuff handfuls of leaves down the neck of his T-shirt. Before I know it, he has turned on me, and I scream loudly as he pushes me onto the leaf pile, where I land and bounce softly, multicolored shimmering leaves falling down over me in the bright autumn sunlight, the sound of Lucy's childish laughter and Digger's barking filling the air.

chapter twenty

The first frosts come too soon, reminding me of all the weeks that you have been gone. Those hazy summer days feel like a lifetime ago now, yet I still feel you with me in all that I do. You are the glowing candle inside the pumpkin I carve for Halloween and place in the front window, the only one on the street with a huge smile on its face rather than a menacing scowl, because you preferred them that way. You are the gloves I wear as I slide my first blackberry pie into the oven, ever cautious that a scalding-hot shelf could give me a nasty burn. You are the warm scarf that I wrap around my neck when I help Ewan in the garden, always aware that a chill autumn morning could lead me to catch my death of cold. You are the whispering breeze as I pick Brussels sprouts, telling me which ones are good and which ones to leave on the stem.

I am everything you ever taught me, even when you thought I wasn't listening.

Working in the garden keeps me busy and makes me feel closer to you. In the past two weeks, I have helped to dig over the empty vegetable plots, built a hibernation box for hedgehogs, strung up bird feeders, pruned the apple trees, and planted tulip bulbs ready to flower next spring. I never knew there was so much to learn. It turns out that gardening really is quite a science.

My back aches constantly, my hands are cracked and sore, but despite the cold and the wet and the pain, I find I am at peace in the garden, working quietly under Ewan's guidance, surrounded by the sound of his humming, the gentle snip of shears, the squeak of the wheelbarrow, and the muffled thuds of a spade against hard soil. I look forward to the days when he comes and I can work alongside him.

In fact, they are my favorite days.

Oh, and you would be pleased to know that we have found a good use for our abundant autumn harvest. After I have taken what I need and distributed some gifts among the neighbors—onions for the major, leeks for Beryl Lampard, rutabagas for Dave Brown—Ewan takes the surplus in his van and drops it off at an unmarked house in town, the address and location of which are kept secret for a very good reason, but which was disclosed to me in confidence by Dr. Bloomberg. It is a shelter for women and their children who are trying to escape domestic abuse. It provides them with somewhere to stay where they can feel physically safe, as well as providing counseling so that they do not have to feel ashamed or isolated, but instead can start to find the strength and confidence to deal with what has happened to them. You always said that a tasty, nutritious dinner was good for the heart as well as the body, so perhaps in our own little way we are helping to heal some broken souls. I like to think so, anyway.

"Isn't it sad?" I say to Ewan one afternoon as we sit on the upturned wooden crate at the far side of the garden. We have just finished dismantling the frames that supported the climbing beans and have packed them away in the shed for winter. Although it can only be about four o'clock, it is starting to grow dark already.

"Isn't what sad?" he asks, gazing distractedly up at the gray sky, reading the clouds for signs of rain.

"The way the summer has to end," I tell him. "The trees lose their leaves, the flowers wither away…"

We both stare out at the brown turned-over earth.

"I don't think it's sad," says Ewan. "It's just part of the cycle of life. Everything going around, keeping moving. That's what it's all about."

I examine the mud underneath my fingernails thoughtfully. Digger comes trotting toward me for attention, wagging his tail, and I lean over to place my cheek against his soft head. My hair has grown long and unruly and hangs over his face as he licks my ear.

"Do you know how the ancient Greeks explained the changing of the seasons?" Ewan asks.

"No," I say with a smile, "but Digger and I both have a feeling that you're going to tell us, don't we, boy?"

Digger barks in amusement.

"Fine, I won't tell you, then," says Ewan, pretending to be offended. "I wouldn't want to bore you."

"Oh, go on!"

"No. Not if you're not interested," he says stubbornly.

"Pleeeease."

"No."

"Go on!" I say, shoving him so that he loses his balance and almost falls off the crate.

"Crikey, woman!" he says, laughing and gathering himself up. "No more digging for you. Any more muscles and you'll be dangerous."

"Tell me the story," I say, elbowing him gently. "You know you want to."

"Okay, but only because you're insisting. It started when Demeter found out that her daughter, Persephone, had been kidnapped. Demeter was distraught and vowed to never rest until Persephone was back home again. She searched the entire world, covering mountains and deserts, seas and forests, and when she discovered that Hades had kidnapped Persephone and taken her to the underworld to make her his bride, her despair turned to anger. In her rage, Demeter decreed that no fruit would grow on Earth until Hades returned Persephone to her, which he agreed to do, but on one condition. Because Persephone had eaten a handful of pomegranate seeds belonging to him, he declared that she would forever have to spend part of the year with him in the underworld.

So, once a year, Persephone is allowed to return to Earth, and when she returns, spring arrives: green shoots appear, trees blossom, fruit grows, and new life flourishes. But when the time comes for her to go back to the underworld, winter arrives: leaves drop, fruit falls, and new growth is suspended until she returns to Earth again."

Digger wags his tail appreciatively and nuzzles his head against his master's leg.

"And that's why we have spring and autumn, isn't it, pal?" Ewan says, giving Digger's head a vigorous rub.

I think about Persephone coming and going, the seasons changing, life and death, love and loss.

"I guess nothing ever stays the same for very long," I say, pulling the sleeves of my sweater down over my cold hands.

"The world has to keep turning," he says. "Six months from now, this garden will be full of birds singing in the trees and flowers blossoming once again."

I shiver in the chill air, wrapping my arms around my body and burying my chin inside my scarf. I know he's right, that in six months' time the garden will be full of life again, but I wonder whether it will ever really feel the same now that my mother is gone.

"She'll always be with you, you know," says Ewan. "All you have to do is close your eyes."

I let my eyelids drift shut, listening to the sound of the breeze playing with the crisp autumn leaves. Wisps of my hair blow gently around my ears, tickling at my cheeks. I can feel the warmth of Ewan's thigh pressed next to mine, the solidness of his body against me.

"She's wherever you want her to be," I hear Ewan say, his voice deep and soothing. "You just have to imagine."

In my mind's eye, an image slowly comes into focus. I can see her there, standing by the apple orchard, her long auburn hair shining in the bright autumn sunshine, thick and luscious as it used to be, her crowning glory. She is strong and healthy, her cheeks glowing and her eyes sparkling with glee. She is smiling at me. In the air I can smell spiced apples, cinnamon, warm chocolate cake, hot vanilla custard, mulled wine, nutmeg…all the scents that ever filled our kitchen on a brisk autumn day. She looks vibrant and happy, full of energy once again. I smile back at her, and she waves. She is wearing the purple cashmere gloves I bought her for Christmas last year, the ones she said she would save for a special occasion and then tucked carefully away in a drawer. I smile and raise my hand slightly, waving back. Slowly, her colorful figure blends with the red and yellow autumn leaves and the sparkling golden sunshine, and the image starts to fade away.

I open my eyes. The clouds are gray and the sky is growing dim. I look toward the apple orchard, where the trees stand huddled in the fading light, their remaining leaves rustling gently in the breeze, their branches already looking sparse. It doesn't matter to me that the orchard will soon be bare, like a huddle of gnarled skeletons against a winter sky. I know that whenever I close my eyes my mother will be there, waving to me, and that it will always be a sunny day.

When I look down into my lap, I find Ewan's hand, rough and warm, enveloping mine.

And it seems like the most natural thing in the world.

It's not like you said it would be. No bolt of lightning shoots across the sky, and no nightingales spontaneously burst into song. I do not find myself engulfed in a dreamy, magical cloud or swept away in a whirlwind of glittering stardust. Instead, I suddenly feel real, as if all the splintered parts of myself have simultaneously come together. I am the child I once was and the adult I am today. I am all of my good points and each of my bad. I am brave but afraid, healed but damaged, strong but helpless. I am everything I have admitted and all that I have denied. The person I am right now in this moment is the product of everything I have ever been—the truth, the lies, and everything in between.

When his lips touch mine, I don't feel myself falling, weightlessly, like you promised.

Instead, for the first time ever, I feel myself become me.

reading group guide

1. The original title of this book was "Nutmeg." Do you think *From the Kitchen of Half Truth* is more appropriate? Why or why not?

2. Do you agree with Meg's following statement to Mark: "I'd rather have fictional memories than no memories at all."

3. What do you think of Valerie's stories about Meg's childhood?

4. Was there any foreshadowing that the fanciful stories hid a darker reality? If yes, what was it, and when did you see it?

5. Meg mentions that embarrassment, anger, and guilt are emotions all teenagers feel. Even though the stories from her childhood are outrageous, do you think Meg's growing pains are relatable? Why or why not? Do you think that, in some respects, she's still an adolescent?

6. Meg joins the science department at her university and studies to become a geneticist. Do you believe that this choice is significant?

7. Ewan: "There's a very fine line between the truth and a lie, isn't there?" Meg: "No, there isn't. One is real, the other is not. It's extremely simple if you think about it." What do you think about this exchange between Ewan and Meg?

8. Meg is baffled that Ewan indulges her mother's fantasies at the beginning of the book. What changes her mind?

9. Each time Meg begins to force her mother to tell the truth about her childhood, her mother's condition worsens. Why? And how does this affect Meg's decision to pursue the truth?

10. Meg's nightmare about the White Giant is recurring and seems to intensify as she gets closer to the truth. Did you have any theories about this nightmare? Did they turn out to be true?

11. What do you think of Gwennie?

12. The second time Meg meets Ewan's niece, she plays make-believe with her. What does this say about Meg's personal growth?

13. After discovering the truth about Meg's father, do you think Valerie's decision to make up stories was justified? Or do you think they did more harm than good?

14. Meg and her mother are very different, but they do have several similarities. What are they, and when do they emerge?

15. When Valerie dies, Meg discovers all of the lives she touched through her cooking and baking. How does this change Meg?

about the author

Maria Goodin graduated from the University of Kent with degrees in French and English. After spending time working in France, she trained as an English teacher and a counselor. *From the Kitchen of Half Truth* is based on the short story "Nutmeg," which won the 2007 Derby Short Story Competition. Maria lives in Hertfordshire with her husband, son, and cat.